Essential
Lies

By

Cindy Conway

*Linda
Thanks for your
support of our profession

Dr Cindy*

First published by Dog Ear Publishing
4010 W. 86th Street, Ste H
Indianapolis, IN 46268
www.dogearpublishing.net

ISBN: 1-59858-214-3
Library of Congress Control Number: 2006933671

This book is printed on acid-free paper.
This book is a work of Fiction. Places, events, and situations in this book are purely Fictional and any resemblance to actual persons, living or dead, is coincidental.

Printed in the United States of America

"The history of the race, and each individual's experience, are thick with evidence that a truth is not hard to kill and that a lie told well is immortal."

—*Mark Twain*

For Steven

Together all things are possible.

Fact:

The research data referenced in this novel is real.

Prologue:

It was one of those rare summer days to remember. Moist air dripping with promise. Brilliant blue skies overhead, lush green grass below. A lazy, barefoot kind of day. Sadie giggled as the grass tickled her toes. Today was her eleventh birthday. It was the kind of day you wanted to last forever. (Be careful what you wish for.) Soon Sadie Jensen would wish this day had never begun. Her life was about to change forever.

It started happily enough. For Sadie, this bright summer day loomed with endless possibilities. She spent the morning in the kitchen helping her mother. Her kitchen duties, you ask? Licking the spoon as her mom made her favorite—German chocolate cake.

Sadie was a lively, plump girl with a riot of red curls spilling down her back and a myriad of freckles dancing across her face. Everything about her was in motion. This was in sharp contrast to her twin, Katie, who preferred to spend time quietly in her room drawing or playing with her dolls. In spite of their differences, the girls shared a strong bond.

It was that very bond that had sent Sadie on her current mission—picking fresh raspberries for her sister. Even at her young age, Sadie instinctively sought to nurture and protect her twin.

Their Iowa farmhouse was surrounded by wild raspberry bushes. Sadie's small fingers efficiently plucked the berries. She developed a rhythm: pick some, eat some, and swat mosquitoes. She reasoned that it was only fair to have a few berries herself—after all, she had to make sure they were ripe.

Looking down at the bowl held by her red-tipped fingers, she frowned. I need some more berries, she thought. She headed for the really good patch near the neighbor's old barn. "This will take her mind off dumb ol' Jeremy and those icky pills," she said. This comment was directed to Susie, a large orange cat currently winding around Sadie's legs.

It was the noise that stopped her. BUZZ. BUZZ. BUZZ. Hundreds of flies swarming by the barn door. It was open. BANG. BANG. BANG. It beat a rhythm on the side of the barn. BUZZ. BANG. BUZZ. BANG. It could have been a cheerful noise. It wasn't.

Deciding to check it out, she headed toward the back of the barn. Then the smell assaulted her. An acrid odor, unfamiliar. Sadie wrinkled her nose. Curiosity tugged at her. Slowly, she walked forward. Little did she know that she'd be walking into the face of hell. Perhaps it was her destiny.

She dropped the berries as she struggled to stand, to breathe. Then, blessedly, she was engulfed in darkness.

Chiropractic College
Trimester One

"The doctor of the future will give no medicine but will interest his patients in the care of the human frame, in diet and in the cause and prevention of disease."

—Thomas Edison

CHAPTER

1

Life tragedies are never easy but most people would agree that if you survived them, they did build character. At twenty-one years of age, Sadie Jensen had already experienced two character-building opportunities. Right now, though, you certainly wouldn't know it by looking at her. Sitting in the classroom on her first day at Chiropractic College, her blue-green eyes sparkled with life. Turning every time a new student entered was causing her red, curly hair to bounce wildly around her shoulders. She'd given up trying to tame it when she was in high school, wisely deciding that there were some battles you just couldn't win.

Okay, she knew it was silly, but she couldn't help herself—she was so excited that she had to do it. Reaching down with her right finger and thumb, she pinched the tender skin on her forearm to make sure this was real and not some wonderful dream.

OUCH!

It was real. Finally, all the years of scrimping, saving, and studying had paid off. She was about to realize her dream of becoming a chiropractor.

Of those life tragedies, the first she never spoke of. The second? Well, that's the reason she was here. It was the only way she knew of to try to make some sense out of her grandmother's death.

Sadie gritted her teeth in an effort to ward off the unpleasant memories. It didn't really work but that didn't stop her from trying. In a way, that small act was descriptive of her nature. Some people might call it "SPUNK"—the ability to act even when the odds were against you. One family friend had likened her to a terrier. Oh, don't worry, he's a dog lover and it was a compliment inspired by her tenacity and loyalty. Come to think of it, *tenacious* and *loyal* are the same words he used to describe his beloved Jack Russell terrier. However you wanted to describe it, spunky or terrier-like, Sadie did possess both traits in abundance

and, thanks to the tutelage of her late grandmother, she'd somehow managed to remain an eternal optimist.

That determination and tenacity also came from her grandmother. Sadie smiled, recalling Elsie's countless tales of Celtic
warriors. "You're a warrior, too, dearie. It's in your blood," she'd
said so often that once—as a child—Sadie had pricked her finger
to see whether her blood looked any different from her classmates'. Much to her surprise, it didn't.

Sadie had always been close to her grandmother, but that
bond had strengthened after her eleventh birthday. From that
moment on, Sadie had practically lived with her. In a way, Elsie
had saved her that summer. Sadie's entire face softened as she
remembered the feel of Elsie's fleshy arms wrapped around her.
Those hugs should have been patented, she thought. Totally
blocking out the outside world, they enveloped you in layers of
love and warmth so powerful that to this day she could still feel
their lingering effects.

Under the watchful eye of her grandmother, she had learned
the love of cooking, using the fresh produce from their garden.
Gardening had also taught her patience as well as the love of the
land and all things natural. That was why she was so excited for
this first class to start. Chiropractic philosophy honored the
body's natural ability to heal itself. For Sadie, becoming a chiropractor was more than a profession—it was a way of honoring
her grandmother's life.

Although she was looking at the blackboard, Sadie didn't
really see it. Instead, she was remembering Elsie's zest for life
and how the endless supply of medications had successfully erad-
icated it. The medical charts said that she had died of a heart
attack, but Sadie wondered how much the medication had contributed to her grandmother's death, especially the Vioxx.

BUZZ. BUZZ. BUZZ.

The sound of the bell brought Sadie back to the present.
Looking over at the door, she saw the professor walk in.

"Good morning everyone. My name is Dr. Hamilton. I will be
teaching you chiropractic philosophy and the history of the chiropractic profession."

"He's cute," Jill whispered.

Sadie smiled. Jill Jones was her roommate. Although they'd
known each other for a short while, they were fast becoming
friends.

Dr. Hamilton was a tall man with silver-gray hair. He was dressed in a well-tailored, gray pin-striped suit covered by a long white lab coat with his name stitched above the pocket. Sadie thought he looked a bit like George Hamilton, except not as tan. The only hint of his true personality peeked out from under the very professional garments in the form of a pink tie.

Sadie smiled when she saw it. Her grandmother would have approved. She had loved the color pink, saying it reminded her of the first blush of dawn. "Each day's a new beginnin'. 'Tis nature's way of givin' ya a new canvas to paint your life's picture," she had said.

Dr. Hamilton stepped in front of the podium. "Today, Americans are in a health crisis."

Sadie looked up as he spoke.

"If you converted the number of people who die from heart disease, hypertension, and diabetes into jumbo jet crashes, you would have roughly 10 jumbo jet crashes every day."

"Wow!"

This came from someone in the back of the classroom. Sadie turned to see a dark-haired, scruffy-looking guy shaking his head.

"That's right," Dr. Hamilton nodded. "According to Dr. Julian Whitaker reporting on a recent Harvard study, 8 million people per year are hospitalized for diseases brought on by drugs that were supposed to improve their conditions. The Harvard study also found that conventional medical care is the fourth leading cause of death in this country, right after killers like heart disease, cancer, and stroke. Adverse drug effects are responsible for about 100,000 deaths per year."

Sadie's entire body tensed up; that was a statistic she didn't have to learn in a lecture. Unfortunately, life had already taught her that one. Right now, all her muscles had joined forces with her in a united protest against such senseless tragedy.

Jill seemed to notice the change in her. "Are you all right?" she whispered.

Not wanting to lie outright, Sadie took a deep breath and nodded her head.

Oblivious to the tension in the fourth row, Dr. Hamilton continued, "If you're 65 or older, risk of drug-induced illness skyrockets. Research from Harvard Medical School found that 9 million Americans over 65, almost one-third of them, are taking drugs that should *never* be taken by the elderly."

BAM! Dr. Hamilton hit the podium with his fist on the word *never*.

Sadie jumped. She wasn't sure whether this was an outward expression of the passion he felt for his subject or an attempt to get the attention of some of the students slouching in the back row. Probably both, she decided.

Dr. Hamilton pulled out a chart from behind his desk. As he held it up, Sadie saw that it was a poster with two pink pills on it. The same pink as his tie, she thought. To the right of the pills was some printing:

> *Such a small innocent looking object, considered by most a solution that is easy to swallow. But think, if given to a healthy person, it will make them sick. Why do we believe it will make a sick person well?*
> *Drugs are not the answer.*

In unison, their heads began to nod as the students read the quote.

"Did you ever stop for a moment to ask yourself why someone gets sick?" he asked in his deep voice.

"Too many drugs?"

This came from someone in the back of the classroom. Sadie turned, looking behind her. Obviously it hadn't come from the scruffy guy. He was looking down at his desk.

"HA!"

Someone in the front laughed at the comment. Sadie turned around. Dr. Hamilton was apparently unperturbed by the outburst. In fact, he was smiling at the students.

"He seems like a pretty cool professor," Jill whispered.

Sadie turned to her left, nodding in agreement. In doing so, she noticed that Jill hadn't been taking notes, she'd been drawing them—and she was good. There was a perfect drawing of Dr. Hamilton holding up his poster.

"Wow," Sadie whispered. "You're good."

Jill smiled at the compliment.

They both looked up as the lecture continued.

"Did you know that if I swabbed your throats and did cultures, I would find pathogenic bacteria?"

Sadie heard murmuring from the back of the classroom.

"Look around," Dr. Hamilton urged. "Even though we may have pathogenic bacteria, no one here is suffering from a disease."

The noise level rose as the students looked around the room. Sadie noticed one big Italian guy begin to look nervous, as though he might come down with something at any moment.

Jill, too, noticed his discomfort. She drew a caricature of him with a thermometer sticking out of his mouth.

"We have constantly blamed bacteria for our ills, indiscriminately giving antibiotics in an attempt to cure them. If you read the newspaper yesterday, you saw the headline: *SUPERBUGS... Antibiotics powerless to stop this trend.*

A blonde-haired girl raised her hand.

Consulting the seating chart, Dr. Hamilton acknowledged her. "Yes, Becky?"

"Dr. Hamilton, I have a question about bird flu. The threat of a pandemic has been in the news lately and I've heard that the United States is spending millions of dollars stockpiling Tamiflu. Does that even work on bird flu?"

"That's a good question, Becky. As I'm sure you're all aware, bird flu outbreaks are spreading, and many researchers are saying that it is not a question of *if* there's a pandemic, it's *when*."

Right now Sadie could think of no other place she'd rather be than here—learning about natural health and natural ways to boost the function of the immune system.

"Current studies have shown that Tamiflu is not the magic bullet that it was hoped to be and yet you're right, Becky, we *are* stockpiling it. In a recent study on people with bird flu treated with Tamiflu, there was a 50 percent mortality rate. Not very promising, I'm afraid."

Dr. Hamilton shook his head, frowning. "For years now, we have looked to the medicine chest for the source of health, but in this class we will focus on maintaining a healthy nervous system and eating a healthful diet."

"That's just what Thomas Edison predicted!" This comment came from a student in the front row, Peter Burger.

"That's right," Dr. Hamilton nodded. "Drugs are not the answer. In 1990, the GAO reviewed 198 drugs that were approved from 1976 to 1985. Unbelievably, 102 of them were found to have side effects serious enough to warrant either withdrawal from the market or marked changes in labeling to warn of increased dangers."

Thinking about the new black-box warnings that had recently been added to psychotropic drugs, Sadie experienced the all-too-familiar sick feeling in the pit of her stomach. *Why couldn't they have issued those warnings earlier?*

As bad as the sick feeling was, she wasn't ready to talk about it. She was; however, ready to talk about something else. She raised her hand.

"Yes . . . " Dr. Hamilton looked down at his seating chart, " . . . Sadie," he added.

"Dr. Hamilton, is it true that there's a link between Vioxx and heart attacks?"

Although she desperately hoped this wasn't the case, she was skeptical. She might be an optimist but she wasn't stupid.

"There is," he nodded. "I know that Merck is facing product liability lawsuits right now. As a matter of fact, there has already been a sizeable sum of money awarded to one of the plaintiffs whose lawyer claimed that Merck had suppressed information about the dangers of the drug."

Sadie's warrior blood began to boil.

"I heard that the company set aside $675 million for litigation costs," Peter Burger said smugly, proud to be able to display what he considered to be his vast intellect.

"He's arrogant," Jill whispered.

Sadie was inclined to agree with her.

Dr. Hamilton ignored the attitude. "That's right, but if the first case is any indication, they'd better set aside some more. The federal judge in Louisiana predicted that the number of Vioxx lawsuits could total over 100,000."

"Wow!"

This came from the big Italian guy. He no longer looked concerned about catching some dreaded disease. Sadie didn't know his name yet but felt compelled to agree with him. She was glad for the large number of lawsuits, hoping that they would help to make a difference in the way the drug companies operated. With that on her mind, she asked another question.

"Did they know that Vioxx would kill people?"

"It certainly looks that way." Dr. Hamilton frowned. "Based on government records, in 2001 Merck tried to patent a drug that would reduce heart attack risks for Vioxx users."

"That's *three years* before the company eventually withdrew the drug!" Sadie nearly shouted, she was so upset. Her grandmother didn't have to die—they *knew*!

"I'm afraid it's worse than that." Dr. Hamilton looked at her searchingly for a moment before continuing. "A researcher testified that Merck knew of the safety risks Vioxx presented a full year *before* the company even began selling the drug."

With that bit of information, Sadie's Celtic blood had passed the boiling point—it was on fire.

WHOOSH.

In what can only be described as a mission of mercy, every available oxygen molecule within Sadie's lungs rapidly evacuated (everyone knows you have to keep oxygen away from a fire). She felt light-headed, but that didn't stop her from resolving to do everything in her power to prevent this from happening to anyone else.

BUZZ. BUZZ. BUZZ.

Class was over. For the time being, Sadie's internal fire was extinguished—replaced by a burning desire to help others. Taking a deep breath, (the oxygen molecules decided it was safe to return,) Sadie walked quietly out of room 201.

— • • • —

At a party, everyone gathers in the kitchen. At Chiropractic College, everyone gathers in the cafeteria, and that's where they were now. The freshmen students were settling into their routine. From the smells, they had learned that the cafeteria, too, had a routine. Today was Friday—the smell was fish.

Sadie was having lunch with her new friends, Jill, Becky, Ellen, and Greg. The green Formica table was chipped from years of wear, but no one seemed to notice. The cafeteria was big, bright, sunny, and, at this time of day, noisy. In addition to the tan cafeteria trays in front of each person, there were stacks of books on each side. At the surrounding tables, the students were busily eating and discussing their classes. At Sadie's table, they were discussing something else—the upcoming freshmen welcome party, which they learned was something of a tradition here at the college.

Putting her fork down, Sadie turned to Greg. "Are you going to the party?"

He nodded. "I'll be there. Save a dance for me," he said with a smile.

"Okay." Sadie noticed that he smiled a lot—she liked that about him.

Their conversation was interrupted by the tinny sound of the intercom. "Dr. Wilson —301. Dr. Wilson —301."

By now they had grown accustomed to the sound of the intercom paging clinic interns. Code 301 meant that a patient was waiting for you. The Chiropractic College had a busy outpatient clinic, providing adjustments for the community at reduced fees. It was a good way for the interns to gain experience, and members of the local community had the opportunity to receive affordable health care.

Dr. Jack Wilson jumped up from the table to answer the page. He was a tall, broad-shouldered man with a quick and ready smile for everyone. At 42, he had the physique of a college freshman. The silver-gray hairs at his temples were the only indication that he was one of the growing number of older students at the college for whom chiropractic would be their second profession. Sadie had heard Jack say that his first profession, banking, was an obligation and that chiropractic was his passion. Sadie felt lucky to have found her passion early on.

"He's cute," Jill said, watching him as he left the cafeteria.

Sadie had to smile. So far, Jill thought most of the guys here were cute, including some of the teachers.

Sitting there in that noisy cafeteria with her friends all around her, Sadie was happy. It was like being a part of a really large family here at the St. Louis College of Chiropractic. Her journey had begun.

CHAPTER

2

After much anticipation, the date of the freshmen welcome party had arrived. Tonight was the night.

Sadie was sitting at the kitchen table, absently rubbing her small feet back and forth across her grandmother's hooked rug as she finished her homework. She was also keeping an eye on the pot of Irish stew simmering on the big, old, gas stove.

The kitchen was Sadie's favorite room in the house. Looking up from her books, she smiled, surveying her handiwork as she recalled what those cupboards had looked like when she'd first arrived. Then, it was chipped paint and stains that had greeted her. Deciding that was one greeting she didn't want on a regular basis, she'd spent hours cleaning them and scraping off the old paint before repainting them light green, the very same shade she remembered so fondly from her grandmother's kitchen. Now that the room was so inviting, she enjoyed spending time sitting at the round, oak table, sipping tea and studying.

"Yum, that smells good." Jill walked into the kitchen and poured herself a glass of water before joining Sadie at the table.

"Thanks." Sadie smiled at the compliment. "We should be ready to eat in about ten minutes and then we can get ready for the party."

"That sounds good to me," Jill said before taking a sip of water. "What are you going to wear?"

"I'm not sure." Sadie closed her book, pushing it to the side. "I don't have anything fancy, just some nice jeans and a top."

"I know!" Jill's eyes sparkled with excitement. "I have all kinds of accessories. Give me ten minutes, honey, and I'll find just what you need to dress up your outfit."

"Thanks, Jill. That would be great." Sadie got up to check on her stew. Lifting the lid intensified the savory smell already pervading the room.

"Wow!" Jill finished her water and put her glass in the sink. "Now I'm really hungry. I'm going to have to watch out so I don't gain weight living with you," she said with a smile. "I'll go get the

jewelry and belts laid out so we can pick out just the right ones
for you."

"Okay." Sadie shook her head, smiling as Jill danced out of
the room. Jill had, up to this point, demonstrated a cavalier attitude toward her studies. She did, however, possess an amazing
talent toward the pursuit of fashion and men, in that order. She
was tall and model-thin with white-blonde, shoulder-length hair. A
native of Savannah, Georgia, she was both beautiful to look at and
beautiful to listen to, speaking in that well-modulated, graceful
Southern manner. For all their differences, the two girls were the
best of friends and both were enjoying their Victorian home.

The home was an eclectic combination of the two girls'
styles. (A sort of shabby-chic that oddly suited the older surroundings.) Hardwood floors, comprising most of the house, were
covered by Jill's faded Persian rugs. The loveseat in the living
room had been donated by Jill's older brother Mark, who had just
finished his residency in radiology at the St. Louis School of Medicine. Next to the loveseat was a tall floor lamp with a hand-
blown, tulip-shaped glass. Sadie had inherited it from her
grandmother. The rest of the living room furniture consisted of
two chairs: a French-style chair from Jill and a large, overstuffed
chair with faded moss-green velvet upholstery from Sadie—
again, a gift from her grandmother. There was also a small stereo
donated by, again, Jill's brother Mark.

As Jill searched upstairs through her endless wardrobe,
Sadie sat down at the kitchen table again. Embedding her toes in
the woolen warmth of the hooked rug, she let her mind wander to
her early childhood days at her grandmother's farm.

"Now all things bein' from this good earth have to be cared
for and respected," Elsie had lectured to her young granddaughter. At that time, eight-year-old Sadie was a small, plump child
full of life and endless questions for her grandmother.

Elsie was a big-boned, big-hearted Scottish-Irish woman
whose skin showed the handiwork of the earth's seasons.
Although Elsie looked to nature (her beloved *Mother Earth*, as
she called it) for her insight and answers, Sadie had looked
instead to her grandmother. To young Sadie, she was more powerful than the wind or rain, brighter than the sun and in some
ways even more mysterious than the moon. Elsie Shaunessy was,
quite simply, the very center around which Sadie's entire uni-
verse revolved.

Sitting there in her St. Louis kitchen might seem to be a long way from the Iowa countryside where she had spent most of her time at her grandmother's farm. But somehow the smell of the stew, the warmth of the rug, and those green cupboards brought it all closer.

"Grandma, why are your kitchen doors painted green?" she'd asked.

"Ooch, my little dearie, 'tis to remind your old grandmother of her roots and to know they're always with you no matter how far you might travel. 'Tis a comfort to me, child, to see the color of my homeland that raised and nurtured me here in the very room where I raised and nurtured my own family. There's a sense of goodness about knowing where you've been and what you're about. Don't be forgettin' it, lass."

The bubbling of her stew brought Sadie back to the present as she jumped up to stir it again. Life and her grandmother's Mother Earth had begun to treat her well. Perhaps she'd gotten her suffering out of the way early on, she thought. After most of the family money had gone to the doctors and hospitals, she'd been lucky to find a wealthy roommate.

Jill's parents owned the St. Louis home, first buying it for Mark and now keeping it for Jill. Uneasy at the thought of her living alone, they had urged her to find a roommate. Sadie's willingness to cook and clean had garnered her a rent-free home to live in. It was close to the school as well as the huge Forest Park, one of the city's centerpieces and even bigger than New York's Central Park, and the open-air market where Sadie had purchased the vegetables for the stew.

St. Louis was proving to be an amazing and exciting city. Two weeks before school started, Sadie's parents loaded up her belongings in the family van and headed for St. Louis. Jill had written to her earlier, finalizing their roommate arrangements as well as giving her directions. Her brother had moved out three months earlier, having finished his residency in May, so the home had been vacant all summer. Sadie shook her head; the memory of that first day's arrival was quite vivid.

"Oh, my!" she'd exclaimed as they were pulling into the driveway. "It looks like a real live gingerbread house!" Her heart sped up at the thought of actually living here. As soon as the van stopped, she jumped out, heading for the front door. Clutching the precious key in her hand, she felt a bit like Cinderella about to enter her castle. Turning the lock, she opened the door.

"PHEW!" What a shock. It was like being greeted by the ugly stepmother instead of the prince. Sadie wrinkled her nose. The combination of the hot, humid St. Louis weather and the three years the house had spent as a bachelor pad was all too evident. (So much for fairy tales.) Sadie's parents were now right behind her.

"It looks like we've got a bit of work to do," Katherine said. Although they hadn't stepped inside yet, Katherine's nose, just as Sadie's had, wrinkled up in protest at the smell.

"I'd better check out the basement," Thomas said, before calmly walking inside. Surprisingly, he seemed oblivious to the smell.

Turning to look at her mom, Sadie saw that she wasn't the only one who was surprised. Katherine's mouth was open as she watched her husband disappear inside the house. Apparently men are immune to strong odors, which is probably what allows them to wear sweaty gym socks with ease. Sadie started to giggle. Maybe the smell was affecting her brain. If so, it was also affecting her mom, who joined in the laughter. After a few minutes, they both had tears in their eyes—whether from their laughter or the smell, it was hard to say.

"Well, we haven't got all day," Katherine said, wiping her eyes as their laughter subsided.

"You're right," Sadie nodded. She knew that her parents could only stay away from their family-owned General Store for five days. "Let's get started."

Luckily, Sadie's mom had brought along cleaning supplies. While her dad was checking out the wiring and plumbing, Sadie and her mom started washing the windows.

After the heavy cleaning was done, it was time for the fun stuff, as Sadie called it. As they listened to the *Irish Tenors* CD, Katherine hung some of her Irish linen curtains on the kitchen windows while Sadie painted the cupboards.

When the cleaning was finished, their remaining days were spent as tourists, enjoying the sights of St. Louis. The obvious first choice was the Gateway Arch, made of stainless steel, it's the tallest monument in America at 630 feet high.

"I'm not so sure about this," Katherine had said as she squeezed into the little passenger car for a jerky, ten minute ride to the top of the Arch. She wasn't exactly afraid of heights, but she didn't enjoy them, either.

Sadie, on the other hand, was enthralled. Looking out of the windows at the top of the Arch, she could imagine her ancestors standing on top of Tara, surveying their surroundings. "It's beautiful," she whispered, looking at the city below.

Although she had admired the view from the top, Katherine was more comfortable below the Arch in the Museum of Westward Expansion.

"Would you look at that," Thomas said, pointing to the life-sized panorama of buffalos and longhorns.

Seeing the pictures of animals on the museum wall made Sadie want to see some in real life. "Let's go to the zoo next."

"All right," her father readily agreed.

They spent hours exploring the zoo. Both Thomas and Sadie loved the Big Cat Country. Ever since she was a child, Sadie had a special fondness for lions. Katherine's favorite was the large bird cage that allowed the visitors to walk inside among the birds. Sadie liked everything about the zoo, but the baby animals were always her favorite. Today, it was a baby gorilla that had caught her eye.

It wasn't until they were back inside the van that they realized how hungry they were.

"Where do you want to go eat?" Thomas asked.

"I know." Sadie leaned forward, grabbing the seat in front of her. "Let's go to the Hill. I read all about it. It was originally settled in the early 1900s by Italian immigrants. It's supposed to have some great restaurants."

"That sounds good to me," Thomas said, turning the wheel as Sadie gave him directions from the back seat.

"It's lovely," Sadie said as they entered the Old World neighborhood. Outside the quaint brick homes, people were sitting on lawn chairs, some even waving as they drove by. Sadie waved back. Children were playing on the small lawns. The tri-color of Italy's flag was represented in the green, red, and white fireplugs along the street.

The smells coming from the nearby restaurant were enough to make anyone's stomach rumble, hungry or not.

"Yum, that smells good," Sadie said as she stepped out of the van.

"It smells like sausage," Thomas said appreciatively as they walked toward the restaurant.

After their meals, Sadie decided that the Hill's glowing restaurant reviews were all true.

"That was the best pasta I've ever had," she said as they left.

"It certainly was," Katherine nodded.

The happy sounds of children playing could be heard as they walked toward the van.

"Good housing, good smells, and good food," her dad said as they drove away. Although he was a man of few words, his concise description summed it up.

Because their time was limited, they tried to see as many sites as possible. Several hours were spent walking through the Central West End admiring beautiful turn-of-the-century homes on tree-lined streets. In the midst of those gorgeous homes was an area of boutiques and sidewalk cafes, where they enjoyed a cappuccino.

One of Sadie's favorite spots was the Missouri Botanical Garden, where they walked through a beautiful Japanese garden as well as an English Woodland garden. Walking down the winding wood-chip path, Sadie thought how much her grandmother would have loved this beautiful place.

Those days spent as tourists were idyllic for Sadie and her parents. This was the first vacation they had taken in a decade. It was good to be able to go out to eat and to hear her parent's laughter. For ten long years, they had been short on laughter.

To help pay the medical bills, Sadie's mom had gone back to work at the General Store. A fine seamstress, her Irish linen and lace curtains were her specialty.

As a young woman, Katherine Shaunessy had a love of creating beautiful things. Whatever she was doing, her mother Elsie had instilled in her that the creation was the important thing. She said that you left a little bit of yourself in everything you made.

"It's just like a thumb print, only it's a wee life print," Elsie would say.

Katherine was a strong, sturdy woman with loving eyes, a generous smile, and dancing hands. She played the piano and the fiddle, painted a little, and sewed a lot. Katherine loved her sewing most of all because it was both practical and beautiful.

Her father had also put in extra hours at the store as well as working on construction projects at night and on the weekends. Thomas was six feet tall and had never weighed over 180 pounds since he had graduated from college. Tall and lanky, with corded muscles as strong as steel, he looked remarkably similar to the dashing football hero Katherine had fallen in love with. Although his business degree helped him to run the General Store, his love was not in the business aspects of the store but in the building that it allowed him. He built chairs, tables, and other furnishings his customers wanted. Anything smelling of freshly cut lumber would put a grin on his face. His hands were as gnarled as a piece of hickory, and due to their constant use, they were strong as well.

Although a very loving couple, Thomas and Katherine had grown quieter and quieter. The stress of working extra hours and worrying about money had taken its toll. (At least that's what they liked to blame it on.) Sadie knew it had more to do with the actual events of the past decade as opposed to their financial consequences. Their normally trusting and outgoing personalities had changed as their belief in doctors turned into uncertainty and doubt.

It had been hard for Sadie, watching her parents change— aging before her eyes. She hoped that in attending Chiropractic College she could help to bury the troubles of the past. She was determined to find the truth. They always said that the truth would set you free. Sadie wasn't sure who "they" were but she certainly hoped they were right.

The sound of the bubbling stew caught her attention. "Wool gathering," she said, referring to her daydreaming. "That's what grandmother always called it." Shaking her head, she smiled as she got up to turn off the stove.

CHAPTER

3

The Leather Bottle was teeming with chiropractic students by the time Sadie and Jill arrived. A Madonna song combined with the smoke to fill the air. Sadie was no fan of alcohol, having learned how drugs of any kind could alter one's personality. She did, however, love music and dancing.

Jill, too, loved to dance and right now she was in search of a partner. Shoulders back, head up, with chiropractic-perfect posture, Jill walked across the crowded bar. Her target? Jeffrey Adams, who already had a grin on his face as her blue eyes caught and held his brown eyes captive.

Sadie watched as they laughed, joking with one another. For Jill, flirting was as natural as breathing. With three older brothers, she'd learned how to relate to men at an early age. Sheltered and protected, she grew up assuming that men liked her and wanted to take care of her. This innate self-confidence, coupled with her striking beauty, had thus far served to justify her beliefs.

Mineral water in hand, Sadie stood with her back to the bar. Surveying the room, she noted that Jill and Jeffrey made a nice couple.

Jeffrey Adams was 28 years old with short-cropped, dark hair. His muscular build was maintained by a daily, hour-long weight-lifting routine.

Sadie sipped her mineral water as she recalled their first official meeting the week before school started. As a Trimester Eight student, he was Sadie's student clinician. All the freshmen had an assigned clinician. Prior to school, they were examined and x-rayed. Throughout the trimester they were adjusted according to their treatment schedule. This was the way upperclassmen gained practical experience while the freshmen received the benefits of the adjustments as well as the experience of being a patient. Doctor-patient relationship training started early here at the college.

Sadie smiled, recalling the sound of his Massachusetts accent as he was taking her health history. "I like the way you add R's onto the end of your words," she'd joked.

"I don't have an accent," he'd replied. "What about your Highland Country brogue?"

For all their laughter about accents, she still recalled how impressed she had been by his skill and thoroughness in conducting the exam. After completing all of the orthopedic and neurological tests, he'd tested the strength of her arm.

"Hold," he instructed.

She did. The muscle was strong.

Then he had her touch a spot on her abdomen; "therapy localize" was the term he'd used. As she was touching the spot, he rechecked her arm.

"Wow! I can't hold it up," she'd said in surprise. "How did you do that?"

"That's a spot for the intestines, the ileo-cecal valve," he'd explained. "The technique I'm using is called Applied Kinesiology. I've been spending extra time studying it."

Sadie was impressed. She hadn't even told him that she'd recently had some intestinal problems. Applied Kinesiology was a subject that she, too, was going to study.

Glancing to her right, she spotted the oddest couple in the center of the dance floor—Paul Santini and Cathy Muncie. He was a short, stocky, New Jersey bull of a man. She was a small, pale blonde with a whiny, breathless voice. She was still unaware that she was referred to as "Wendy Whiner" by her classmates.

Paul was at school because he wanted to be the first Italian doctor in his family. The fact that he was already having difficulties with his studies prompted much gossip as to whether it was his family's connections that had gained his admission, as opposed to his transcripts. "I'll make them an offer they can't refuse," was quoted in Brandoesque fashion as the reason he'd been accepted.

A self-proclaimed "lady-killer," he wore black shirts unbuttoned enough to reveal a heavy, gold necklace. His famous *Playboy* collection and habit of telling dirty jokes had earned him the class nickname of "Sanporno." (He was secretly pleased with this title.)

Cathy with a "C," as she was quick to point out, was a petite five foot two inches tall. Her shoulder-length blonde hair was coarse—dried out from endless colorings. She had a prominent nose and a large, pouty lower lip that had immediately pouted in

Paul's direction. They had been the class' odd-couple ever since. Her classmates ungraciously said that the only reason she had entered chiropractic college was to meet a man. Mission accomplished.

"Would you like to dance?"

The question brought Sadie back to the present moment in a hurry. Turning, she saw it was one of her classmates, Greg Stanish, who had asked.

"I'd love to!"

Greg was tall and lanky with curly brown hair and rich brown eyes. "Your eyes remind me of a Hershey bar," she'd blurted out the first time they'd met.

"And yours remind me of Loch Ness," he'd replied. That had invariably turned into references of the Loch Ness monster.

"How well do Hershey bars dance?" she joked, using their private nickname.

"Well, you little monster, I'll just have to show you, won't I?" he answered.

As they walked toward the dance floor, Sadie recalled one of their earlier conversations. "What made you decide to become a chiropractor?" she'd asked. (She didn't have the heart to tell him the full reason for her career choice.) Instead, she told him of her grandmother's decline following a stressful incident. The stress, in turn, had aggravated her arthritis, which led to the Vioxx prescription. Sadie had felt comfortable enough to share her suspicions that her grandmother's subsequent heart problems had been due to her medications.

"And you were probably right to think that. I'm sorry about your grandmother," he'd said before answering her original question. "I decided to come here after hurting my shoulder in a hockey game. A chiropractor was the only one who helped me. My dad didn't want me to see "one of those quacks," insisting I see his friend, an orthopedist, who put me on muscle relaxants. After weeks of not sleeping, I begged my mom to take me to see my friend's chiropractor. She finally did when my dad was away on a business trip."

Sadie recalled how shocked she'd been to learn that Greg's dad was the Vice President of Zena Pharmaceuticals. Greg had told her that his dad had fully expected him to become a psychiatrist and climb the Zena corporate ladder. It was then that Greg had shared his views on psychiatry with her. "I just don't buy it," he'd said. "Medicine's entire premise is that diseases are a manifestation of diseased tissue. If psychiatry is a medical specialty, then where is the diseased tissue? Psychopathological conditions are bogus," he'd said. At least you know you have a diseased lung if you're diagnosed with emphysema." Sadie agreed. "What did he say when you told him you were going to become a chiropractor?" she'd asked.

"He was really mad when I applied to Chiropractic College— even threatening to disown me. Then, it was strange; he got really nice when I started going out with Jennifer and seemed to accept my decision."

She shivered as she recalled that remark. Something about Greg's dad didn't seem quite right. Sadie's grandmother had always called her a "fey young lass" when commenting on her remarkable intuitive powers.

"Are you cold?" Greg asked, putting an arm around her.

"No," she shook her head.

"Let's dance," he said, pulling her close.

At first they seemed to be an odd pair on the dance floor, his six-foot frame dwarfing hers. Somehow her fire and spirit added the illusion of size to her frame, making the pairing work. Already the best of friends and study partners, they danced effortlessly, as if they'd known each other for years.

— • • • —

It was 2:00 a.m. Saturday morning and the girls were in their kitchen having tea. Sadie's small hands gripped the cup for warmth as she stared into space.

"What are you thinking?" Jill asked, putting her cup down.

Sadie looked up from her reverie. "All of tonight's singing and dancing made me think about something my grandmother used to say: "A penny for your thoughts; a song for your troubles." She said that communication was the solution to all the problems of the world and the more joyful the communication, the better."

Jill smiled. "I would have liked to have known her."

"Oh, Jill, she'd have loved you. I know she's looking down at me right now and she's happy for me."

"She probably is," Jill agreed naively.

Sadie smiled at her friend, wondering whether she should tell her more about her current relationship with her grandmother.

"Brrr," Jill said, searching for her teacup. "I just got a chill."

Reaching for the teapot, Sadie decided not to say anything else. Some things are better left unsaid.

CHAPTER

4

Monday morning came early for Jill as her snooze alarm went off for the second time.

"Hurry up, Jill, we've got Anatomy lab this morning," Sadie called.

"Don't remind me! The thought of that place makes me feel like I'll lose my breakfast before I've even had it." Jill groaned as she rolled out of bed.

Contrary to her protests, the air in the Anatomy lab smelled remarkably fresh considering the quantities of formaldehyde present. The modern dissecting lab was just one of the college's impressive features. The steeply sloped circle of chairs provided everyone with a good view of the center table. TV monitors throughout the room allowed the students to watch the instructor perform delicate dissections before they began performing them on their own cadavers.

A hush fell over the room. The students' eyes were riveted to the metal table.

"It gives me the creeps," Jill whispered.

CLANK!

Both girls jumped as they turned their attention to the center of the room. The cadaver had appeared. The cameras were on. Time to watch and learn, Sadie thought.

This person, the class learned, had died from congestive heart failure. The lab teacher seemed dwarfed by the amphitheater-like classroom as he delivered this bit of information.

"He looks like a mortician," Jill whispered. Sadie grinned in agreement.

Professor Cox had been dubbed "Underdog," by the upper classmen. (The nickname suited him.) "The rates of congestive heart failure have doubled over the past decade, with about 400,000 cases each year being newly diagnosed," he said as he stood quietly and began his lecture.

"Recently, we are seeing an epidemic of heart failure. I believe this is a result of the cholesterol-lowering drugs currently being taken by millions of Americans. As you know, statin drugs block the action of an enzyme that is used to produce cholesterol in the liver. As with any drug, there are also side effects. In addition to blocking the cholesterol-producing enzyme, they also block about twenty other essential biochemical pathways crucial for cardiovascular health.

"One of the most dangerous side effects of statin drugs is that they deplete the body of Coenzyme Q10. CoQ10 is important for both heart health and energy production. Low levels are associated with fatigue, accelerated aging, and many chronic diseases including heart failure. The fact that statin drugs have so many deadly side effects has been known for years. As a matter of fact, the drug companies even knew how to prevent some of them yet they did *nothing*!

That got everyone's attention.

"Patients with heart failure have decreased levels of CoQ10. It has been demonstrated that the lower the CoQ10 level, the greater the problem. One double-blind study showed that patients experienced a 40 percent drop in blood CoQ10 levels while taking statin drugs. Peter Langsjoen, M.D., a noted cardiologist, has written about this problem in *The Asia Pacific Heart Journal*."

Professor Cox quietly placed his hands on the podium before continuing. "What is the most disturbing is that the statins don't produce the beneficial results promised. This was written in the December 12, 2001, issue of the *Journal of the American Medical Association*."

As Sadie watched Professor Cox, she recalled Jill once saying that if they ever did a wax model of him, you'd have a hard time telling which was which. Sadie was inclined to agree with her. One thing was certain: No one would ever accuse him of being hyperactive. With a minimum of motion, he surveyed the class. "Can someone tell me the names of these statins?" he asked.

"Lipitor, Zocor, Mevacor, and Provachol," answered Peter Burger. Peter sat in the front row of every class. This was probably good because it prevented him from seeing the students in the back row roll their eyes every time he spoke. Even though the semester had just started, they were already annoyed by his constant need to impress the teachers.

"That's right, Peter. Some of the other side effects related to these drugs include liver toxicity, extreme muscle fatigue, weakness, and pain. Can anyone tell me some natural ways to lower your cholesterol?"

Professor Cox surveyed the raised hands, this time calling on Greg.

"People could add garlic, soy, and flaxseed to their diet. Niacin is also useful for lowering total blood cholesterol."

Professor Cox nodded to Greg before continuing. "As you may know, Merck was the pharmaceutical giant that brought the first statin drug to the market back in 1987."

Not them again, Sadie thought, gritting her teeth. Jill looked over, patting her arm for comfort.

"Three years later, Merck received two patents for Mevacor and other statin drugs with up to 1,000 mg of CoQ10 added to their formulations. According to the patent, this is 'for the avoidance of myopathy as well as the amelioration of myopathy.' As you all know, cardiomyopathy is a common cause of congestive heart failure. Merck's second patent is for a similar formulation to prevent liver damage."

"I don't get it," Paul Santini said, looking confused. "If they added the CoQ10 to the drugs in 1990, then why are we in the midst of an epidemic of heart failure?"

"Because even though the company held the patents to the combination drugs, they didn't make them available to the public. Until recently, the pharmaceutical company hasn't even educated physicians about the use of CoQ10 when utilizing statin drugs," answered Professor Cox.

"That's outrageous!" Sadie exclaimed. "The drug companies *knew* their drugs blocked CoQ10 production. Knowing this was a serious health risk; they got patents for drugs with improved formulations containing CoQ10 and *deliberately* withheld them from the public!" She shook her head in frustration. "By holding the patents, didn't they prevent other pharmaceutical companies from developing improved drugs as well?"

"I'm afraid that is true," said Professor Cox sadly.

"And they call us *quacks*!" exclaimed Paul. For once the entire class thought he'd said something intelligent.

"Merck is having some problems of its own right now," Professor Cox informed the class. "I just heard that there was a settlement in the first Vioxx lawsuit. The jury awarded the plaintiff over $250 million dollars."

"Wow!" Paul's jaw dropped at the mention of so much money.

"Good!" Sadie said, hoping that would make drug companies more careful in the future.

Evidently the rest of the class felt the same way. The professor known as Underdog had their full attention and respect.

Jill touched Sadie's arm. She looked over, reading the two words Jill had written in her notebook. PRODUCT LIABILITY. Sadie nodded in agreement.

"Now let's get back to the dissection of the heart." As he dissected, Professor Cox continued to ask questions. "What are some other contributors to heart failure?"

"Diabetes, hypertension, smoking, obesity, and inactivity," said Greg.

Professor Cox continued the routine of asking questions as he performed the dissections. "What vitamin deficiency has been linked to heart failure?"

Peter Burger answered, "Vitamin D deficiency has been found by German researchers to be linked to heart failure, probably due to its role in regulating calcium."

Sadie didn't hear the rest of the lecture; her mind was still reeling with the news of the lawsuit. Not only had the drug companies caused her grandmother's death, they were causing numerous fatalities *every single day*—all in the name of profit.

Although the rest of the lab was interesting, the hot topic for the rest of the day was the conspiracy of the pharmaceutical giant. That, and product liability. Lying to the public to protect profit margins troubled even the most jaded students within the class.

CHAPTER

5

Sunlight filtered through a canopy of red and yellow leaves. Sadie was fascinated by the interplay of lights and colors—nature's very own kaleidoscope. The crisp air carried with it the woodsy smell of leaves. Breathing deeply, Sadie smiled, relishing the sights and smells of fall. She often spent her lunch hours here on this very bench, nestled in the school's park-like setting. One hundred manicured acres in the suburbs made the St. Louis Chiropractic College one of the most beautiful in the nation.

HONK. HONK. HONK.

Sadie looked up from her reading to watch the geese: A perfect V-formation passing through a nearly cloudless sky. Her grandmother would have loved it here, she thought. She'd often said that the colors of the autumn landscape reminded her of a patchwork quilt. Pumpkin carving and canning preserves had filled her weekend visits with her grandmother. So vivid was her memory that she could actually smell the cinnamon and spice that had been ever-present in her grandmother's kitchen.

"There you are!" Greg said, before sitting beside her on the park bench.

"Hi, Greg." Sadie moved her books to give him more room. "Are you going to the Halloween dance?"

"No." Greg shook his head. "Jennifer wants to go to the movies instead. She said she doesn't know anyone here and she feels left out at all the school functions."

Sadie thought that if Jennifer made an effort to be nice she might enjoy herself more. As a child, Sadie had been told often enough that if you can't say something nice about a person, then don't say anything at all. Calling upon that early wisdom, she managed to keep this thought to herself. For weeks she'd been hearing "Jennifer Stories" and it was really starting to bother her. In an effort to please her, Greg was now working at a local restaurant, earning extra money to allow him to take her to all the places she preferred. The stress of work and studies as well as trying to keep Jennifer happy was starting to show. Greg had dark circles under his eyes. Normally cheerful and outgoing, he now seemed tense and preoccupied. She missed his easy laughter.

Sadie knew that Jennifer's family and the Stanishes were friends. Both men worked for Zena Pharmaceuticals. Jennifer's brother was in medical school studying to be a psychiatrist. *Everything Greg's father could want.* She didn't like it. If Greg had been struck by Cupid's arrow, who pulled the string? Her bet was on Greg's dad.

CRUNCH. CRUNCH. The sound of leaves crunching and rustling underfoot interrupted her thoughts. It was Jill, walking through the lane toward them.

"Hi, guys."

"Hi," Sadie and Greg replied in unison.

Looking at his watch, Greg stood up. "I'd better go," he said. "I've got to call Jennifer before class." Cell reception was never good under the trees in the knoll.

Sadie sighed as she watched him retreat through the tree-lined path.

"You know, you should be dating him, not Jennifer," Jill stated matter-of-factly. "He doesn't love her; he just thinks he does."

Sadie may have been the "fey one" but she was amazed by her friend's insight. She'd been thinking the same thing herself. "I'm worried that he's dating her to please his father," she said, sharing her concerns with Jill.

"I think you're right," Jill agreed. "Mark knows Jennifer's brother; he said he doesn't really like him. There is something about that family . . . " she said, shaking her head. "The problem is—that girl has him wrapped around her little finger." She pulled an apple from her Gucci purse and took a bite before continuing. "Mark said that she was engaged to a guy in his class. I guess she worked to help him through school. As soon as graduation was in sight, he dumped her."

"What a jerk!"

"I know," Jill nodded. "Mark said the guy even bragged about using her to get through medical school. He called her his 'wifey meal ticket.' Anyway, she hooked up with Greg right after that."

"I didn't know that," Sadie said, shaking her head. Even though she didn't have the highest regard for Jennifer, no one deserved to be treated like that.

"I'm telling you, Sadie," Jill said, waving her apple for emphasis, " you two are perfect for each other."

"Tell that to Greg," Sadie said, only half jokingly.

"Sadie, girl, we are going to make him see the light!" Jill's sky-blue eyes sparkled with determination.

"Now you sound like a preacher," Sadie joked.

Jill grinned.

"I don't know, Jill. I mean, we're just friends—really!" (This was said in an effort to convince Jill as well as herself.) *"Really!"* she added for emphasis. Sadie didn't know Greg's parents, but she did know that she wasn't the type of person they'd approve of for their son. *I can't believe I'm actually considering this.* "Jill, really, we're just friends!" *There, that ought to quiet those thoughts.* Her heart felt all fluttery. After her recent work in the lab dissecting the heart, she wasn't sure whether she was ready to start examining her own too closely.

"Sure you are," Jill said knowingly, arching her eyebrows as she looked at Sadie. "You can keep telling yourself that, but I see the way you look at him. I see the way he looks at you, too. I know!" she said, jumping to her feet. "How about the Halloween dance?"

Sadie didn't have a chance to interrupt as Jill continued formulating her plan.

"Maybe we could get him to take you. I could put you in a really cute costume . . . " She looked at Sadie appraisingly. "Believe me, if you let me dress you, he'll wonder why he ever looked twice at Jennifer." Jill was warming to her subject now. There was a definite gleam in her eyes.

Sadie recognized that look. Reaching out, she grabbed her hand. "Jill, I don't want to confuse him; besides, he's already planning to take Jennifer to the movies." Actually, Sadie was the one who was confused. Choosing to ignore that fact, she continued, "He's my friend. I don't want to do anything that would jeopardize our friendship. Sure, I think about more of a relationship, but I don't know if he does."

"He would if you let him."

"I just don't want to mess up the best relationship I've ever had with a guy before. It would kill me to lose his trust."

"You *are* in love with him!"

Sadie looked down for a moment. "Please, Jill," she begged.

"All right. I won't do anything to tip the scales in your favor although I know it's for your own good. His, too! You'd both be better off together. Instead, he's killing himself trying to make her happy, and you're spending every weekend with your books." Frowning, Jill shook her head.

CRUNCH. CRUNCH.

"Shush, here he comes," Sadie whispered hurriedly.

Deep in thought, Greg wound his way slowly down the path.

"What's bothering you?" Jill asked bluntly.

"Jennifer is going out of town. She canceled our date."

"Well then, you can go to the Halloween dance." Ignoring her earlier promise, Jill decided not to ignore the hand of fate. "Jeff and I will go with the two of you. It will be fun."

So much for renting *Dead Poet's Society*, Sadie thought. It was obvious that Jill already knew the meaning of *carpe diem*.

THUMP. THUMP. THUMP. Her heart beat faster at this turn of events. *I wonder if they can hear it?* Taking a deep breath, she hoped to quiet the pounding. THUMP, THUMP, THUMP. *And the beat goes on.* Now she had a pounding heart *and* a Sonny and Cher song to contend with. Opting for plan B, she decided to ignore them both.

"Okay," she said as calmly as possible.

"Now, we've got to figure out what we are going to wear," Jill said.

Sadie was glad that Jill was back to her favorite subject— fashion. It took the heat off of herself.

Jill eyed Greg appraisingly. "I know! You can be Captain Pelvis. We'll put the plastic pelvis upside down on your head; it will make a great mask. All we need is a cape with a big 'P' on it and you're set!"

"HA!" Greg threw back his head and laughed. "Great idea, Jill. Captain Pelvis it is."

BUZZ. BUZZ. BUZZ. The sound of the bell put an end to the costume planning.

"It's time for class." Greg grabbed Sadie's books as they headed back inside. Jill walked behind them. Luckily, Sadie missed seeing the gleam in her eyes as she watched the two of them.

CHAPTER

6

Sadie had to admit it—Jill looked good as a witch. Her white-blonde hair gleamed against the jet black of her costume. Standing in front of a full-length mirror, lips puckered, she was applying crimson lipstick as Sadie entered her room.

"You look great," Jill said, deftly applying her lipstick at the same time.

"How do you do that?" Sadie asked. "It takes all my concentration to get that stuff on. There is no way I could actually *talk* at the same time. I'm impressed."

"It's just practice, that's all." Jill smiled before turning to face Sadie. "Do you think Jeff will like it?" she asked anxiously.

"Definitely!" Sadie nodded. "How are things going with you two, anyway?"

"Well . . . " Jill paused, trying to sound nonchalant. "We're keeping it casual."

"Really?" Sadie was skeptical.

"Oh, Sadie, I really do like him. He's the first guy who makes my throat go dry when I talk to him. At first it was easy—I was just flirting. Now that I know him, it's different. I'm worried that he'll graduate soon and we'll still be here at school. I wish I knew how he felt about the two of us." Her words rushed out in a tide of emotions.

"Jill, I'm sure he likes you!" Sadie said loyally. The more Sadie had gotten to know her roommate, the more impressed she'd become. Jill had started out with a "fashion first" mentality. School had changed her. The more she learned about chiropractic, the more dedicated she'd become. Sadie thought that Jeff's influence was also responsible for the changes she'd noticed in her friend.

"Thanks, Sadie." Jill said, walking over to her. "Let's get you fixed up. You're going to knock the socks off Greg tonight!"

Peering into the mirror, Sadie turned from side to side. "Are you sure this Grecian Goddess thing isn't a bit much?"

"Nonsense," Jill said, with a firm shake of her head. "When it comes to knocking a man's socks off, there is no such thing as too much." Jill grabbed a brush. "All we have to do is finish your hair and make up; the rest is perfect."

Sadie wasn't fully aware of the truth of Jill's words. She did look perfect. The white tunic dress showed off her curves while the gold belt emphasized her tiny waist. Thanks to Jill's magic touches with her brush and bobby pins, Sadie's hair was now a cascade of red curls. Soft, wispy tendrils framed her face.

"There!" Jill said with a smile. "Now you're ready to make an entrance."

KNOCK. KNOCK. KNOCK.

"They're here!" the girls said in unison.

Suddenly nervous, Sadie smoothed an imaginary wrinkle from her dress. In that moment, she recalled something her grandmother used to say: "Time's a-wastin', dearie. There's too much life ahead of ya to be draggin' your heels." With newfound confidence, Sadie marched to the front door. "Here we go, Grandma," she said as the door swung open.

"HA!" Sadie's surprised laughter greeted Greg. "I knew you were going to be Captain Pelvis. I just didn't realize how funny it would be." Shaking her head, she continued staring at his costume.

"Hasn't anyone ever told you that it's not polite to stare? Besides, you're hurting my super-hero feelings," Greg said with a grin.

"Come in." Sadie said, glad that her brief bout of nervousness was over. All the earlier tension was forgotten.

Captain Pelvis was followed by Batman—Jeff's chosen costume for the evening.

"It looks like we're being escorted by two caped crusaders," Sadie joked.

"I told him there was no way that I'd dress up like Robin," Jill said as she headed out the door.

Sadie laughed as she followed her friend, completely missing Greg's look of surprise. His wide-eyed wonder may have been hidden behind a plastic pelvis, but one thing was certain—he was definitely impressed.

Inside, the auditorium had been transformed into a Halloween fantasy. Mr. Bones, the skeleton from the anatomy lab, was now reclining in a coffin near the entrance. Trees covered in cobwebs and twinkle-lights illuminated the corners of the room. A container of dry ice was already creating a dense fog. The crepe-paper cut-outs hanging in the windows seemed to curl up as the eerie shroud of mist crept across the dance floor. Overhead, the ceiling now resembled the night sky.

"It looks like a scene from *Harry Potter!*" Sadie said, still gazing at the Milky Way.

"It does," Greg nodded.

Jack-o'-lanterns covered the tables of food and refreshments lining the east wall. Hundreds of bats circled overhead. The rest of the auditorium was left open, serving as the dance floor. Sadie noticed that several of their friends were already dancing.

"Oh, my, look at that!" Sadie pointed to dozens of upperclassmen who had dressed up as sperm. Currently they were swarming around Cathy Muncie. "Paul doesn't look too happy."

"I'll bet he wished he'd thought of that as a costume instead of coming as the Godfather," Jill said.

As usual, Cathy and Paul drew attention. She was dressed in a form-fitting cat suit and she was purring at the attentive sperm that were flocking around her. It was hard to know where to look—there was so much activity. Swarming sperm, dancing ghosts, and goblins . . . Sadie was struggling to take in all of the sights.

"Hey, look over there!" Greg pointed to their teachers. Dr. Hamilton was dressed as Dracula. He was drinking V-8 juice and talking to the best-dressed professor of the evening—Underdog! Professor Cox, whom everyone had dubbed Underdog, had actually chosen that character as his costume.

"I guess he's aware of his nickname," Sadie remarked.

"He is," Jeff said. "A guy from our class told him at the end of our freshman year."

"Priceless!" Jill said as she looked approvingly at her professors.

"Would you look at that!" Greg shook his head as he pointed out their classmate, Peter Burger. "Is he even wearing a costume?" Peter, the annoying class know-it-all, had come as a radiologist. He wore a long, white lab coat over his suit and was carrying an 8-x-10 cervical x-ray.

"He definitely went all out," Jill observed dryly.

"HA!" Jeff laughed when the next song started. It created quite an outburst within the auditorium. Not only were the sperm swarming around Cathy, they were writhing on the floor as well. Paul was scowling at them as he stood nearby.

"He looks like he'd like to fit them all with concrete slippers and drop them in the river." Greg started laughing as he continued watching them. Their frenzied activity increased as the song lyrics got to "a little bit louder now."

Sadie, too, was laughing. Initially the students had cleared the dance floor as they watched the sperm's antics. Now, as the song cried out "shout," the students did—shouting as they all stepped onto the dance floor. Sadie and Greg joined in the action. She waved to Jill, who was holding on to the brim of her hat as she was whisked away by the caped crusader.

A slow song finally mellowed out the sperm. Greg pulled Sadie close as they started to dance. Their bodies molded together as one. Staring into each other's eyes, they circled the dance floor, moving effortlessly to the music. As the dance continued, Sadie was beginning to think that Jill's Grecian Goddess scheme had some merit. She could feel the heat of Greg's muscles; it felt as though she were melting into his arms when . . . BUZZ. Greg looked down, reaching for his cell phone.

"I've got to take this. I promised Jennifer that I'd take my cell phone with me," Greg apologized as he walked toward the hallway in search of a quieter place to talk.

"Damn!" Sadie muttered to herself as she stood all alone on the dance floor. Even the sperm avoided her. "Well, Grandma," she asked, "what do you think now?" Elsie's' ever-present voice, however, was strangely silent. "Never mind." Sadie shook her head. "I already know what you'd say—I'm beholden to no man." Squaring her Grecian Goddess shoulders, she headed for the refreshments.

That is where Greg found her when he returned. Watching him approach, Sadie felt the pit of her stomach drop. Then she felt something else—the cold chill that preceded one of Elsie's visits.

"Ooch, dearie," Elsie said, "there's no such thing as a pit in your stomach—you know that."

"Very funny, Grandma." Sadie whispered. "Where were you a few minutes ago?"

"Come on now, girlie. You're beholden' to no man," Elsie said before leaving.

"I know that already." Sadie rolled her eyes. Still, the exchange—as exasperating as it was—managed to put a smile on her face.

"I'm so sorry, Sadie. I've got to go," Greg said. "It's Jennifer; part of her trip was cancelled so she's coming home early. I have to go pick her up at the airport." Greg looked down at her. Sadie thought his eyes looked sad, but she wasn't sure whether the plastic pelvis was playing tricks on her.

"That's okay, Greg," she said, placing her hand on his arm. "There are lots of people here to dance with. Go on and get Jennifer."

"Thanks." Greg gave her a brief hug before turning and walking out of the auditorium.

Sadie felt that her heart wanted to follow him. With an effort, she tugged it back where it belonged. I just want him to be happy and I don't want to do anything to jeopardize our friendship, she thought resolutely. With that decided, she turned, rejoining the party.

— • • —

Later that evening, Sadie sat alone in her kitchen, sipping tea. She idly ran one hand over the oak table, caressing it. Then, with both hands capturing the warmth of her mug, she looked around her. The candles on the table illuminated the light-green cupboards. Flickering shadows were dancing across her mother's Irish lace curtains. With her grandmother's hooked rug below her, she felt the presence of her family all around her. She smiled when the chill hit her.

"I'm glad you're likin' me old rug," Elsie said approvingly.

"I do." Sadie nodded.

"Concentrate on your blessings, dearie," her grandmother instructed. "To be sure there will be sorrows and troubles, but don't you be lettin' them take ya down. We're survivors, aye, and dreamers, too. No dreams of the future can be fashioned strictly from the sorrows of the past. Look ahead, lassie. Look ahead and live."

"That's easy for you to say."

"Ooch, now you're jokin' with me and that's a fine thing," Elsie said as she continued her spiritual pep talk. "To be sure, there are winters of the heart, but for every winter comes a spring. The only place to live is in the present, dearie. In the present—while you're creatin' your future."

"You're right," Sadie agreed, taking another sip of her tea.

"Of course I am, lassie. Now you jump in there and play the game of life. No spectator sittin' on the sideline a-mopin' can create

a future. No, that takes livin'—powerful livin'. In the end it does-
n't matter if your heart was broken or your body was tired. What
matters is—did ya live? Did ya play the game of life?"

"You're right, Grandma." Sadie was grateful for this insider
information.

"Now don't ya be disappointin' me, girlie," Elsie said before
leaving.

Sadie sat there, thinking about her grandmother's words.
She smiled as she finished her tea.

— • • • —

It was in the kitchen where Jill found Sadie the next morning. A
pot of Irish oatmeal was simmering on the stove. The smells of
coffee and cinnamon filled the air.

"I can't believe you're making breakfast! Oh, honey, I'm so
sorry. I feel like it's all my fault." Jill gave Sadie a big hug.

"It's okay, Jill. I'm fine. Really!"

"Really?" Jill was now holding her hands as she stood there,
searching for the truth.

"Well, I'm going to be fine, Sadie amended. "I had a long talk
with my grandmother. She helped me put things into perspective."

Jill looked at her searchingly for another moment. Satisfied,
she dropped Sadie's hands.

Hands free, Sadie stirred the oatmeal. She was glad that
she'd recently explained Elsie's visits; it helped to have one less
thing to explain this morning.

"I don't understand this Celtic thing you have going on but
it sure seems to be working for you. You really *do* look okay," Jill
said with some astonishment. "What did she have to say?"

"She told me that in order to survive I had to live, so that's
what I'm doing—living! Here, have some oatmeal," she said,
spooning the thick oatmeal into a blue ceramic bowl.

"Live?" Jill laughed. "That's quite a thing for a dead grandmother to say."

Sadie started giggling. When you put it that way, it *did*
sound funny.

Somewhere in the heavens, Elsie smiled at the sound of
their laughter.

CHAPTER

7

Dr. Hamilton's philosophy class gave Sadie something besides the Greg and Jennifer saga to think about. They had already learned the early history of the chiropractic professions. Apparently, a janitor named Harvey Lillard had been working in a cramped area when he felt something give in his back. Immediately thereafter he was deaf. Early accounts said that he could neither hear the sounds of the wagons on the street nor the ticking of a timepiece. Dr. D.D. Palmer, the founder of chiropractic, examined him—finding a vertebra out of place. After giving Mr. Lillard a specific adjustment in September of 1895, his hearing was restored to normal.

"Wouldn't it be great if they could do a 'reverse-adjustment' when Cathy starts whining?" Jill had said. "That way, we wouldn't have to listen to her."

Sadie recalled biting her lip to keep from laughing out loud in class. As she thought about it, there *were* times when a "reverse-adjustment" (temporary, of course) would come in handy.

Today, Dr. Hamilton was departing from his recent historical lectures, choosing to focus on children instead.

"I still visualize him as Dracula," Jill whispered to Sadie as Dr. Hamilton began his lecture. Sadie smiled—it *had* been quite a costume.

"Did you know that in 1993 the most frequent diagnosis for emergency room visits was not heart attacks or gunshot wounds? It was for otitis media—earaches. Although this continues to plague children, parents are finally starting to be informed about the risks associated with the overuse of antibiotics. Since the local news featured another segment on ear infections last night, I decided that today's lecture would focus on the philosophy of chiropractic care for children. First of all, what causes an earache?"

"Swelling of the tissues that line the middle ear, which prevents the normal drainage of the Eustachian tube," answered Becky Holter. "The congestion causes pressure on the eardrum, which can be very painful."

Becky was from Edgar, Wisconsin, where her family owned a 300-acre dairy farm. When Paul Santini had learned that she had been once named Alice in Dairyland, he laughed, referring to her has "Miss Milk Queen" or "that cow lady."

Alice in Dairyland, a one-year, full-time contract position with the Wisconsin Department of Agriculture, is one of Wisconsin's most recognizable spokespersons. Since its inception in 1948, the women who have won this prestigious title have traveled nationwide to promote not only the dairy industry so prevalent in Wisconsin, but all of the other agricultural products generated within the state such as cranberries and honey. Crowned in the month of May, Alice starts her reign by kicking off the popular June Dairy Month events.

Paul was known to say, albeit grudgingly, that "the only good thing to come out of Wisconsin was the Green Bay Packers."

Becky was a 5-foot, 4-inch, blue-eyed blonde who looked as though she had stepped right out of a Norman Rockwell painting.

"You must have a perpetual milk moustache," Cathy Muncie had said on their initial meeting.

Becky was very interested in working with children and babies. She had told the girls that she intended to pursue a Diplomate status in Pediatrics after graduation.

"Wow! That's more than 300 additional hours of study, isn't it?" Sadie had been impressed when Becky had mentioned her plans.

"Yes, but it's worth it," Becky had replied.

Now, whenever the subject of babies or children came up, Becky's hand was in the air even faster than Peter Burger's.

"Who can tell me what the studies show regarding the use of antibiotics to treat ear infections?" Dr. Hamilton asked.

Peter won the hand-raising race this time.

"*The Journal of the American Medical Association* published a study showing that children who were treated with amoxicillin for chronic earaches experienced two to six times the rate of recurrence as compared to children receiving a placebo."

"Thank you, Peter." Dr. Hamilton began pacing in front of the podium. "Unfortunately, in a review of antibiotic therapy for acute otitis media, poor evidence was found to support the use of antibiotics for children under two years of age."

Dr. Hamilton stopped in front of the podium, surveying the class. "Can anyone give me some reasons, physical and neurological, why some children could be predisposed to ear infections?"

"Birth trauma," Becky answered. "The forces of 90 to 120 pounds of pressure exerted on the spine can affect the nervous system. According to Dr. Viola Frymann's research, approximately 90 percent of all infants show some biomechanical stress from birth."

In an effort not to be out done by the "milk queen," Peter shot his hand into the air. "According to Dr. Gutmann, blocked nerve impulses resulting from subluxations in the upper cervical region contribute to many clinical conditions." (This pronouncement was followed by the usual eye rolling from the back row.)

"Very good, Peter." Dr. Hamilton walked to the blackboard and wrote a name, "Patricia C. Brennan, Ph.D.," before continuing. "As you may know, chiropractic adjustments have been shown to improve immune functions. According to Dr. Brennan's research, the activity of two types of white blood cells can be enhanced using spinal manipulation. With this enhanced function, these white blood cells are more efficient at killing harmful bacteria."

The sounds of pens on paper as the students took notes now accompanied Dr. Hamilton's lecture.

"Recently, a study was published in the *Journal of Clinical Chiropractic Pediatrics* concerning the role of chiropractic care for children with otitis media. Of the 332 children who participated, their condition was resolved in an average of five office visits."

Sadie looked over to her left. Jill was drawing a picture of a smiling baby receiving an adjustment. Jill's love of drawing made her think of how much Katie had loved to draw. With an effort, she returned her attention to Dr. Hamilton.

"Antibiotic use sets off a vicious cycle by encouraging the overgrowth of a common yeast, *Candida albicans*. *Candida* creates toxins that weakens the immune system and irritates the nervous system, causing a whole host of symptoms as well as predisposing the child to developing food allergies and hyperactive behavior. Nearly 90 percent of hyperactive children studied had a history of three or more ear infections. If we have enough time, I'll cover one of the research scandals regarding antibiotics at the end of class." Dr. Hamilton paused a moment, rubbing his chin as he recalled the tainted research study. Then, with a brisk shake of his head, he resumed lecturing.

"First, I want to follow up on this link between early antibiotic use and hyperactivity. The United States consumes 90 percent of the world's supply of Ritalin. This makes one wonder if it's only American children who are suffering from a 'Ritalin deficiency'? Believe me, it's not just chiropractors who are alarmed by this trend. Stanley Turecki, M.D., has also said that Ritalin is overprescribed. Stimulant medication prescriptions have shown a 250 percent increase, just within the last few years!" Dr. Hamilton was so obviously irritated by this subject that he was once again beginning to resemble his Dracula character.

"This huge increase corresponds to the fact that in 1980 the American Psychiatric Association gave the label ADHD to a group of subjective childhood symptoms. These included fidgeting, talking excessively, and difficulty waiting their turn . . . ."

"That's outrageous! Those things aren't symptoms of disease," Sadie said, shaking her head. "They are normal childhood behaviors!"

"That's right, Sadie, and it's exactly the same thing that Dr. Julian Whitaker has said. As a matter of fact, the Citizen's Commission on Human Rights has been working for quite a while now to inform the public of these facts."

Sadie wrote down the letters "CCHR" in her notebook. She put a star next to them with the notation, "check on Web site."

Dr. Hamilton continued, "One of the only long-term studies of the effects of drug therapy for ADHD, the *Satterfield Study*, found that 43 percent of the boys followed were later arrested for felony crimes. The study also found juvenile delinquency rates to be 10 to 20 times greater within this group as well."

"How could psychiatrists know about the harmful effects of these drugs and keep right on prescribing them?" Sadie asked. Her earlier distrust of psychiatrists was growing stronger.

"That's a very good question, Sadie," said Dr. Hamilton. "Far too many research studies are either tainted or hidden from the public. It will be up to each of you to educate your patients so they can make informed decisions regarding their health. Let's suppose you have a patient who does not want his or her child on stimulants. What would you suggest as natural alternatives?"

Peter's hand shot into the air. "You could tell her not to give her child sugar because according to a study in the *Journal of Pediatrics*, it's linked to overly aggressive behavior. The study also showed a 10-times increase in adrenaline levels in children who consumed sugar, resulting in difficulty concentrating, irritability, and anxiety."

Jill leaned over closer to Sadie, "Where does he get all this information?"

"I'm not sure." Sadie shook her head. "He's like a walking encyclopedia."

Jill immediately started drawing an encyclopedia. Sadie watched as she drew lips, legs, and then began drawing a long, white lab coat. Sadie smiled. Paul Santini's comment turned her attention back to class.

"So you're saying that you just clean up a kid's diet—eliminate sugar, soft drinks, and junk food—and that will help?" Paul had a habit of summing up Peter's research studies. He was demonstrating a remarkable aptitude for bringing Peter's lofty proclamations down to their simplest form. For this, the class was grateful, especially the back row, who could be seen grinning each time he successfully took the wind out of Peter's sails.

"That's true, Paul. As a matter of fact, since the Feingold study on nutritional management for hyperactivity came out in 1973, the AMA has known that hyperactive patients improved by dietary changes alone. Who can give me some more nutritional recommendations for children labeled with ADHD?"

"You should supplement with omega-3 fatty acids," Becky answered.

Sadie raised her hand. "Zinc should be supplemented because zinc levels in children with ADHD have been found to be significantly decreased."

Sadie was in a nutrition and AK study group, led by her clinician, Jeffrey Adams. Jill, too, was in her study group. Sadie wasn't sure whether Jill was a part of this group because she was interested in these subjects, or Jeff. Whatever the reason, the study group was having a big impact on both girls.

Jill was the next one to raise her hand and give an answer. "Magnesium, calcium, and B-6 help reduce nervous system irritability."

"A 1979 study found that B-6 was found to be more effective than Ritalin," Becky added.

"I don't get it," Paul said, shaking his head in disbelief. His heavy gold chain shook in protest. "Why don't the kids just get adjusted, take vitamins, and eat a good diet? Why do we even have a Ritalin problem? Some of the studies you mentioned are really old. Doesn't anyone read them?"

Wow! The class's impression of Paul Santini shifted. Maybe he was smarter than they thought.

The class was nearly over and the tainted research story had yet to be told. A long, thin-arm rose in the air. "Dr. Hamilton, you mentioned antibiotic research scandals earlier. Do you have time to tell us about that?" asked Ellen Rivers.

Ellen was 5 feet 10 inches tall and very slender. Everything about her was long and thin. She'd been dubbed "horse-face" by some members of the back row. An accomplished equestrian, she *did* have a slight resemblance to the animals she loved so well. She had long, thin brown hair and lively brown eyes. Her parents owned a farm in Troy, Missouri.

In addition to studying regular human chiropractic, Ellen wanted to get certification for giving chiropractic adjustments to animals. She had told the girls earlier that one of the main reasons she'd enrolled in Chiropractic College was so that she could later become certified by the *American Veterinary Chiropractic Association.*

Ellen's love of animals was already legendary. During the first week of school, she had told them about her golden retriever, who had become paralyzed in his hind legs. One veterinarian suggested putting him to sleep, while another suggested chiropractic. After only a few adjustments, Andy, her beloved golden retriever, was walking again. In that moment, Ellen's career path had been chosen.

"Thanks for reminding me, Ellen." Dr. Hamilton leaned against a table in the front of the room. "Back in 1986, two scientific studies were forwarded to the *New England Journal of Medicine.* Both were concerning the use of antibiotics for the treatment of ear infections and both were based on the same set of data, but that is where the similarities end. One study, written by a doctor whose lab received $1.6 million from pharmaceutical companies, found the drug amoxicillin to be effective. The second paper, written by a researcher receiving no money from the pharmaceutical giants, did not find any drug to be effective. Which one do you think got published?"

"The first one," Greg answered.

"Exactly." Dr. Hamilton nodded. "Let me tell you the background story," he said as he leaned forward on the podium.

The class leaned forward, too. Even the back row didn't seem as slouched as usual.

"Well, in 1980, Dr. Charles Bluestone set up an Otitis Media Research Center at the Children's Hospital in Pittsburgh. He appointed Erdem Cantekin to be his research director. Cantekin, a biomedical engineer, was a full, tenured professor in the

Department of Otolaryngology at the University of Pittsburgh Medical School. The two began working on a federally funded study of treatment options for otitis media. In 1983, Cantekin voiced his ethical concerns to his department chairman, more specifically his concerns about mixing public and private financing. He was uncomfortable doing studies whose funding came from pharmaceutical companies trying to promote their drugs. Cantekin decided not to participate in any more clinical studies funded by pharmaceutical companies, but he did continue his work on the federally funded project. The clinical trial had over 1,000 subjects enrolled. Halfway through the study, however, it was stopped with the claim the drug's efficacy had already been proven."

"What happened to Cantekin's research?" Sadie asked.

"Cantekin submitted his paper to the *Journal of the American Medical Association*. Initially, they agreed to publish it, but something happened."

"What?" Paul asked.

"Apparently the academic bureaucracy got nervous. In an attempt to retain the goodwill of the pharmaceutical companies, they began publicly demoting Cantekin."

"Why were they so concerned about the pharmaceutical companies?" Paul asked as he leaned forward with his elbows on his desk, thoroughly caught up in the study.

"They were concerned because during a five-year period, they had received over $3.5 million in grants from the pharmaceutical companies."

"If they were so worried, why didn't they fire him?" Paul asked. (This was the most interaction Paul had shown during class.)

"They couldn't fire him because he had full tenure. Instead, his office was moved from the hospital to the attic of a local supermarket. All of the computer data from the study mysteriously disappeared."

"Did his research ever get published?" Greg asked. (Paul wasn't the only one wrapped up in the story.)

"Yes, it did. Five years after he had initially submitted his paper, it finally appeared in the *Journal of American Medical Association*. That issue of *JAMA* also contained an editorial entitled *The Cantekin Affair*, looking for outlets for whistle-blowers such as Cantekin within the scientific community.

"Ironically, in 1990 there was a huge study conducted by an international group of researchers with nearly 4,000 participants. The results of their study were consistent with Cantekin's earlier research findings, which showed that the drug was not effective."

For once, even Paul Santini was speechless.

CHAPTER

8

Sadie was in her room, packing her suitcase. "I can't believe it's Thanksgiving already," she said to herself as she placed a carefully folded sweater on top of her jeans. Ellen had invited them to spend the holiday with her family. Becky Holter would be there as well. They had decided to return home on Saturday in order to study. This trimester would soon be ending, and the prospect of finals had already begun to dictate their activities.

"Are you almost ready?" she asked, calling out to Jill, who was in her bedroom next door.

"Not quite," Jill answered. "I'm wondering what to wear to a farm—most of my clothes are city clothes."

Sadie shook her head and smiled. "I'll come help you."

Finally packed, they put their suitcases in the back of Jill's car and began their journey to Ellen's farm in Troy. The morning air was crisp. They could still see their breath as the car warmed up. Although the skies were gray, no snow was predicted. It was a perfect day to travel.

"I'm glad we have some time together," Jill said turning the wheel as she merged onto the interstate. "It seems like we've been so busy lately that we haven't had time for a nice long talk. So . . . what's up with Greg?"

Sadie frowned. "I'm worried about him, Jill. Just the other day, he got a call from Jennifer and had to rush off. I ended up finishing his part of the dissection myself. He is even missing some of his hockey practices."

"He really is running on a short leash," Jill remarked. "He's trying to keep up with his studies, work, and keep Jennifer happy. That's a lot to deal with. I know he doesn't want to let you down either, Sadie. He's so busy running in circles lately that he's in danger of losing sight of things that really matter."

"You're starting to sound like my grandmother!" Sadie looked over and smiled at her friend.

"Ha!" Jill laughed. "Maybe your Celtic stuff is rubbing off on me."

"Maybe." Sadie looked out of the window. Unaware of the scenery rolling by, she stared straight ahead, deep in thought.

"What?" Jill asked, breaking the silence.

"I'm not sure, Jill. It's just an odd feeling I have . . . "

"A sick feeling or a premonition feeling?" Jill asked.

Sadie smiled. "I guess you'd call it a premonition feeling. It's something about Greg's dad. Greg doesn't talk about him a lot, but when he does . . . " Sadie paused, searching for the right words.

"Does it make your hair stand on end? Give you goose bumps? Anything like that?"

Smiling at Jill's rapid-fire questions, Sadie nodded. "Something like that," she answered.

"Well, it's got to be weird for Greg having a dad who's the Vice President of Zena Pharmaceuticals. That alone would certainly be enough to make my hair stand on end."

"I know," Sadie nodded. "There's something about that company that I just don't like. I did some research."

"What did you find?" Jill asked as she turned off the interstate onto a two-lane highway.

"They have a history of dealing in deadly drugs. Sadie frowned, shaking her head slightly before continuing. "Did you know that in the early 1900s, Zena produced cough medicine laced with heroine?"

"What?" Jill gasped. Wide-eyed, she glanced over at Sadie before turning her attention back to the highway. "You're kidding me!" she said, still stunned by the news.

"Oh, that's not all," Sadie said, shaking her head. "I found out that in 1945 a research chemist went over to Germany to tour the I.G. Farben pharmaceutical plant . . . "

"Wait a minute," Jill interrupted "wasn't that the firm that made the gas used in Auschwitz?"

"That's right." Sadie nodded her head.

"Oh, my God!" Jill hit the steering wheel with the palm of her hand. "Talk about dealing with the devil!"

"That's what I thought," Sadie said. "It's creepy to think that a company could actually be evil and that Greg's dad *works* for it." Sadie shifted in her seat before sharing the rest of her findings with Jill. "Apparently this chemist brought back the formula for a drug called Dolophine—named after Adolph Hitler. Zena became the major manufacturer of Dolophine."

"I've never heard of it," Jill said with a shake of her head.

"That's because they changed its name to Methadone." With her index finger pointed, Sadie gestured to the dashboard as she spoke.

"Methadone! That's what they give to heroine addicts, isn't it?"

"It is, Jill. From what I've read, it's even *more* addictive than heroine!"

Jill shook her head in disbelief. "I'll bet that chemist moved up the corporate ladder."

Sadie nodded. "He became Zena's Executive Director of Product Development in the 1950s.

"Wow! I can't believe they pushed heroine *and* methadone."

"They pushed LSD, too," Sadie said sadly, sickened by her research findings.

"Really? Jill's jaw dropped. "I knew that in the 1960s the psychiatrists were pushing LSD," she said, shaking her head. "I guess they had to get it somewhere."

"It's scary, isn't it? I read that in the 1950s the chemists at Zena were looking for ways to mass-produce LSD for the CIA."

"I don't believe it!" Jill shook her head. "Who needs the "X-Files" when you've got real life?"

Sadie nodded. "You're right about that."

"It seems as though you've turned into a super sleuth. What about tainted research? You know, stuff like Dr. Hamilton was talking about. Did you find anything like that?" Jill asked.

"I did, and I only had time to research a few drugs like Darvon and Oraflex."

"Oraflex . . . " Jill looked over at Sadie, "wasn't that an arthritis drug?"

"It was. I couldn't believe it, Jill, but they had information on its side effects—possibly even deaths! They were later forced to plead guilty to criminal charges for withholding that information from the public."

"Lying bastards!" Jill wasn't one to mince words.

Sadie nodded in agreement. "Do you remember Diethylstilbestrol?"

"DES?" Jill asked. "Isn't that the drug that caused all the birth defects?"

"That's right. It was put on the market to prevent miscarriages before it was even tested on pregnant laboratory animals."

"No!" Jill vented her frustration on the steering wheel. "That doesn't seem right. You'd think the FDA would regulate things better." Jill shook her head. "Didn't I read that DES also caused cancer?"

"Yes. Apparently actions were being taken to ban the use of DES as a fattening agent for cattle because even small amounts caused cancer."

"So the cows were better off than the women," Jill said.

"Well, not if you factor in the trip to the slaughterhouse."

Jill grinned. "Yeah, I guess you're right."

Interstate had given way to two-lane highways, and now they were turning onto a gravel road. The tires crunched beneath them as the surface changed.

Jill glanced over Sadie. "Are we headed in the right direction?"

"Yes. According to Ellen's directions, the farm is ten miles down this road. The driveway will be on our right." In need of some lighter conversation, Sadie changed the subject. "Okay, now that we know where we're going, what's been going on with you and Jeff?"

Jill took a deep breath before answering. "He's been pretty busy lately. You know he'll be working with another doctor during his tenth trimester, so he's trying to get everything ready. Sadie, do you know Dr. Andrews?"

"Dana Andrews? Sure, I see her billboard when I come home from the farmer's market."

"That's her. Lately, Jeff has been meeting with her. He's thinking of interning with her," Jill frowned. "I don't like it, Sadie. Not only does she have a huge practice, she's drop-dead gorgeous, too. Let's face it, she's exciting and successful and I'm a first-trimester student."

"Jill, I know Jeff, and he won't be seduced by success."

"Yeah, but what about her?" Jill said, turning the steering wheel.

Their arrival at Ellen's farm prevented Sadie from giving Jill any further reassurance.

Woof! Woof! Woof! The loud barking nearly drowned out the sound of the wheels crunching along the gravel driveway.

"Hey, look!" Sadie pointed to the golden retriever running toward them. "That must be Andy!"

"The dog that used to be paralyzed?"

"Yes," Sadie nodded. "He looks good now."

Andy was running toward the car, barking and wagging his tail as he greeted the girls. When they got out of the car, Sadie noticed that his muzzle was flecked with gray hairs. "Hi, boy." She paused to scratch his head. Then, after grabbing their bags, they headed toward the white farmhouse.

"It smells good in here," Sadie said upon entering. The smells of turkey, sage, and cinnamon reminded her of her grandmother's kitchen. She felt instantly at home.

Ellen's mom hugged the girls as she greeted them. "Ellen has told me so much about you both. I feel as though I know you already. I'm so glad we can spend the holiday together," she said warmly. It was easy to see where Ellen's looks came from. Donna Rivers was tall and thin as well—an older version of Ellen, really.

"Hello! Hello!" their greetings were interrupted as Ellen and Becky came running down the stairs. "Let's take your things upstairs; then we can help mom." Ellen grabbed Jill's overnight case and headed upstairs. "You two are in the blue room," she said, opening the door to reveal a pale-blue room. Inside were two brass beds covered with white quilts.

"It's lovely," Sadie said as she looked around the room. The sloped ceiling was made of bead board that had been painted white. With the sunlight streaming in, the attic bedroom looked warm and cozy.

"It's next to my room," Ellen said.

"We share the bathroom," Becky informed them.

Downstairs, Donna enlisted their help for the meal preparations. Sadie was in charge of sweet potatoes. Jill was chopping celery and apples for the cranberry salad. Becky was mashing potatoes, and Ellen was making her famous green bean casserole. The turkey and stuffing detail was all Donna's.

Woof! Woof! Woof! Andy let them know someone was arriving. It turned out to be Ellen's father and brother.

"Smells good!" they said in unison the minute they stepped inside the kitchen. Ellen's brother tried snitching some turkey.

"You go wash up," Donna said, swatting his hand away from the bird. "We're almost ready to eat."

"The whole family is tall and thin," Jill whispered as she helped Sadie carry plates to the dining room table.

"Shush," Sadie said, grinning. (They were.)

The official Thanksgiving feast began as everyone sat down to a table full of food. The oak table looked beautiful in the flickering light. In addition to the food, it was covered with candles. Long, tapered-candles in the center as well as votives at every place setting combined to create a magical glow. It was then that

Ellen formally introduced the girls to her father, Tom, and her brother, Troy. As Jill's eyebrows arched, Ellen was quick to interrupt any comment. "I know, Troy lives in Troy, but we didn't live here when he was born. We moved here when he was two years old."

"Kids were sure quick to tease me," Troy said. At seventeen years of age, he looked more like a basketball player than the talented rodeo-rider he actually was.

Ellen, too, had gone to rodeos and competed as a barrel racer when she was in high school. No longer barrel racing, she now preferred show jumping.

They soon found out that the entire family thrived on activity and they all were accomplished equestrians. The girls learned that Tom used to be a rodeo rider as well. It was at a rodeo where he had met Donna, who had been the barrel-racing champion that year.

"I can't wait to show you the horses!" Ellen said excitedly. "Hey!" she said, spooning more potatoes onto her plate. "Let's go on a trail ride after we eat."

With that decided, the mounds of food quickly disappeared. Even though they were thin, the Rivers family all had healthy appetites.

"I've never ridden before," Jill said as they headed toward the barn.

"Don't worry," Ellen reassured her, "I've got just the horse for you. Troy, saddle up Maggie."

Maggie was a fifteen-year-old chestnut quarter horse. "She makes me think of 'My Friend Flicka'" Jill said, reaching out to touch the white blaze on her forehead. Maggie nickered in appreciation. "She likes me." Jill seemed to relax after that.

Ellen smiled as she watched Jill bonding with her horse. Satisfied that Jill was all right, she turned to Sadie. "I'm putting the English saddle on your mare, Sadie. Her name is Duchess. That way, you can take a few jumps along the trail if you want to."

"What?" Jill looked panic-stricken when Ellen mentioned jumping.

"Don't worry, Jill," Ellen said. "Maggie won't try to jump; she'll walk next to Troy's gelding."

"Okay." Jill looked happier after Ellen's reassurances.

Becky was given a bay thoroughbred gelding to ride. He, too, was wearing an English jumping saddle.

"I'm glad I have something to hold on to." Jill said, referring to the fact that both she and Troy were riding with western saddles. Unaccustomed to riding, she was gripping the saddle horn tightly. Normally, Troy was a daredevil on horseback, and his gelding, Cutter, loved to jump. Today, however, he kept his horse at a quiet walk. The chance to ride close to someone as pretty as Jill was making the sacrifice of no jumping worthwhile.

The horses' hoofbeats were pounding out a rhythm over the rolling pasture. The smoky smells of a nearby wood fire filled the air. Geese were honking overhead. Nature's symphony, Sadie thought. "I can see why you love it here, Ellen."

"I do," Ellen said. "When I graduate, I want to practice here, adjusting people three days per week and animals three days a week." Ellen's eyes lit up with excitement over her future plans.

"I'm going back to Wisconsin when I graduate," Becky announced.

"I'm not sure where I'll end up," Jill admitted. "How about you, Sadie—back to lower Iowa?"

"I don't think so," Sadie said, keeping the memories to herself.

As they rode on, the rolling hills had given way to a clearing. This was Ellen's jumping course.

"Jill, you and Troy can ride around the outside of the pasture," Ellen said, turning her horse to face them. "We'll let our horses do some jumping."

"That's fine with me," Jill said, still holding on to the saddle horn for safety.

With that, the girls touched their legs to their horses and galloped off. Ellen led the way, hair flying as her sixteen-hand chestnut gelding soared over the first jump. Close behind them, Sadie's laughter filled the air as she and Duchess flew over the three-foot fence.

"That was fun," Becky said after they had completed the course.

Tired and happy, they headed back to the barn.

"Whew!" Jill said, stretching her arms above her after she finished brushing Maggie. "Grooming horses is as much work as riding them."

"Just think of all the calories you're burning," Sadie said, grabbing a soft brush to finish grooming Duchess. After a bit more brushing, the horses were all taken care of and their saddles were once again hanging in the tack room.

"I can't believe I'm hungry after eating all that turkey," Jill said as they were walking back to the house.

"It's the fresh air and exercise," Becky said as she opened the kitchen door. "Wow! That smells wonderful!" Spicy smells filled the kitchen.

Two pumpkin pies, fresh from the oven, were cooling on the kitchen table. Ellen's parents were sitting, side by side, having coffee. Upon the riders' arrival, Donna began slicing the pie. As soon as they washed up, everyone gathered around the table, enjoying the pie and discussing their ride. Things were never boring (or quiet) at Ellen's house.

"Thanks for inviting us," Sadie said carrying her empty plate to the sink. Becky and Jill added their thanks as well.

"You're welcome," Donna said with a warm smile.

With the dishes put away, the girls climbed the stairs to their bedrooms.

— • • • —

It was early the next morning when Sadie called to Jill, "Wake up."

"What?" Jill asked sleepily.

"Wake up. Look outside—it's snowing!"

Huge snowflakes were landing on the windowpane. (What is it about the first snowfall that brings out the child in us?) Whatever it is, Sadie was enthralled, watching the snowflakes in a state of child-like wonder. They reminded her of her mother's curtains, little patches of lace sliding ever so slowly down the windowpane, putting on such a beautiful show before melting. Sadie wasn't the only one enjoying the snow. The horses were galloping in the pasture below. She could easily spot Duchess—jet black against the white snow.

It was the smell of coffee and bacon making their way upstairs that finally convinced Jill to get out of bed.

Becky and Ellen were already downstairs, drinking coffee. Donna was frying bacon and making waffles.

"Yum!" Troy said as he walked inside the kitchen. He'd been outside helping his dad feed the animals. His cheeks and nose were still pink from the cold. He rubbed his hands together before grabbing a mug of coffee. Tom came in right behind him and he, too, headed straight for the coffee pot.

"We're all going on a sleigh ride today!" Ellen said. "It's a tradition. We go into the woods for a Christmas tree."

"That sounds like fun," Sadie said, joining them at the table.

"Breakfast is ready," Donna announced as she took the bacon off the stove. Everyone gathered around the table for a hearty, family-style breakfast.

"I love this maple syrup!" Ellen said after tasting her waffles. "Thanks for bringing it, Becky."

"You're welcome. We make it every year," Becky said, swirling her own waffle piece in the syrup.

As soon as the breakfast dishes were put away, the girls bundled up and headed outside. Tom had hitched up two huge, brown Belgian horses to the wagon. Their breath made smoke rings in the frosty air. The horses, Molly and Dolly, were wearing sleigh bells around their necks. A festive jingling-sound began as soon as they started trotting toward the woods. Soon, everyone was singing carols.

Things quieted once they entered the woods. The huge pine trees blocked out the wind and the thick layer of needles below muffled the sounds of the horses' hooves. The scent of pine filled the air. Overhead, hundreds of tiny shafts of light penetrated the thick branches.

"It looks like an outdoor cathedral," Sadie said in a hushed tone.

"It *is* awe-inspiring, isn't it?" Ellen tilted her head taking in the view. "When we were kids, Troy and I used to think this was heaven."

"As in . . . *died and gone to heaven*," Donna added.

"Remember that, Troy?" Ellen smiled. "When his dog died, mom and dad told us he went to heaven. So . . . we both ran back here to look for him."

Troy grinned sheepishly at the memory.

The appearance of a perfect Christmas tree put an end to their reminiscing. "Look at that tree," Tom said, pointing to the beautiful spruce tree straight ahead. "It looks like a good one."

"I think you're right." Troy jumped out of the wagon to help his dad.

After cutting and loading the tree onto the wagon, they turned the horses, heading for home.

— • • • —

Decorating the tree was a joyful activity accompanied by the sounds of Bing Crosby singing *White Christmas*. Troy had twinkle lights spread across the living room floor. Andy was sniffing them and wagging his tail, letting Troy know they were working. Boxes of tissue-wrapped ornaments were being unpacked.

Pop! The stone fireplace came to life as Tom lit a fire. The crackling initially threatened to drown out the background sounds of Bing Crosby. Eventually it quieted, acting as an accompaniment rather than a threat to the legendary crooner. The smell of the wood smoke mingled with the scent of pine. They were happy smells, evoking happy memories.

Sadie recalled tree trimming with her grandmother. Elsie would carefully unwrap each ornament. She could still see her gnarled fingers caressing the crisp white paper as she uncovered her treasures. Elsie had said that life came full circle. Sadie smiled, watching the activity in the living room. This was definitely a full circle moment.

Later that evening, Sadie, Becky, and Jill were piled on the sofa eating popcorn and watching *It's a Wonderful Life*. Ellen was sprawled on the floor with Andy, who was also eating popcorn. Red-orange embers glowed in the fireplace.

"Ellen, thanks. This has been such a great holiday." Sadie put her popcorn bowl on the end table. "I wish we didn't have to leave in the morning," she said wistfully.

"It *has* been great," Becky agreed. "It felt like home," she said, before reaching for another handful of popcorn.

As the girls discussed the highlights of their holiday, it was Jill ("I'm afraid of horses") who surprised them. "I really liked Maggie," she said as she reached for a nearby glass of water.

"I'm glad you guys could make it." Ellen shifted to a sitting position. "I haven't had much time to get to know a lot of people, with studying and helping out here. I didn't know if I'd ever make friends after the 'horse-face' incident."

"Those guys in the back row are jerks," Sadie said. "Don't listen to them."

"Yeah, they're jerks," echoed Jill and Becky.

Ellen smiled. "I like you guys."

CHAPTER

9

With the festivities of the Thanksgiving holiday in the past, the inevitable onslaught of finals week loomed in the future. Finals—the word was spoken in hushed tones as if an increase in volume would increase their difficulty. No one wanted that! Finals—ssshhh!

Sadie and Jill were both hunched over a stack of books in the back row of the library. Jill stretched her arms before turning to face Sadie. "Do you think they'll ask us about the anti-trust suit?"

"Definitely!" Sadie nodded. "When a federal judge finds the AMA guilty of conspiring to destroy the profession of chiropractic, you know it will be on the test." Looking down at Jill's notebook, Sadie watched her as she drew a picture of a woman in robes holding a gavel in her hand. Underneath it she wrote: "Judge Susan Getzendanner—1987—GUILTY." Sadie shifted in her chair. "Don't forget that this wasn't the first time the AMA was convicted of violating anti-trust laws."

"That's right," Jill nodded as she put her pen down. "I still find it hard to believe that they actually formed a committee to eliminate our profession. It's amazing that a professional organization would deny hospital privileges to any M.D.s who accepted referrals from a chiropractor." She shook her head, sending her white-blonde hair on a rapid journey around her neck and shoulders.

"What about Kentuckiana?" Sadie frowned at the thought of how those early prejudices had affected the institution.

Kentuckiana is a special facility set up by a chiropractor, Dr. Lorraine Golden, that provides free care to indigent, multi-handicapped children. Prior to the lawsuit, there was also a pediatrician who was contributing her time to help these special children. Unfortunately, the Kentucky Medical Society informed her that it was unethical to associate with a chiropractor, threatening to revoke her hospital affiliation if she continued to do so.

"Denying help to a bunch of children for the so-called '*good of the profession.*'" Sadie's eyes narrowed. "Some profession."

"Honey, take it easy; this is no time for the revenge of the Celtic grandmother," Jill said, flashing Sadie a mischievous smile. Jill understood some of Sadie's frustrations with the medical profession as well as her unusual bond with her grandmother.

"You're right," Sadie nodded as they resumed studying.

— • • • —

Finals fever spread through the school like an epidemic. The students now resembled battle-weary veterans under siege. The dark circles under Greg's eyes were even more pronounced. Jill was thinner than normal. Sadie rarely had time to "chat" with her grandmother. Studying occupied every waking moment. Deciding to join forces, Sadie, Jill, Greg, Ellen, and Becky were currently in the back room of the library.

"Which subject should we review first?" Greg asked.

"I'm the most concerned about Anatomy and Physiology," Jill said, reaching for her Anatomy book.

"Me, too!" Sadie agreed.

Looking at the huge pile of books in front of them, Becky sighed. "I think they're all going to be tough."

"I think you're right." Ellen grabbed her Anatomy book. "I'll need to spend some extra time in the Anatomy lab, too." The others nodded in agreement.

"Okay, let's go through our outlines and we can quiz each other." Sadie looked at her notebook. "What's the most common form of cancer in men?"

"Bronchogenic." Greg rubbed his temples. "Why do people smoke when they know all of the risks?"

"I don't know." Jill shook her head. "I went on a blind date once with a guy who smoked. He gave me a good night kiss and it was like kissing an ash tray!" Frowning, Jill's brows puckered at the memory.

Carrying on, Becky asked the next question. "Where do you palpate for tenderness of appendicitis?"

"That's McBurney's point," Ellen said. "I'll never forget that because Troy had to have an emergency appendectomy." She tilted her head, recalling the memory. "Okay, my turn for a question." She looked down at her notes. "We'd better pay attention to referred pain; they really stressed that. Here's one. What causes pain to be referred to the mid-back?"

Greg shuffled through his notes. "I got it—pancreatic cancer. How about two things that can refer pain to the knee?"

"Herniated disc in the lumbar spine," Sadie answered.

Jill completed the answer, "Osteoarthritis of the hip. If we could take our test as a group, we'd do great!"

"I wish we could." Becky smiled at the thought.

Ellen flipped to Chapter Ten in her anatomy book. "We can't forget the spine itself. Did you know that giraffes have seven cervical vertebrae just like we do?"

"Really?" Sadie looked over at Ellen. "With such a long neck, you'd think they would have more."

"I know," Ellen said. "I've been studying animal spines in my spare time."

"I'd like to borrow some of that spare time," Jill said.

Sadie looked at her watch. "It's time for the anatomy review," she said, jumping up from her chair. "Let's go. I don't want to miss it."

Even though this was an optional review class, the lecture hall was packed. Professor Cox and Dr. Rodriguez, the Anatomy and Physiology professors, were both giving them some last-minute study tips.

Dr. Rod, as he was known by his students, was a short, round, good-natured Puerto Rican. Pursuing knowledge with the same vigor he devoted to the pursuit of happiness had made him very popular with the students. He was a published author in peer-reviewed journals and encouraged his students to do the same. Such a well-rounded lifestyle as his wasn't usually found within the halls of academia.

Professor Cox stepped up to the podium first. "The lab practical will cover the dissections as well as in-depth questions of each area."

Several students groaned. Sadie looked over at Jill, who had written "INCREASED DEGREE OF DIFFICULTY" in her notebook. She grinned.

Professor Cox ignored the groaning and continued, "For example, if we're examining the abdomen, we might go over things like the boundaries of Hesselbach's triangle or its clinical significance."

Sadie made a notation in her notebook: "HESSELBACH'S TRIANGLE-INGUINAL HERNIA." Looking over, she saw that Jill was drawing a picture of a guy wearing a truss. With a smile on her face, she shook her head. *Typical Jill.*

Professor Cox pushed his glasses back up his nose as he surveyed the class. "Who can tell me the most common malformation of the digestive tract?"

"Meckel's diverticulum," said Terry.

The class was stunned. (Oh, they knew the answer; it was where the answer came from that startled them. The back row! Terry Hart had actually answered a question!)

"Maybe the end of the world is coming," Sadie whispered to Jill.

Jill grinned. "You could be right; we've just witnessed two miracles at once. Peter didn't answer first and Terry did."

Terry was the kind of guy who had probably been nicknamed "bean pole" as a kid. Age hadn't changed him all that much. Still tall and thin, he had shaggy black hair and wore dark glasses all the time. So far, his only class contribution had been to become the unofficial leader of the back row.

Apparently Professor Cox's surprise extended all the way to his glasses, which had stopped their customary downward descent while Terry was speaking. His voice seemed to freeze them in their tracks. "Very good, Terry. What is its clinical significance?"

"If it becomes inflamed, it can cause symptoms mimicking appendicitis," Terry answered.

Because of his dark glasses, it was hard to tell whether he registered the surprise of his classmates. If he did, he didn't show it. He sat, slouched as usual, as if that were the only position that allowed his tall frame to fit within the confines of the auditorium seating.

Now it was Dr. Rod's turn at the podium. "The final will contain patient-oriented essay problems. Let's go over some examples to familiarize you with the exam style." He cleared his throat before continuing. "A wife is awakened by the unusual sound of her 50-year-old husband's snoring. She looked over and noticed he was sleeping with his right eye open. That morning she noticed that the right side of his face was drooping. He had trouble eating breakfast because his food kept dribbling out of the right side of his mouth."

Sadie wasn't sure that she wanted to see the kind of picture Jill would be drawing as a result of that description, so she kept her eyes focused on Dr. Rod.

"Frantic that her husband had suffered a stroke, she took him to the doctor. Who can identify the probable cause of this man's problem?"

Peter Burger's hand sprang into the air. (The back row was betting that he'd have some sort of acromio-clavicular problem by spring. They figured that the amount of force he used to propel his arm upward might eventually dislocate his shoulder. They were saving that injury, however, for his senior year.) "A lesion of Cranial Nerve VII," he answered.

Jill leaned over toward Sadie. "Anyone else would have just said Bell's Palsy," she said, referring to the common name for a problem with the facial nerve.

Sadie nodded. "I know."

Dr. Rod moved from behind the podium, which had dwarfed his short stature. "We also want you to be able to correlate various physical examination findings. For example, what is the term for a person's gait characterized by a falling of the pelvis toward the unaffected side with each step?"

"That is a gluteus medius limp," Peter said. He was on a roll.

"That is correct," Dr. Rod nodded. "Now I'd like to add some nutritional aspects to our discussion. First of all, the gluteus medius muscle can be paralyzed by injury to the superior gluteal nerve or by a disease such as poliomyelitis. Can anyone tell me how diet relates to polio?"

Sadie was glad that she was in Jeff's nutrition study group. She'd read a book by Dr. Benjamin Sandler called *Diet Prevents Polio*. Dr. Sandler, an M.D. from North Carolina, advocated no sugar in the diet. In his community in 1948 there were 2,402 cases of polio. The following year (even though statistically polio was on the rise), there were only 214 cases of polio in his hometown. The reason? The members of his community had been following the Sandler diet. Confident that she knew the answer, she raised her hand. "When you eliminate sugar, you decrease your risk of contracting polio."

Dr. Rodriguez nodded. "Very good. How much sugar does the average American consume?"

Jill, too, was in the study group and this was an easy question for her. "Over 130 pounds of sugar per year."

"Excellent. What nutritional deficiencies could cause one to crave sugar?"

Not to be outdone by the girls, Peter answered rapidly, "Chromium and Vanadium."

"Okay, that's how the test will be structured," Dr. Rodriguez explained. "We will cover the anatomy, muscular and neurological, and then go to clinical significances and end with nutritional correlations. Any questions?"

"Could we go over one more of the patient-essay type problems?" Ellen asked.

"Sure," Dr. Rodriguez nodded. "Why do people in Alaska and Canada frequently develop shin splints after the first big snow of the season?"

The class was silent. Dr. Rodriguez looked to the back row.

"Like he'll get an answer there," Jill whispered.

But wait. He did get an answer!

"Because when you use snowshoes, you have to use the anterior tibial muscle," said Ken Davis. The ski bum of the back row, Ken was from Northern California.

Amazing! Not only did Ken answer a question, he managed to do so without using the word "dude." Another miracle. Maybe the end-of-the-world theory had some merit.

BUZZ. BUZZ. BUZZ. The bell rang without the sky falling, so that was probably a good sign. At the sound of the bell, everyone started hurrying toward the door. Jill, however, slowed her pace when she noticed Greg approaching. Since he was looking in Sadie's direction, Jill decided to give them some time alone.

"Let's get something to eat," Greg said, grabbing Sadie's books and heading down the long hallway to the cafeteria.

Faced with chocolate-brown eyes as they sat together, Sadie felt the familiar force of attraction. "Tugging at your heart strings," Elsie would have said. An apt description, she thought. It wasn't so bad during class because there were other things to focus on. It was the one-on-one that got to her—as now. Finals were already enough to make her heart beat faster, and now this. For some distraction, she took a bite of her cheese sandwich. "How are you doing?" She couldn't help noticing how tired he looked.

"I'll be glad when finals are over." Greg stretched his arms. "I'm trying to get more time to study. Jen wasn't too happy when I told her I couldn't see her for a while." Greg yawned. "Now if I could just get Dad to stop calling all the time."

There it was—that awful feeling that something wasn't right. She seemed to get it every time Greg's dad was mentioned. Looking down, she noticed goose bumps covering her arms.

"It's funny," Greg said reaching for his sandwich. "Dad *never* called me when I was in undergraduate school."

There it was again—that awful feeling. Sadie felt as though she couldn't breathe. Doing a quick differential diagnosis, she came up with three possible causes for her current symptoms: 1. Greg's nearness (he smelled of Bay Rum aftershave.); 2. She had a rib out of place, causing some type of intercostal neuritis; 3. There was something fishy about Greg's dad. If it were a multiple-choice question, she'd choose all of the above.

"Well, I guess we should join the rest of the gang in the library," Greg said as he finished his sandwich.

CLOMP. CLOMP. CLOMP. The rhythmic sound of their footsteps on the tile floor turned her attention away from Greg's dad. She thought instead of their dances at the freshman welcome party. Her relationship with Greg had been easier then—before these new feelings had intruded.

The beautiful sadness of longing for something, or in her case—someone. Sadie sighed.

"What are ya pinin' for, darlin'?" Elsie asked.

"Nothing," Sadie muttered under her breath. Elsie's brief appearance had helped, though. It was good to know she was still out there.

If Greg noticed their brief exchange, he didn't comment on it.

CHAPTER

10

A well-worn vinyl booth at the local Denny's restaurant was providing refuge for the girls. It was ten o'clock at night. Sadie and Jill were sitting across from Becky and Ellen. Four grand-slam breakfasts had just appeared on the table in front of them.

"Do you think we're ready?" Ellen asked as she stabbed her fork into her pancakes.

"I think so." Sadie began swirling the eggs around on her plate. Looking to her left, she made sure that Jill was eating. The bulky sweater she was wearing over her corduroy trousers failed to hide her thinness.

Sensing Sadie's stare, Jill took a bite of her food. "Well, there's not much more we can do now."

"We'll do just fine." Becky took a sip of milk. She was from the "Dairy State" and proud of it. (Actually, Cathy Muncie's quip about her having a perpetual milk mustache wasn't entirely untrue.)

Jill, too, had noticed Becky's fondness for milk. "You'll never have to worry about taking calcium supplements."

Becky smiled. "Not only do I believe in the power of milk," she said, referring to the popular ad with the slogan *I believe in the power of food*, "but did you guys hear about the nutritional experiment they did at the Central Alternative High School in Appleton?"

The girls shook their heads.

"No?" Becky looked across the table. "Maybe it just made the news in Wisconsin."

"What did they do?" Sadie leaned forward, always eager to learn about nutrition.

"It's so cool," Becky said. "They took out all the vending machines and hired Natural Ovens to create a healthy lunch program."

"That's a great idea!" Sadie said.

"I know." Becky nodded in agreement. "Apparently the school used to have a lot of disciplinary problems."

Ellen shifted to her left, facing Becky. "Did the lunch program help?"

"Yes. It was incredible! Get this . . . ." Becky leaned forward and began gesturing with her hand. "Since starting the program, they've had no drop-outs, no one expelled, no students found doing drugs, no concealed weapons, no suicide—*nothing!*"

"Wow!" Ellen said.

Sadie dropped her fork.

Jill looked over at her briefly. Satisfied that Sadie was all right, she turned her attention back to Becky. "With all the violence you hear about, you'd think every school would have a healthy lunch program."

"I know." Becky reached for her milk glass.

Ellen shoved a fork-full of pancakes into her mouth. It was while she was chewing that something (or someone) came to mind. "Hey, where's Greg these days?" she asked, pointing her empty fork at Sadie.

"Well . . . " Sadie looked down, pushing her food around at a rapid rate. "He's working, and I guess his dad has been bugging him a lot lately." (Her plate now resembled a Picasso.) Although Sadie was unaware of the artistic qualities of her uneaten breakfast, her friends weren't. "He's having a hard time," she added quietly.

Becky's eyes widened in understanding. "You *like* him!"

Sadie looked over at Jill.

"Don't look at me." Jill lifted her hands in protest. "I didn't tell anyone." With that, Sadie's secret was now confirmed.

"You can't let him know!" Sadie's words tumbled out faster then she'd intended.

"Don't worry," Becky said reassuringly.

"I won't tell him," Ellen promised.

"When did all of this happen?" Becky was now ignoring both her milk and her breakfast.

Sadie sighed. "Around Halloween."

"You two have a lot more in common than he has with Jennifer." Ellen poured herself a cup of coffee. She took a sip before adding, "she seems kind of snooty to me."

"I don't want to do anything to mess up our friendship," Sadie said as she reached for her teacup.

Jill laid a hand on her arm. "Honey, look around you. Things have already changed between you two or else he'd be sitting here right now."

Becky and Ellen nodded in agreement.

"I guess you're right," Sadie admitted. "You know Grandma used to say that you could solve any problem with communication." She paused, recalling the memory. "I just realized that lately I've been so worried about what to say that I haven't been saying much of anything!" She brightened up and actually began eating her breakfast. Pausing with her fork in mid-air, she continued, "No wonder things have seemed strained. Well, that stops now!" She nodded her head for emphasis.

Jill patted her arm. "Good for you!"

Becky put her fork down. "You know, Sadie, you just made me realize that I've got some more communicating to do myself."

Sadie looked up, "You do?"

"Yes," Becky nodded. "When I go home for Christmas, Roger and I are going to have a long talk."

"Who's Roger?" Sadie asked.

"My boyfriend."

Jill's eyes widened in surprised. "I didn't know you had a boyfriend!"

Becky had everyone's attention. "He's a dairy farmer. I've known him forever. I still have the first Valentine's card he gave me when we were in grade school. We dated all through college. Then, for some reason, we decided to cool things off since I was going to be gone for such a long time."

"Is that what you wanted?" Ellen asked.

"No!" Becky shook her head. "You know, now that we're discussing it, I think he might have felt intimidated, knowing I'd be in a big city with lots of doctors. He was probably worried that he might hold me back somehow. That crazy nut!" she said with a grin.

"What does he look like?" Jill was eager to spend a few moments on a subject other than finals. Besides, affairs of the heart were much more interesting than actually *studying* the heart.

"Well . . . " Becky's eyes started to sparkle. "He's six feet tall with light-blonde hair. Kind of like yours, Jill. He has the cutest blue eyes." Her face softened as she described him. I think he's the most handsome man I've ever seen."

"He sounds wonderful, Becky." Sadie leaned forward, grasping her friend's hands. "I'm so happy for you!"

"Thanks." Becky smiled. "I can't wait to get home for Christmas."

Noticing Ellen's wistful expression, Jill asked, "What's on your mind?"

Now Ellen looked embarrassed. "It's silly, really. I was wishing I had someone waiting for me as well."

"You could easily have anyone you want, Ellen." Jill looked at her friend appraisingly. "All you have to do is apply yourself."

"Maybe I need a makeover," Ellen joked.

"I'd *love* to give you one!" Jill said quickly before Ellen could back out. "After finals I'm taking you to a fabulous hair salon. Oh, this will be so much fun! Let's see, we'll cut your hair and give it some highlights. I've got some volumizing shampoo . . . "

Sadie and Becky starting laughing. Admittedly, they were both sleep deprived, but there was something about Jill's intensity and Ellen's bewilderment that struck them as funny. Once they started, it was hard to stop. Sadie was laughing so hard she had tears in her eyes. Two booths down, an older couple turned to see what was so funny. When they shook their heads as if to say "nothing," Jill and Ellen started laughing as well.

"Oh, that felt good." Sadie wiped her eyes. "I think I'll sleep well tonight."

"I'm not sure I will. I feel all tensed up." Ellen shrugged her shoulders, attempting to ease the tension.

"Take some extra magnesium and drink some chamomile tea," Sadie advised.

"I will." Ellen scooted out of the booth. "We'd better get going."

As if to mock her earlier prediction of getting a good night's sleep, the nightmare came back in full force. For Sadie, talking about sleep was like tempting fate, something she was usually careful not to do. The fact that it hadn't been haunting her recently must have made her careless.

BEEP. BEEP. BEEP. Sadie heard the sound of Jill's alarm clock. BEEP. CLANG. The clock hit the floor. Sadie smiled. Today she knew how Jill felt. The dream had kept her up most of the night.

An hour later, the girls were driving up the tree-lined hill to campus. Sadie could see Paul and Cathy walking past the ivy-covered brick building toward the front entrance. To her left, in front of the out-patient clinic, was a life-sized sculpture of Mark Twain sitting on a park bench. It was customary for the freshmen to have their pictures taken while seated next to the legendary figure. Sadie had sent one home herself during her first week at school.

Greg caught up to them as they were entering the building. Impulsively, Sadie gave him a hug.

"What was that for?" Greg asked.

"Luck. Although you won't need it." Sadie grinned at him. With that, all traces of the tension that had been straining their relationship evaporated. She felt better after last night's discussion.

Noticing the change, Greg put his arm around her shoulder, giving her an affectionate hug. "Let's go kick some finals butt!"

Happy and confident, Sadie sat down for the Anatomy and Physiology final. She was neither happy nor confident two hours later as she slowly made her way out of the classroom.

Apparently she wasn't the only one. Glimpsing Peter Burger's face on the way out, she noticed that all traces of smug arrogance had been wiped clean. He looked shell-shocked, as though he'd just come through a disaster. In a way, he had. Sadie thought it was a safe bet that she didn't look much better.

With the next final starting in just thirty minutes, the class milled about in the hallway. Too tired to venture much further, they looked at one another, shaking their heads and shrugging their shoulders. No one had any idea how they had done. Many, hoping for a passing score, were now concerned since this test counted for 50 percent of their grade.

Sadie looked up at Greg. "How did you do?" she asked, marveling that her vocal chords were still working.

"I'm not sure." Greg shook his head." Let's get something to drink before the Histology final." He put his hand on the small of her back, propelling her toward the cafeteria.

After a few sips of tea laced with honey, Sadie was feeling better. "I still can't believe how hard that test was."

Greg nodded. "I know," he said, staring deeply into her eyes.

It's as though he's searching for something, Sadie thought. *The answer to his anatomy test? True love? Himself?* She wasn't sure. Right now it didn't matter. Whatever that look was for, it had energized her. She smiled, showing both dimples.

A few minutes later, they were joined by Jill, Becky, and Ellen, who were still showing the effects of the exam.

Jill was amazed that Sadie looked so refreshed. "How can you look so good after that?" she asked. It was only after asking that she noticed the cozy familiarity between Sadie and Greg. Then it all made sense.

"Have some tea," Sadie replied.

"Tea?" Jill smiled in understanding. "Sounds good to me."

BUZZ. BUZZ. BUZZ.

Everyone jumped up. It was time for the next exam. Shoving Styrofoam cups into metal trash cans, they marched down the hallway.

On and on it went. Test; fatigue; tea. By the end of the day it had become a routine. Tomorrow that routine would include their lab practicals.

— • • • —

The next day, the students looked much the same as they had before—like shell-shocked soldiers. Only Ken Davis, the ski bum from the back row, seemed unfazed. He was wearing his trademark sunglasses and a tee shirt stating: "THE LUMBRICALS ADDUCT THE THIGH."

One by one, as people read Ken's shirt, they started laughing. (Everyone knew that the lumbricals were tiny finger muscles that had absolutely *nothing* to do with leg movement.) Soon the entire class was laughing as they stood in the dim hallway outside the Anatomy lab.

CREAK.

Instantly the laughter ended as Professor Cox opened the door to the anatomy lab. One by one he was taking people inside, in alphabetical order. Peter Burger was ushered inside. The sounds of nervous pacing replaced the earlier laughter.

CREAK. The door opened again, allowing the smell of formaldehyde to escape into the hallway. Ken walked inside.

"Nice shirt!" Professor Cox's comment could be heard as the door closed shut.

"Underdog is pretty cool," Jill said, leaning forward so that Sadie and Becky could hear her.

Sadie was glad Jill's last name was Jones, because she was right behind her in line. Becky was in front of her with her blonde hair pulled back into a ponytail. It had taken only one incident of bending over a cadaver looking for a nerve and finding your hair instead to realize that ponytails were a requirement for anatomy lab.

One by one, the students exited the lab, giving no hint of what was inside. Their faces were frozen and expressionless. Who needs Botox when you have finals? Sadie thought.

"Sadie Jensen."

Momentarily startled, she didn't start moving until Jill pushed her on the shoulder. Becky gave her a brief smile as she walked by. Inside, Professor Cox pointed to ten cadavers. "There are three tags on each body. You will be asked to identify each structure and answer related questions. All set?" Professor Cox peered at her from behind his glasses.

She nodded.

They walked over to Leroy first. Good, this one will be easy, Sadie thought. This was her cadaver. Right now he felt like an old friend.

Professor Cox pointed to the first tag.

Easy. "Stomach." Sadie's own stomach seemed to relax after identifying her first structure.

Professor Cox turned to face her. "What causes ulcers?"

"The *H. pylori* virus." Sadie was feeling more confident.

"How many people are affected with it?" Professor Cox was writing her responses as he asked new questions.

Making a mental note to hug Jeffrey Adams for teaching the nutrition study group, she answered, "More than half of all the U.S. population as well as 80 percent of the flocks of chickens are affected with the *H. pylori* virus."

"What else has *H. pylori* been associated with?" Professor Cox stopped writing and waited for her answer.

Think. Think. Breathe. Think. She gave rapid-fire orders to her tired brain. "Oh! *H. pylori* also appears to trigger strokes." Taking a deep breath, Sadie gave her overworked brain some much-needed oxygen.

"Very good, Sadie."

On and on it went. Identifying structures and answering questions. They went from cadaver to cadaver, ending up with the fattest cadaver of the group—Big Bertha. During dissections, "Gross!" and "Ick!" could be heard from Bertha's group as they waded through layers of adipose tissue. On one such occasion Jill had leaned over, whispering, "Now I know why they call it *Gross* Anatomy."

"Can you tell me a correlation between weight and vasculature?"

"It takes a mile of capillaries for every one pound of tissue in your body," Sadie answered. With more than three hundred miles of capillaries, Bertha's red blood cells could qualify for frequent-flyer miles.

"That's it." Professor Cox put his pen down and they walked to the door.

PHEW! No more questions. Sadie gave Jill a big smile on the way out.

11

It was "makeover morning", and once again the girls were gathered at Denny's. "A big breakfast for a little money" was Ellen's explanation for her choice of restaurants.

Looking across the table at Becky, Sadie asked, "Did Underdog ask you about the thymus?"

"No," Becky said, shaking her head as she reached for the salt shaker. "Why's that?"

"Oh, he asked me its weight in kids versus adults. I was hoping he'd ask you the same question." Sadie's pride in her friend's knowledge of pediatrics was obvious.

"Girls, finals are over." Jill reached for her coffee mug. "Today's makeover day and it's my present to you, Ellen."

"What?" Surprised by Jill's generosity, Ellen didn't know what else to say.

"Merry Christmas," Jill said with a smile. After taking a sip of coffee, she added, "It's also for giving us such a terrific Thanksgiving holiday. After breakfast we're going to Plaza Frontenac."

Ellen's jaw dropped, adding length to her already long face. (Not a good look for her.) Plaza Frontenac was an upscale shopping center near Ladue—the heart of "old money" in the St. Louis area. This was the type of mall where Saks and Neiman Marcus replaced the usual anchor stores of Sears and JC Penney. "Really?" Ellen's jaw finally closed. "I've lived here all my life and I've never gone inside."

"Well, then it's about time you did!" Jill's eyes sparkled with pleasure. "By the way, I'm treating you all to manicures and pedicures. I wouldn't have made it through the first trimester without you guys."

Becky gave Jill a warm smile, "I don't know what to say."

"Me, either," said Ellen.

"You're the best friend and roommate I could ever have!" Sadie gave Jill a hug—not the easiest thing to do within the confines of a booth.

Christmas at Plaza Frontenac was like something out of a King Midas fantasy. (There were no blown-up Santas here.) At Frontenac, everything was pristine white and glittering gold. Elegant. Christmas for the upper class. Inside, white packages tied with gold ribbon rested under trees tastefully decorated with golden globes.

"Oh, my," Sadie said, pointing to the center of the mall. Thousands of white poinsettias (housed in golden pots, of course) surrounded an antique sleigh, which was sitting on a bed of pine boughs.

Ellen stared, open-mouthed, at the opulent decorations.

"Pretty, isn't it?" Jill said before grabbing Ellen's arm and propelling her toward the entrance of Saks.

"We're going in there?" Ellen asked. For once, her long legs were having trouble keeping up with Jill.

"Of course we are. They have a great salon. That's where I have my hair done." Jill led the way, giving Becky and Sadie a view of the back of her perfectly cut, white-blonde hair.

Fresh flowers filled the softly lit salon. Relaxing music playing in the background contributed to the spa-like atmosphere. The girls were ushered inside for manicures and pedicures.

With one person working on her hands and another on her feet, Sadie decided that this was the perfect way to celebrate the end of finals week. "I can't believe I've never done this before!" she said when the pampering ended. Looking down, Sadie admired the red polish on her fingers and toes. "Thanks, Jill."

"Yes. Thanks, Jill." Ellen wiggled her coral-tipped toes. This was a first for her as well.

Jill was getting the white tips to complete her French manicure. "I used to get my nails done every week but I haven't been here since September. There didn't seem to be much reason since we spent half our time in latex gloves."

"You're right about that," Sadie nodded. They *had* spent a lot of time wearing gloves. It was going to be nice to have a break from the lab.

"Jill, this was such a nice present," Becky said as she waved her fingers to help them dry. "Thanks. I can't wait to show Roger!"

"I'm glad you're going to talk to Roger." Red nails now dry, Sadie got up and put a hand on her friend's shoulder. "I know that everything will work out for the two of you."

Becky smiled at Sadie's earnest expression. "I hope you're right."

"Okay, girls, let's get Ellen to the hair salon." Jill led them into an adjoining room.

"Hello!" They were greeted by a small-boned man with black hair and goatee.

"Henri, hello!" Jill gave him a kiss. "This is my friend Ellen. I'd like you to give her auburn hair with highlights. What do you think about a shoulder-length bob?"

Henri ran his fingers through Ellen's thin hair. "Yes," he said nodding in agreement.

Draped in a gold cape, Ellen's wide-eyed expression resembled a deer in the headlights. Looking like a runway model, Jill stood with her hands on her hips as she explained the "look" she had in mind for Ellen.

Sadie smiled, observing the scene and wondering what her grandmother would think about this place. The last time they'd gone to a beauty parlor (they weren't called salons back then), black vinyl capes had protected their clothes. There was no soft music, either. Instead the parlor was filled with the sounds of gossiping voices and frequent bursts of hissing from aerosol cans. With hairspray coating every available molecule of oxygen, the air itself was stiff and rigid.

Do they even use hairspray here? Sadie wondered.

"Darlin', even though they're havin' a bit o' money, they'll still be needin' to tame those fly-aways."

There she was! Sadie smiled. Elsie had imparted her celestial salon wisdom and quickly vanished. Perhaps she, too, felt awed by so much glamour and glitz.

Henri interrupted her musings. "Come back in two hours and you will not recognize her," he said with his French accent.

The girls decided to spend their time shopping as they waited for Ellen's metamorphosis.

"Let's go to Williams Sonoma!" Sadie said, clasping her red-tipped fingers in anticipation. Her red curls bounced merrily down her back as she bounded into the store. "Oh, look at these pots!" Sadie reverently stroked the Le Creuset cookware.

Becky and Jill nodded politely. Watching Sadie dance from aisle to aisle was more entertaining than looking at the pots and pans.

After thoroughly inspecting everything in the store, Sadie returned to her friends. "Let's go to Pottery Barn next!" she said, her blue-green eyes sparkling with excitement.

Pottery Barn held more appeal for Becky and Jill. Once inside, they, too, began shopping in earnest.

Sadie rushed over to a green velvet sofa. "Oh, my grandmother would have loved this." She paused a moment to stroke the plush velvet armrest before something else caught her eye. "Candles!" she said as she hurried to the display.

"She's like a kid in a candy store," Becky said, watching her friend sniff one candle after another.

Jill nodded. "She's pretty much always that way—full of life. As though she's living for herself as well as for her grandmother. (Jill didn't know the half of it.)

"I'm going to get one of these for Mom," Sadie said, choosing a scented pillar candle from the shelf.

"That's a good idea." Becky selected one for herself.

"I might as well join you," Jill said. "They do smell good."

Packages in hand, the girls headed back to the salon. They couldn't quite believe their eyes when Ellen appeared. The transformation was remarkable.

"Oh, my! Ellen, you look beautiful!" Sadie said.

"You really do!" Becky couldn't stop staring.

Jill looked at Ellen, raised her eyebrows, and smiled. Henri had done exactly what she'd asked.

Ellen smiled back. "I know—no more horse face!" She threw her arms around Jill. "Thank you so much!"

"Oh, honey, I always knew you were beautiful." Jill ran her fingers through Ellen's hair. The cut added width to her face, and the volumizing shampoo made her hair seem much thicker.

Ellen smoothed her hair back into place. "The color is close to yours, Sadie—we could be sisters," she said.

"I know." Sadie nodded. Looking down, she rubbed at the gooseflesh on her arms. It quickly disappeared. Good, she thought. Time to change the subject. "Let's go to Whole Foods for lunch."

Jill grabbed her purse. "That sounds good to me—I love their salad bar."

"Me, too," Becky said. "The only Whole Foods store we have is in Madison. We don't get there very often, usually only for the Dairy Expo." Becky, who had been following Jill, nearly ran into her when she stopped abruptly.

Turning around, Jill asked, "The Diary Expo? Are you serious?"

"Yes, I am serious." Becky nodded. "It's a big event in Wisconsin."

Jill smiled, shaking her head. "Don't let the back row hear about that."

Ellen laughed. (She wasn't the close-mouthed type.) Ellen had an unaffected "horsey" laugh, displaying every tooth in her mouth. She didn't try to hide it behind her hand, either. She laughed joyfully, inviting everyone to join her, and so they did.

Whole Foods was as busy as usual. Sadie lingered over the floral displays before joining her friends at the salad bar. She was surprised to see Paul Santini pouring dressing onto his salad. "I didn't know you came here, Paul."

"Yeah, I like it here. According to the *Lancet*, men who eat organic foods produce over 40 percent more sperm." This tidbit of information was delivered with an air of nonchalance, as though it were the kind of thing he talked about every day. Perhaps it was. Then, just as calmly, he and his salad headed for the check-out counter.

Sadie's blue-green eyes were still wide with surprise as she watched him walk away. She began giggling the moment he was out the door.

"I can't believe that guy." Jill shook her head. "You can bet he didn't read the *Lancet* article."

"Maybe Cathy told him about it," Ellen suggested.

"Probably." Jill stabbed her fork into a tomato.

Becky looked over at Ellen. "He didn't even notice your makeover." She shook her head.

"Probably too busy counting his sperm," Jill said.

"Ha!" Ellen's horse laugh followed.

The girls were seated within the large, Whole Foods eating area. With the sunlight streaming in, vases of fresh flowers on the tables, and the artwork on display, it had a cozy atmosphere. Salads and herb teas filled their table. Even Becky was having tea.

"I'm not that sure about soy milk," she'd said, opting for the safer choice of herb tea with honey.

"I love this place!" Sadie munched on a carrot stick as she looked around. "It's the best! Great food. Juice bar. Organic produce—nothing harmful." She smiled before continuing. "Plus, it has tons of flowers—it's beautiful!"

Jill nodded in agreement. "It *is* hard to think of this place as a supermarket."

Sadie put her fork down. "My grandmother would have loved it here. She was an organic gardener way before it became popular. She used to tell me that one day pesticides would ruin agriculture."

Becky looked up. "She was right. It's already happening in California."

"What's happening?" Sadie asked.

"Pesticides have wiped out the local honey bees so the almond growers have to import bees to pollinate their trees." With that, Becky reached for some honey to add to her tea.

Jill looked up in surprise. "I didn't know that."

"I'm so glad we're all going to be chiropractors!" Sadie said. "No drugs, nothing unnatural; what a great way to help people."

Ellen put her teacup down. "You're right. I'll choose natural healing and a natural lifestyle any day."

Jill poked at her salad. "We just have about a million more tests, National Boards and State Boards, plus a successful internship before that's a reality."

Sadie remained undaunted by the years of study still ahead of them. "Well, at least the first trimester is done." Her Celtic blood was useful, allowing her to step into a world of dreams and possibilities while temporarily leaving behind the harsh realities of life.

Walking through the aisles of the Whole Foods Market, the girls searched for items to take home for Christmas. A wheel of aged cheddar cheese from California was going home with everyone except Becky.

"There's no reason to buy this when Wisconsin already makes the best cheese," she said, choosing a bottle of sparkling cider instead.

It was late afternoon before they returned to their house. Time to start packing for Christmas vacation. Both girls were leaving in the morning. After Sadie was finished packing, she went to help Jill, who was having some difficulty. She was packing for a warm Christmas in Savannah followed by a New Year's ski trip to Vail.

"So, you're having dinner with Greg tonight?" Jill continued folding her blue-and-white sweater as she spoke. "Where is he taking you?"

"West Port Plaza. We're eating at Robata's of Japan." Sadie began folding the clothes that were draped over a chair. Right now the room resembled an exotic flea market. Cashmere and silk, scarves and socks, all on display.

"Wow! That's fancy," Jill said, placing her sweater in the suitcase.

"It's not as fancy as it sounds." Sadie finished folding the clothes on the chair. "He has one of those dinner coupons—buy one, get one free. It expires at the end of the month."

Jill smiled. "Big spender."

Sadie looked at her watch. "Oh, I'd better get ready."

— • • • —

West Port Plaza was an assortment of shops, restaurants, and hotels all located on forty-two acres. There were lakes and fountains, trees and flower gardens, making the outside of the shops as interesting as the inside. The walkways and open courtyards were beautifully decorated for Christmas. The Old World elegance appealed to Sadie. It was as though West Port Plaza had been created with couples in mind.

At Robata's, tableside chefs prepared your food while you watched. It was an elaborate and entertaining production. "I'm so glad you're here." Greg's chocolate-brown eyes focused on her, ignoring the chef's masterful production. Bite-sized bits of vegetables were already sizzling nearby.

"Me, too," Sadie said with a smile.

"I've missed you, Sadie." Greg grasped her two small hands between his.

Sadie watched as her new red nails were hidden from view. Looking up, she was surprised by the frank admiration in his eyes. This was the way a man looked at a woman. Sadie thought it was, well—primal. She was now hoping her hands wouldn't start sweating.

"Sadie, I want to tell you something."

Sadie's heart skipped a beat. Although they'd just ordered, she no longer felt hungry. She now felt as though her stomach were stuffed full of lead. It didn't matter how small those vegetables were chopped; she was certain she wouldn't be able to get them down.

"I broke up with Jennifer."

What? He broke up with Jennifer! Her brain appeared to have imposed its own five-second delay. Probably to protect her in case the news was disturbing. *He broke up with Jennifer!* Suddenly, the lead in her stomach disappeared. The vegetables looked wonderful—they were the best-looking vegetables she had ever seen. Laughter bubbled up inside her.

"Oh, Greg. I'm so happy!"

"Me, too!" Greg squeezed her hands, releasing them only when steaming plates of food were placed in front of them.

Sadie took a deep breath. "Yum, that smells good."

Greg nodded. "It does."

Reaching for her fork, Sadie found chopsticks instead. Looking over at Greg's plate, she watched as he singled out a piece of chicken, bringing it all the way up to his mouth without mishap. *Okay, I can do this.* After her second unsuccessful attempt, she decided to change her grip. Apparently the claw-hand technique was unworkable. Focusing her efforts on a water chestnut, she managed to capture it between the two wooden tips. *Ha!* Carefully she inched it toward her mouth. *Steady. Okay, here it comes.* No! Open-mouthed, Sadie watched as the water chestnut plunged back onto her plate, landing next to some peas. She started giggling as she realized she was no match for those tiny vegetables.

"Here, let me help you." Placing his right hand over hers, Greg helped her to master the art of eating with chopsticks. Soon, she was using them with ease. (Even the peas were afraid.)

They were sipping tea when their fortune cookies arrived. "What does yours say?" Sadie asked, reaching for her cookie.

"Beware of a wolf in sheep's clothing." Discarding the strip of paper, he bit into his cookie. "How about yours?"

"The waters are always stormy before they are calm." She frowned. "Whatever."

Greg laughed. Deep, rich, male laughter filled the restaurant.

Late that night, as Sadie burrowed under her covers, she thought about her perfect day. There was a smile on her lips as she drifted off to sleep.

Oh yes, West Port Plaza had been created with couples in mind.

TRIMESTER TWO

"Look well to the spine, for this is the requisite for the cause of disease."

—*Hippocrates*

CHAPTER

12

Grey skies, which managed to look charming when combined with sparkling Christmas lights, now looked bleak and desolate. It was as though the sun itself were exhausted after the holidays, unable or unwilling to muster enough energy to illuminate the sky. Today was Sunday, January 4,, and the St. Louis landscape was windswept and barren. This is no reflection on St. Louis. Most places are desolate in January—unless you live in the South. People from the northern climates are an optimistic lot. Some might call them stoic—keeping firmly in mind that spring will follow winter. It's their climatic version of "this too shall pass."

Sadie was definitely one of the optimistic ones, splurging on several hyacinth plants. Their rich, sweet scents were already creating a spring-like atmosphere within the house. Having arrived several hours earlier, she had already put away the groceries and unpacked her clothes.

"*And where will the frail birds fly if their homes on high have been torn down . . . ?*" Sadie was singing a popular song from *Riverdance* as she puttered around the house. She was anxious to get back to school tomorrow to see Greg. He had called regularly until shortly after Christmas. Since then, she hadn't heard from him. She paused as she looked at her new dishtowels, her mother's hand-made Christmas gift to her. They really do suit this kitchen, she thought. Covered with bright-red cherries and a black-and-white checkerboard border, they complemented her green cupboards perfectly. Her momentary concern over Greg's silence was replaced by the joy of her simple Christmas presents. After all, she'd see Greg tomorrow. I'm sure he was busy with his family, she thought. Satisfied, she once again began singing.

Joyful sounds greeted Jill as she walked into the house. Sadie was still singing. "Hey, Sadie," she shouted, as she took off her coat.

"Jill!" Sadie gave her friend a hug. "I didn't hear you come in."

"I guess not," Jill said with a smile. "For a moment there I was wondering whether this was our house or the set of *Riverdance.*"

"Ha!" Sadie laughed. "Sit down and tell me all about your holidays!" Sadie poured two cups of tea before joining her at the kitchen table.

"It was wonderful!" Jill reached for her cup. "We had a great Christmas at home. At first, Mark kept telling me I should switch to medical school . . . you know—become a 'real' doctor."

Sadie shook her head. It was still hard to believe that some people could be prejudiced against something as helpful and natural as chiropractic. "Did you tell him how many credits we're taking?"

"I did." Jill sipped her tea. "You know, he was surprised to find that the total clock hours of chiropractic school were over 250 more than medical school. I told him I *will* be a real doctor!"

"Good for you!" Sadie nodded in support.

Jill smiled. "The amount of schooling got his attention, but I think it was details from the anti-trust suit that really won him over. He couldn't believe it when I told him about the memos from the AMA instructing its members to raise doubts in their patient's minds regarding chiropractic."

"Did you tell him about the AMA document stating that all chiropractors were 'rabid dogs'?" Sadie leaned forward, resting her elbows on the kitchen table.

Jill nodded. "I did. I also told him that chiropractors weren't allowed to join country clubs with medical doctors and that school nurses would tell classrooms full of children that chiropractors were 'quacks.'"

Sadie shook her head and gripped her mug a bit tighter. "How about the plans and efforts of the AMA to destroy chiropractic education? Did he know about that?"

"He didn't, but he does now!" Jill grinned. "I told him all about C.W. Post College, and I told him about Attorney McAndrews telling the court that it was the first time in this century that there was such an organized effort to prevent the education of any group. You know, Sadie, for the first time I think Mark understands why I'm going to Chiropractic College. I think my parents do as well." Jill smiled before finishing her tea.

"Oh, Jill, that's great!" Sadie smiled. "I know they were all a bit skeptical at first. I'd say this calls for a celebration." She went to the pantry, bringing back a bottle of sparkling cider, a loaf of freshly baked Irish soda bread, and a wheel of cheddar cheese.

Jill eyed the cheese. "I hope that's from Wisconsin," she said with a grin.

Sadie smiled, recalling their Whole Foods trip. "Actually, it is." She began slicing it.

"Good. We don't want Becky to alert the Dairy police."

Sadie didn't have to turn around from the counter to know the expression on her friend's face. "You're awful!" she joked.

Jill got up to help Sadie with the food. "I can't wait to see everyone. What about Greg? Did he call you?"

Sadie frowned. "He did at first but I haven't heard from him since the day after Christmas."

"I'm sure he's been busy with his family." Jill bit into the fresh bread. "My God, that's good! If you weren't going to be a chiropractor, you'd make a great chef."

"Thanks." Sadie smiled. It was good to see Jill looking healthy and enjoying food again. The vacation had been good for her. The mountain sun had bronzed her skin and the gauntness that had plagued her during finals was gone.

Jill helped herself to another slice of bread and a wedge of cheese. "Did you find out anything more about Greg's family? I know you had a bad feeling about his dad."

"I still do." Sadie frowned. "Greg told me that after he told his dad about his plans to become a chiropractor, his dad threatened to disinherit him. Greg said they had a huge fight. Afterward, he stormed out of the house and went to the club." Sadie smiled at Jill. "Can you believe I'm dating someone who has a membership to a country club?"

Jill smiled. "Yes, I can. Believe me, country clubs are no big deal. What happened at the club?"

"Well, he was really shaken up and Jennifer helped him out."

"Aha! So that's where she enters the story." Jill took a sip of cider. "I always wondered how those two hooked up; they never seemed to be well suited for each other."

Sadie nodded. "I know. Greg started dating her right away. He really felt like she cared about him, not his inheritance, especially since there wasn't going to be one anymore. Not only did his dad cut him off, he disowned him!"

"That would definitely make him vulnerable." Jill set her glass down.

"It did. He moved in with Jennifer since his dad had thrown him out of the house."

"Nice dad." Jill shook her head. "When did they patch things up?"

"I get the impression that Greg didn't want to talk to his dad. It was only after Jennifer kept begging him that he agreed to a meeting."

"That must have been some meeting," Jill said.

"That's the weird thing, Jill. Greg said his dad did a 180—something his father *never* does. Not only did he support his decision to come to Chiropractic College, he was fine with him living with Jennifer. Greg said he actually encouraged it—'a practical solution' is what he said."

"So they both came here from Indiana and set up house."

Sadie nodded.

"I see what you mean about Greg's dad—he does seem to run hot and cold." Jill reached for her cider. "At least everything worked out." She raised her glass. "To us."

Sadie raised her glass to meet Jill's. "To us."

KNOCK. KNOCK. KNOCK.

"I wonder who that could be?" Sadie opened the door. "Becky! Come in."

Jill was nibbling on some cheese as she walked into the living room. "I promise, it's from Wisconsin."

"What?" Becky asked.

"Never mind." As Sadie was taking Becky's coat, she noticed the sparkling diamond on her left hand. "Becky!"

Unable to contain her excitement, Becky whirled around with her ring finger extended. (Naturally a group hug followed the display.) First, Sadie grabbed her hand; the ring was beautiful. Then she threw her arms around Becky. "Oh, I'm so happy!" Becky said, now clinging to both Sadie and Jill. They spent several minutes that way, as only girls can. Hugging, crying, and laughing in celebration of a very female rite of passage.

As soon as the initial excitement died down, Jill's desire for details surfaced. "Okay honey, tell us everything," Jill instructed.

Becky smiled. "Well, I went to talk to Roger."

"Was it romantic?" Sadie asked. An incurable romantic herself, she wanted things to be beautiful and special for her friends as well.

"Actually, it was in the milking parlor, but it was romantic to us." Becky smiled at the memory. "I told him that I loved him and it didn't matter to me if he was a doctor, dairy farmer, or a rocket scientist."

Sadie leaned forward. "What did he do?"

"He stopped milking and grabbed me, swinging me around. He said he loved me, too. Then, right there in the center of all the cows, he asked me to marry him!" Becky jumped up and hugged her friends again. "I'm so excited. I couldn't wait until school tomorrow to tell you."

"I'm glad you didn't," Sadie said. "How about Ellen; does she know?"

Becky grinned. "She must have gotten some Celtic powers from you, Sadie. She called me within ten minutes of Roger's proposal."

"Oh, Becky, I'm so happy for you!" Sadie's eyes sparkled with her excitement. "I can't wait for tomorrow. It's going to be a great year!"

Jill grinned. "Don't let the back row know that he proposed in the milking parlor. As a matter of fact, I don't think you should advertise that to Paul or Cathy, either. I wonder if they're still together?" She shook her head at the thought. "That's definitely a good reason to get up tomorrow."

Sadie looked over at Jill and grinned. She knew her friend was not fond of 8 a.m. classes, saying that it just wasn't civilized to get up so early.

"Don't worry," Becky said. "I can handle the back row as well as Paul and Cathy. What did they call me? Miss Milk Maid?" Becky looked down and frowned.

Sadie knew she wasn't frowning over being called Miss Milk Maid. "Becky, what is it?"

"Oh, I hope it's nothing. Ellen said that Troy was sick. She wasn't sure what was wrong, but she sounded concerned."

"Oh, honey, don't worry. I'm sure he'll be fine." Jill patted her shoulder.

"Yes, I'm sure he'll be fine. We can send him some vitamins," Sadie said.

"You guys are the best," Becky smiled. "I'd better go. I've got some more unpacking to do and I want to pick up some groceries so I'll be all set for our first week back."

"Good night." Sadie waved goodbye to her friend. She smiled as she closed the door. I can't wait for tomorrow, she thought.

CHAPTER

13

Second-trimester students were entering the Nutrition classroom. Soon, every chair was occupied—except Greg's. Sadie turned, checking the doorway—no Greg. Looking up at the clock, she frowned. Two minutes until roll call. Where could he be?

The St. Louis College of Chiropractic was very strict regarding attendance. Unlike other professional schools, you not only had to pass your exams, you also had to physically attend your classes or you would not be allowed to graduate.

CLICK. CLICK. CLICK.

The second hand inched forward. Sadie was worried.

CLICK. CLICK. CLICK.

Greg came rushing in.

Whew! Sadie sighed in relief.

"That's it; roll call," said Professor Jack Gutman. Resembling a young Clint Eastwood, he stood in front of the podium calling out their names.

Jill leaned over, whispering to Sadie, "It's like having Dirty Harry doing roll call."

Sadie grinned at the analogy.

Class began abruptly. "What do Alzheimer's disease, ADHD, depression, and dyslexia have in common?" The students soon learned that he had a brisk, no-nonsense style of teaching. Undaunted by the rapid-fire questioning, several hands went up, Sadie's included.

"Patients with these disorders also have deficiencies in omega-3 fatty acids." For some time now, Sadie had been doing her own research on this subject. She discovered that they're called essential fatty acids because the body can't produce them, yet it requires them for normal functioning. She learned that 80 percent of Americans are deficient in these essential fatty acids, harming not only the brain but also the heart, blood vessels, immune system, and joints—literally every cell and organ in the human body.

"That's correct." Professor Gutman nodded. "There have been many studies documenting their health benefits. Stepping out from behind the podium, he continued, "A British clinical trial showed that supplementation with essential fatty acids reduced ADHD-related symptoms in children. Seasonal affect disorder is much less common in Iceland than in other northern countries due to their high consumption of fish. There have been two long-term Dutch studies that found a 60 percent decreased risk of dementia in those who consumed a high intake of omega-3 fatty acids from fish."

Becky raised her hand. "Why don't they give essential fatty acids instead of poisons like Ritalin and Prozac?" Turning in response to her question, nearby classmates also noticed her new engagement ring. There were several smiles in the fourth row.

Before Professor Gutman had a chance to answer, Paul Santini cut in, "That's because they can't patent fish oil." Paul definitely knew all about the bottom line—money.

"Unfortunately, Paul, you're absolutely right." Professor Gutman shook his head. His frustration at the business-side of the health care industry was evident.

Cathy Muncie smiled, placing her hand on Paul's forearm.

Jill turned, facing Sadie with her trademark raised-eyebrow expression. Sadie nearly laughed out loud. That was one question answered. Paul and Cathy were still together.

Professor Gutman resumed lecturing. "As you know, fish oil contains the omega-3 fatty acids EPA and DHA. EPA is a natural anti-inflammatory, so it's good for pain control."

Sadie clenched her teeth, wishing she'd begun her essential fatty acid research earlier. Instead of Vioxx, her grandmother could have taken fish oil. Shaking her head, she turned her attention back to the lecture.

"EPA is very beneficial for the cardiovascular system because it prevents platelets from sticking together, it relaxes the arteries, and lowers triglyceride and cholesterol levels."

Jill leaned over. "People should be on fish oil instead of statin drugs."

Sadie nodded in agreement.

"Since the brain is 60 percent fat, it shouldn't be surprising that a lack of omega-3 fatty acids can impair mental functions. DHA is crucial to the proper development of the brain and nervous system. This is so important for the development of an infant's brain that it has been added to infant's formula in most countries throughout the world. Unfortunately, only recently has the United States followed suit."

Professor Gutman began pacing. "As critical as DHA is to an infant, it remains an important component of cognitive function throughout life. Omega-3's also reduce the risk of some types of cancer, improve insulin sensitivity, protect against macular degeneration, and relieve the pain of arthritis. It's amazing that something natural, with so many health benefits, is not already as well-known as Prozac, Ritalin, and a whole host of other drugs."

BAM! Professor Gutman's fist hit the podium. He shook his head, momentarily lost in thought. The burden of educating a public that readily believed the myriad of drug ads was definitely the hardest part of his job.

Sadie raised her hand. "Wouldn't you think that with the huge increase in the use of psychiatric drugs that are supposed to control depression and violence, these things would be decreasing instead of increasing? Instead, the United States has the highest rate of violence of all the industrialized countries in the world." Sadie felt very strongly about this. One of the things she had often discussed with her grandmother was the alarming trend of increased psychiatric drugging of children.

Becky was just as passionate as Sadie on this issue. "In the United States, child homicides have tripled and suicide rates have quadrupled!" She looked down, shaking her head in aggravation. (It wasn't until one of those head shakes focused her attention onto her new engagement ring that she began to calm down.)

"It's the typical American diet that's making people crazy."

Wow! This statement came from the fifth row—Jackie Adams. It was surprising to hear from her; she usually kept to herself. Dubbed "Nature Girl" by the back row, she was in her late 40s, with long, graying hair restrained in a perpetual ponytail. Her narrow feet were encased in Birkenstocks all year long. Disillusioned with the medical life, Jackie had quit her nursing career to become a chiropractor. The reading glasses, which hung from a chain around her neck, had bounded forward and then slapped back onto her chest following her forceful outburst.

Her glasses heaved forward again; apparently she wasn't finished. "Food used to be natural. Now people eat prepackaged meals stripped of all vital nutrients. Today, instead of fruits and vegetables, the average American consumes over 200 pounds of sugar and artificial sweeteners every year. Teenagers drink soda pop instead of milk."

Sadie turned to see Becky, smiling after that comment.

Jackie continued, "Even parents who try to give their children healthful food are sabotaged when they send them to schools that are earning millions by having vending machines and fast food served on the premises."

She shook her head; her glasses were getting a workout today. "I don't understand why the increasing use of mind-altering drugs is considered normal. Why isn't anyone properly investigating the link between what we eat and how we think, feel, and act? The FDA should be held accountable for allowing the food industry to alter our food supply. It's destroying our brains!"

As Jackie's glasses settled back into their normal resting place, the back row had to admit that Nature Girl had made some good points.

"Thank you, Jackie," Professor Gutman looked relieved. Here was some evidence that he wasn't alone in his fight for nutritional reform.

Feeling the pressure to perform, Peter thrust his arm upward—at a gravity-defying speed. If they could have held up cards, the back row would have given him a perfect ten. (Their bets that he would have a shoulder problem by spring now seemed to be a certainty.) "I think Linus Pauling was correct when he said, 'It is now recognized by leading workers in the field that behavior is determined by the functioning of the brain, and that the functioning of the brain is dependent on its composition and its structure.'"

Whew! The girls were definitely giving Peter a workout. Was it mental exertion or anxiety that had painted his face an alarming shade of beet red?

"I find it interesting that the rates of depression have been skyrocketing since World War II." Jackie Adams pressed her lips firmly together in a prim pout before continuing. "That coincides with the ending of the Victory gardens and the advent of frozen and prepackaged foods."

Jackie was no longer the silent Nature Girl. Now she was another force for Peter Burger to reckon with—his very own force of nature.

During this discussion, two things were becoming noticeable. Peter's cheeks were getting redder and Professor Gutman was developing a true Dirty Harry glint in his eyes as he looked with pride at his students.

Paul Santini shook his head. "I don't get it."

"He never does," Jill whispered.

Sadie grinned.

Paul continued, "If your car doesn't run, you don't give it some psychological label and inject drugs into the engine—you give it the fuel it needs. It should be the same with kids. How can the brain make hormones and stuff without the proper fuel?" With his eyebrows puckered together, Paul looked genuinely confused as to the plight of the normal American student.

Jill leaned over to Sadie and said, "It seems like he got it right this time."

Sadie nodded in agreement.

While the back row knew that lots of things didn't make sense to Paul, they had to admit that this didn't make sense to them, either. Amazingly, it seemed that Paul Santini was actually getting smarter. Apparently those essential fatty acid supplements really work.

Professor Gutman smiled. "The brain cannot make hormones and neurotransmitters without proper nutrients. One of the things we'll be studying, Paul, is the nutritional requirements of the brain."

Turning his attention to Jackie, he continued. "You are right, Jackie. Our diet is the *one* major change we've noted, and we are seeing how this has altered the physical states of our brains. Not only has it altered the states of our minds, it has profoundly affected our moods."

BUZZ. BUZZ. BUZZ.

For once, even the back row was sorry to hear the bell signaling the end of class.

Sadie stood in the hallway waiting for Greg while everyone was filing through the doorway. She was shocked at how pale he looked. Dark circles shadowed his eyes. Reaching out, she grabbed his hand. "Let's have some tea."

"That sounds good." Greg hugged her. The tension in his muscles was palpable.

Sadie's chest felt heavy. Something was wrong—very wrong. The hallway to the cafeteria seemed endless. CLOMP. CLOMP.

CLOMP. Even his footsteps sounded heavy.

"Now, dearie, don't ya go borrowin' trouble," Elsie advised.

"Okay, Grandma, but trouble is obviously trying to find me," Sadie muttered under her breath.

"What's that?" Greg looked down at her.

"Nothing." She sat down, grateful for the support of the cafeteria chair while Greg got their drinks. Green tea with milk and lemon for her and strong black coffee for him.

Sadie gripped the mug, savoring its warmth as well as the fresh scent of lemon. "What's wrong?" She searched his face, looking for clues.

He grasped her small hands, staring at them for a moment as he recalled holding them this very same way at Robata's. Slowly, his eyes moved up to hers. Sadie held her breath. "Jennifer is pregnant."

14

"**W**hat?" Jill's reaction when Sadie told her the news was much the same as Sadie's had been—she was stunned.

"That's what he said. Jennifer is pregnant and he has to do the right thing." Sadie sighed; even the familiar surroundings of her kitchen failed to soothe her.

"What are you going to do?" Jill searched her face.

Slumping forward, Sadie shook her head, "What can I do?"

"You can fight for him." Jill's blue eyes burned with intensity.

Sadie shook her head.

Jill walked around the table, giving her a hug. "Oh honey, I'm so sorry."

"Me, too." Sadie cried on her friend's shoulder.

The week was long and stressful for Sadie. Thankfully, the course schedule was full of labs and lectures that had kept her busy. Finally—it was Friday! Somehow she made it through the week. Becky and Ellen were on their way over with a large pizza. Although she rarely ate pizza, tonight it sounded good.

KNOCK. KNOCK. KNOCK.

Yeah, Sadie thought. The cavalry had arrived.

As the pizza disappeared, Sadie's spirits began to lift. As usual, talking with her friends helped.

Ellen reached for another slice of pizza, pausing in mid-air as she brought it up to her mouth. "I still can't believe he's going to marry her." She shook her head before biting into a slice of pepperoni.

Getting over her initial anger at Greg, Becky decided to act as peacemaker. "Well, you do have to give him credit for being honorable and responsible. Not every guy would do that."

Sadie looked up. "I know; that's one of the things I love about him."

Becky nodded. "I can't imagine what this must be like for Greg. Wanting to be with you but feeling burdened by his responsibilities to Jennifer. I'm sure he's hurting, too."

"You're right." Sadie nodded her head. "I've been so focused on my own sadness that I didn't really see things from his viewpoint. I guess deep down I knew that he didn't mean to hurt me. He's trying to do the right thing. Even if it's hard for both of us." Rising from her chair, she gave Becky a hug. "Thanks."

"You're welcome," Becky said, patting her on the shoulder.

Watching the exchange, Jill smiled. This was the most emotion Sadie had shown since hearing Greg's startling news. Thankfully, she was looking and sounding more like herself.

"Now I feel bad that I didn't talk to him all week." Ellen shook her head, causing her newly auburn hair to swirl momentarily before returning to its new, sleek shape.

Her week had been full as well. First, there had been all of the compliments on her makeover. The back row had actually wolf-whistled when she walked into the anatomy lab. (No one had ever wolf-whistled at her before.) Staring at her for a full minute, Cathy Muncie had walked away—speechless! (Maybe that's why the back row was so pleased with her.) The entire week's worth of compliments, however, had paled beside the grief in her friend's eyes. She couldn't recall ever experiencing so many emotions in the span of one week. In addition to the happiness from so many compliments was her concern about Sadie and the struggle to sort out her mixed feelings for Greg. Finally, on top of everything else was the nagging worry about Troy's health.

"I guess you're right; maybe we were a bit hard on him," Jill said, warming to the "other person's viewpoint" philosophy.

Finishing her pizza, Becky wiped her hands. "We all temporarily forgot that, above all, Greg's our friend, too!" She threw her crumpled napkin into the empty pizza box.

"You're right, Becky. He needs our support." Sadie felt relieved. Having made a decision, she no longer felt stuck in the emotions of the past week. It was one thing to feel sad, she thought, but quite another to feel like a prisoner of your own emotions. Thankfully, with the help of her friends, she'd been set free of that self-imposed jail cell.

"Well, we may all be friends, but we're girls first." Jill summed things up with her unique brand of Southern wisdom. "It was only natural that we would take your side over Greg's."

"I know." Sadie yawned. "I don't think I could have made it through this week without your support." The tension of the past week was receding, leaving in its place an overwhelming exhaustion.

"Honey, go on up and get some rest," Jill said, watching as Sadie tried to suppress another yawn.

"Do you mind?" Ever the proper hostess, Sadie didn't want to abandon her friends.

"Go!" Ellen pointed in the direction of the stairs.

"Yes." Becky nodded. "Get some sleep."

"Okay. Thanks, you guys." Sadie headed off to bed. She was fast asleep by the time her friends began to make their plans.

"What can we do to help her?" Becky asked. Now that she was engaged, she wanted a "happy-ever-after" feeling for all of her friends. Even her combined concern for Sadie and Troy couldn't extinguish the joy she felt in being engaged to Roger. Smiling, she could still remember receiving that first Valentine's card. She had been only twelve years old and very excited about the upcoming Valentine's party. Her excitement soon vanished when one of the cows she was milking before school decided to kick her. She remembered pleading with her mom to let her stay home. The tragedy of a toothless smile didn't sway her mom— she'd gone to school. Tragedy had quickly changed to triumph when Roger shyly handed her the card. He didn't even care that she'd lost a tooth that morning!

"We need to find someone else for her." Jill leaned forward as she laid out her plan.

"Do you think that will work?" Although Ellen was thoroughly impressed with Jill's makeover skills, she still wasn't sure about matchmaking.

As if she could read her mind, Jill continued, "It's not crucial that the match-up works; we just need to get her mind off Greg."

In hushed tones, Jill filled her friends in on details from Sadie's past. (The ones she was aware of, that is.) "Her grandma got sick and died when she was in high school. She doesn't talk about it much but I know that she was spending so much time helping her that she didn't go to any of the school dances. Then, when she was in college, she worked at her parent's general store to help pay the bills. She really hasn't dated at all."

"I didn't know that," Ellen said.

"Me, either." Becky shook her head.

Privately, Ellen thought that she and Sadie now had one more thing in common. She hadn't dated much, either. Unfortunately, "horse face" hadn't started in Chiropractic College—it had haunted her since grade school. That was one of the reasons she loved horses so much—they don't care what you look like. She had gone to a horse show instead of her school prom. No big loss either, she thought.

"So," Jill continued, "I think Greg is the first guy she's ever been serious about. What if it's just because he's her first real boyfriend? I think she needs to go out with someone else so she has a comparison. You know how Sadie is; she loves everyone."

Ellen nodded in agreement.

Becky was deep in thought. Having loved Roger her whole life, she had a different perspective. She knew that once you found your soulmate, that was it. Whether he was the first guy you dated or the tenth, it didn't matter. As she recalled all her observations of Sadie and Greg, she couldn't help thinking that they belonged together. Maybe they'd come to that realization if Sadie dated someone else. It might jar them both, she thought. "This just might work," she said, warming to the idea.

"We could check out the Trimester Ones to see if there are any potential candidates." Ellen, too, had jumped onto the matchmaking bandwagon.

"That's a great idea, Ellen. On Monday, start checking them out." Jill's eyes sparkled in anticipation of the start of her plan.

Looking over at Jill, Ellen couldn't help thinking how unusual it was to hear orders of any kind coming out of such a model-perfect mouth. Southern belles, she thought, really were made of steel. Buried deep within her was another thought—a hope, really. The unspoken hope that she, too, could find romance.

"Sadie has worked her whole life, always putting the needs of others above her own." Jill ran her hand through her hair, tucking a few strands behind her ear. "In a way, that's what she's doing now with Greg." Jill frowned. "I never told you all this, but she's still working. She does all the cooking and cleaning in exchange for her rent."

"Really?" Ellen's jaw dropped. Thanks to her new bob, it didn't lend itself to her old horse-face comparisons.

Jill nodded. "At first I thought—great. I don't cook and I don't like to clean. But then, when I got to know Sadie, I wanted her to be able to live here without the responsibilities of cooking and cleaning. I remember one day when I came home early to help out with the cleaning." Jill shook her head.

"What happened?" Ellen asked.

"She very politely told me to stop." Jill leaned forward. "She said, 'a bargain is a bargain.'"

"She is proud and honorable," Ellen said.

"Just like Greg," Becky said, strengthening her belief that they belonged together.

Jill stood up, grabbing the empty pizza box. After throwing it in the trash, she turned her attention to Ellen. "How's Troy?"

Ellen frowned. "Mom took him in for tests. We're still waiting for the results. It's so hard. He just lies around. That's not like him."

"I'm sorry, honey." Jill remembered Troy's exuberance from their Thanksgiving visit. She, too, was having a hard time imagining the lively seventeen-year-old with no energy. She frowned at the thought.

"When will the test results come back?" Becky was worried as well. Troy was like a brother to her.

"We should know something this week." Ellen yawned. "I'd better be going."

The yawn was infectious; now Becky was yawning. "Me, too."

"Thanks for coming," Jill said as she escorted them to the door.

Upstairs, Sadie was tossing and turning. The dream was a familiar one, but that didn't mean it was pleasant. For Sadie, it was an unspoken, unwelcome companion. Taking great lengths to hide it from her friends and family, to this very day it still remained a secret. When she was younger, not wanting to burden her parents, she had hidden under eye concealer in her nightstand. Even now she was careful not to leave her room without its necessary camouflage. She also slept with a fan running, even in the dead of winter, to muffle any noises.

The events of the past week had triggered a sadness deep within her. Hidden by day, it was only at night—in her dreams—that it resurfaced. Suddenly, Sadie sat upright, captured by the force of the dream. "Katie!" she cried.

CHAPTER

15

Grudgingly, January had given way to February. The sun shone with renewed purpose—the days were getting longer. The last vestiges of mid-winter blues were being formally banished. Mardi Gras, St. Louis-style, was in full bloom. Second only to the famed Mardi Gras celebration in New Orleans, St. Louis hosted a large, rowdy party, filling the streets of the historic Soulard neighborhood.

Part of the Mardi Gras celebration included a Pet Parade and the ever-popular Weiner Dog Derby. The sight of those Daschunds running for charity, cheered on by their wildly enthusiastic (dare we say obsessed) owners, was enough to make anyone smile.

Miles away in the Nutrition classroom, that is exactly what Sadie was doing—smiling. Thanks to her friends, her life seemed to be getting back to normal. She had worked things out with Greg. Although she knew she wanted more of a relationship, as did Greg, they had come to an understanding. Thankfully, they were still friends.

I can't believe I actually have a date this weekend, Sadie thought. Evidently, Ellen had searched the entire freshman class, finding what she called "the perfect male." Sadie smiled again before letting her mind wander to more serious issues: Troy and Greg.

She was worried about Greg's future with Jennifer. Deep down she had felt all along that Jennifer was trying to trap Greg. Now she had. Greg was going along with the plans to marry her at the end of the trimester. The fact that his dad was not only all for the wedding but also planning it and paying for it just didn't seem right. *How could a man threaten to disown his son for going to Chiropractic College and suddenly become ridiculously happy over an unplanned pregnancy? It's as though Jennifer isn't the only one setting a trap,* Sadie thought. She made a mental note to talk to Jill about it more after class.

Troy was another matter. According to Ellen, ever since he'd helped in a friend's ginseng fields, he'd complained of headaches. They hadn't been bad enough to draw attention to them over Thanksgiving, but since then they'd gotten progressively worse. In addition to the headaches, he was tired all the time—spending most of his time on the couch instead of outside riding Cutter. So far, the doctors hadn't come up with a definite diagnosis. One even suggested Prozac, claiming he must be depressed. According to Ellen, her dad had hit the roof at that suggestion.

"Like hell I'll put him on that suicidal poison!" Tom had shouted before stomping out of the office.

Sadie knew that Tom was right. There was something physically wrong with Troy. *But what?* Before she had time to form an answer, Professor Gutman stepped up to the podium.

"Today we're going to talk about trans-fatty acids (TFAs)," he announced. "As you know, trans-fats are found in margarine and any other partially hydrogenated oils. This would include processed snack foods, peanut butter, cookies, crackers, cakes, fried foods, most breads—basically your typical American diet."

Shaking his head, Paul interrupted, "So a peanut butter sandwich is loaded with TFAs?"

"That's right," Professor Gutman nodded. "We know that trans-fatty acids impair the formation of the brain tissue. Since they are readily transmitted through the placenta, pregnant women should *never* consume trans-fatty acids!"

As usual, once another classmate spoke up in class, Peter was compelled to add even more information. His hand shot skyward.

"Peter?" Professor Gutman acknowledged him.

"According to Dr. Walter Willett of Harvard's School of Public Health, it is estimated that Americans consume at least 20 percent of their daily fat intake from TFAs. The consumption of these unnatural fats kills about 30,000 people every year."

"Thank you, Peter." In addition to the rest of the class, Professor Gutman was now aware of Peter's need to answer any and all questions posed to the class. As an instructor, he valued that trait, but privately, he was worried. The need to be right as a freshman was going to be hard to maintain for the next eight trimesters.

"If you recall from your organic chemistry . . . "

"UGH!" Jill groaned.

Turning, Sadie smiled at her friend's look of horror at the mention of chemistry.

" . . . the chemical structure of a trans-fatty acid has been altered from the flexible, chemically active cis configuration to the trans shape. This altered shape doesn't fit into any of the fat-requiring structures of the body. It also blocks out the essential fatty acids, preventing them from being utilized by the body."

Professor Gutman started pacing as he spoke. "As you know, TFAs have been linked to some serious diseases. They have devastating effects on the cardiovascular system. The *New England Journal of Medicine* did a study in 1990 showing that TFAs raised total cholesterol levels and 'bad' LDL cholesterol while lowering the healthy HDL cholesterol."

"I think it's criminal that the medical community has known about this all this time. Instead of telling people to consume fish oil and get rid of trans-fatty acids, they allow an epidemic of high cholesterol to occur, all the while making billions on bogus cholesterol-lowering drugs!" Jackie Adams was visibly shaking, she was so angry. It was easy to see why she'd decided to quit her nursing career.

"Unfortunately, greed is a strong motivator." Professor Gutman frowned. "As Peter stated earlier, Dr. Willet estimates 30,000 deaths each year to be TFA-related. He has also found TFA consumption to be linked with breast cancer and prostate cancer. It's amazing that all these conditions as well as diabetes, infertility, obesity, and immune dysfunction have all been linked to TFA consumption and yet the FDA does *nothing* to ban them."

BAM! His fist hit the podium. "Now we're seeing a *huge* rise in violence in our schools. In addition to the side effects from psychiatric drugs, the consumption of TFAs also plays a roll."

Sadie clenched her teeth. Those psychs and their drugs, she thought, shaking her head. Meanwhile, Jill was drawing a little boy in a jail cell. Sadie looked over to see that the bars were made out of prescription bottles. How true, she thought, before turning her attention back to Professor Gutman.

"We know that when trans-fatty acids are taken into the brain, they displace DHA, causing the brain to make DPA." He paused before adding, "DPA is *not* supposed to be in human brains. Primate brains have DPA."

Paul Santini was obviously still upset by the fact that peanut butter sandwiches were loaded with TFAs. (Maybe he

had eaten a lot of them and was now worried.) Whatever the reason for his concern, something about "primate brains" put him
over the edge. "*What?*" His thick, bull-like torso expanded in outrage.

"Wow! That's like the incredible Hulk," Sadie whispered to
Jill.

"Yeah." Jill pointed to the sketch she'd drawn of him with
his shirt ripping off.

"That was fast," Sadie whispered, smiling at the caricature.

Paul's outburst continued, "You mean we're making a bunch
of kids with monkey brains?"

Although they were outraged at the deceitful lies being told
to the American public, some of the students started laughing. It
wasn't every day that you heard "monkey brains" being shouted
in a thick, New Jersey accent. The back row was definitely beginning to warm toward Paul. (Who wouldn't like a guy proud to be
called "Sanporno"?)

"That's right, Paul," Professor Gutman continued, "DPA
causes aggression and poor socialization skills. Additionally,
Crawford Studies show that although as a race we are increasing
our body size, our brain size is actually decreasing."

"A nutritional de-evolution," Sadie said out loud as she realized the full impact of Professor Gutman's words.

"Exactly." Professor Gutman nodded. "We are severely damaging our children and ultimately the very future of our society."

Thinking about how her grandmother had stressed the
importance of eating organic foods, she shared her feelings with
the class. "It's sad that the United States has totally gone astray
on one of the most important fundamentals determining the
quality of life—that is, the very quality of its food supply."

"You're right, Sadie." Professor Gutman nodded in agreement. "The marketing strategies of the food-processing companies have been so successful, so pervasive, that we no longer find
it strange to see someone drinking coffee or soda instead of
water. Most people don't even think it's unhealthy."

Walking toward the front row, he continued. "So many of the
health problems plaguing our society are preventable. I want to
stress the fact that it's not enough to learn to give a good adjustment. No! You have a moral obligation to educate your patients
so we can reverse the dwindling spiral that we're on."

BUZZ. BUZZ. BUZZ.

Once again, the class was sorry to see the lecture end.

— . . . —

With only thirty minutes before x-ray lab, Sadie grabbed Jill and headed for her favorite outside bench. The sun was shining. After the dreariness of January, it felt good to be outside. The crisp air already held the promise of spring. Placing her books on the bench, she remained standing.

"What can we do to help Greg?" she asked, not wasting any time on preamble. She needed Jill's advice. The overwhelming urge to help Greg had hit her during class. Sensing her urgency, her heart was pounding—ready for action. Unable to stand still, she started pacing in front of the bench.

"Honey, you're making me dizzy," Jill said as she stood up. "Have you talked to him?"

"A bit." Sadie stopped pacing.

"There has to be some way to expose her. That girl's a gold digger for sure." Jill stomped her feet to keep warm. (Fifty-eight degrees was still cold to a Southerner.)

"Jill, that's it!" Sadie said. "That's what's been bothering me!"

"What?" Jill went from feeling cold to feeling confused.

"Money!" Sadie shook her head. "That's what doesn't make sense. I know Greg isn't taking money from his dad for school or living expenses—even though he keeps offering it."

"Just because he isn't right now doesn't mean that he won't once the baby comes. Jennifer could still see him as her meal ticket. Besides, his dad is paying for the wedding." Jill rubbed her hands together.

Sadie hadn't thought about that. Frowning, she shook her head. "Something about the money is bothering me."

"Well, maybe it's bothering Greg, too. Talk to him."

"You're right." Sadie nodded.

HONK. HONK. HONK.

Looking up, Sadie watched as a flock of geese circled the campus pond.

Jill, ever the city girl, ignored the geese as she ignored the traffic noises of the city. "I wonder if it's even Greg's baby."

Sadie's jaw dropped in surprise. "I don't trust her but surely she wouldn't make up something like that!"

"I wouldn't be so sure." Jill's eyes narrowed. "I know! I'll have Mark check into things. He knows her brother; maybe he can help us."

"Oh, Jill, that's a great idea!" Sadie smiled before checking her watch. "We'd better head back for class."

Radiology reminded Sadie of putting together a crossword puzzle. Each piece was significant, and it took a sharp eye to find the hidden pattern.

CLICK. The main lights were turned off. An eerie glow filled the room with the x-ray view boxes now providing the only available light. The class, as with the subject itself, had a definite pattern. Two students stood in front of each view box looking at an x-ray with an arrow to point out what they should observe. On the bottom right was a card listing the x-ray findings. Sadie and Jill were lab partners.

"It's easy when they have the answer already typed out for you," Jill said, pointing to the card that read Pott's Disease—Tuberculosis of the spine.

"I know." Sadie nodded.

Walking to the next viewing station, Sadie extended her right hand, preferring to cover the answer so that she could figure out the puzzle for herself. "That definitely looks denser," She said, still squinting at the radiograph.

"What does the card say?"

Sadie moved her hand.

GROUND GLASS APPEARANCE:

Notice a slight increase in density throughout this radiolucent lesion.

The most common disorder associated with this ground glass appearance is fibrous dysplasia.

"Fibrous dysplasia," Sadie said.

"Too bad they won't come into our office like this," Jill said pointing to the typewritten information card.

Sadie had to smile. (That *would* be helpful.) "Yeah, too bad."

After reviewing all of the radiographs, Sadie walked to the row of tiered desks and took her seat. Again, this was all part of the pattern. First, you walked around the perimeter of the room, stopping at each view box. Then you took your assigned seat for the slide presentation. The humming of the slide projector filled the room as the students sat, waiting.

CLICK. The first slide was in place and Dr. Dawson began his lecture. "Today we're going to discuss neoplasms. This is very important to you all because the most common site of metastasis from any organ is to the spine. Always look closely at the vertebral bodies for any sign of cancer."

Sadie recalled reading about the "winking owl sign" representing osteolytic metastatic carcinoma destroying a single pedicle on the vertebral body.

Although the puzzle aspect of radiology intrigued her, the classroom itself was another story. It depressed her. She made it a point to study in the radiology lab with another classmate. The one and only time she had done so alone had left her feeling cold and edgy—reminding her of being in the hospital before her grandmother's death. As if that weren't bad enough, that night she'd been haunted by the dream again. No, she thought, pushing back the memory. For Sadie Jensen, radiology was a team event.

CLICK. Sadie looked up at the screen. "Is this x-ray normal or do you detect cancer?" Dr. Dawson looked at the class, his eyes protected by large, thick glasses. The lenses magnified his features, giving his face an odd, perpetually distorted look.

The term *absent-minded professor* was often used to describe Dr. Dawson. Although prone to absent-mindedness in his day-to-day affairs, his mind was razor sharp when it came to radiology. He might not be able to see his car keys in broad daylight, but give him the fluorescent glare of an x-ray view box and he could pick out a metastasis at twenty paces. The man was a radiology wizard.

Peter was confident that he knew the answer. "Normal," he replied.

The rest of the class nodded in agreement. (Although it was usually a safe bet to agree with Peter.)

CLICK. Next slide.

"Wow! That looks bad," Sadie whispered to Jill.

"This is the same patient—six months later," Dr. Dawson informed them.

What? That can't be right, Sadie thought. That x-ray looked normal. In the front row, she could see Peter squirming in his seat.

CLICK. Back to the first slide.

"That still looks normal to me," Jill whispered to Sadie.

"I think so, too." Staring at the slide, Sadie kept looking for something that she could have missed earlier. Her heart sped up at the prospect of missing a diagnosis. It was scary. Even after seeing the second slide, this one still looked normal to her. From the murmurs she heard around her, she could tell that the rest of the class felt the same way.

CLICK. Second slide—scary.

"You were right, Peter. The first slide *is* normal."

WHEW! The class breathed a collective sigh of relief. Even in the dim light you could see the color come back to Peter's face. Now that the shock of possibly being wrong was wearing off, he felt brave enough to ask the question that was on everyone's mind. "If we didn't miss cancer on the first x-ray, what destroyed the bone mass on the second x-ray?"

That's a good question, Peter." Dr. Dawson faced the class, looking a bit like a bug under a magnifying glass. The fluorescent lights from the view boxes created shadows under his eyes, which were then distorted by his thick glasses. "The second slide shows the same patient—after taking steroids."

"Wow!" Paul exclaimed.

"I wonder if he ever took any," Jill whispered.

"Whether he did or not, you can bet he'll tell his patients not to," Sadie whispered back.

"That's for sure," Jill said as the overhead lights came on. That, too, was part of a pattern, signaling the end of the class.

CHAPTER

16

Spring was fast approaching. It was Friday, March 5, and St. Louis had given them a beautiful 70-degree day to enjoy. With the bedroom windows opened, Sadie's linen curtains were now rustling in the breeze. Sniffing the air, she smiled. It smelled of spring—of life. That wonderful combination of rain and chlorophyll, hyacinths and jonquils—spring.

Humming to herself, she was getting ready for her date. Well, not a date really—more like a friendly group outing. Ellen and Becky, Jill and Jeffrey Adams, and Sadie and Danny Durbin.

"HA!" She laughed. The song she had been humming was *Danny Boy*. "It's a good thing Jill didn't hear that," she muttered to herself.

The girls had been trying to schedule this outing for several weeks now, but Ellen had been rushing home every Friday to check on Troy. Still no news. Finally, Becky convinced Ellen that it would do her good to relax for one night. Jeffrey and Danny would be picking them up in a few minutes. Becky and Ellen were meeting them at Gian-Tony's on the Hill. Ellen was a huge fan of Italian food. Gian-Tony's motto of gourmet food without the gourmet price appealed to her.

Sadie smiled, thinking about her friend—always searching for a bargain. She, too, was excited to get back to the Hill. She hadn't been there since her parents had brought her to St. Louis. It seemed like ages ago and yet she could still recall those wonderful smells.

The heavy moisture of that August day had been laden with the fragrances of fresh-baked Italian breads and simmering sauces with just the right amount of tomatoes and oregano. Then, when you thought it couldn't get any better, came the smell of sausage. The entire neighborhood smelled like a giant outdoor kitchen. A family kitchen, she thought. Her stomach grumbled at the memory.

It was after 6:00 p.m. when they arrived at the Hill. The smells were every bit as good as she remembered. Jeffrey's older

SUV was parked next to a sleek, black BMW. The Hill was open for business. Inside, Becky and Ellen had a table waiting for them. Appetizers were waiting as well. Sadie watched Danny as he dipped his ravioli into a red sauce. He was tall and thin with red hair and freckles.

"Wow! That's good!" Danny turned to Sadie. "Do you come here often?"

"No," she said, shaking her head. "Actually this is only the second time I've been to the Hill. I came here with my parents before school started last year."

"It's hard to get away with schoolwork and labs." Ellen reached for another ravioli as she spoke.

"Yeah, there is already a lot of studying to do." Danny nodded in agreement.

"How are you doing in Underdog's class?" Becky asked, using the universal nickname for Professor Cox.

"He's tough." Danny set his fork down. "Plus, our cadaver must weigh nearly 300 pounds, so it takes twice as long to do any dissection. We spend most of our time picking through all that fat." Danny had just summed up the luck of the draw when it came to cadavers—everyone hoped for a thin one.

"We're lucky because Leroy is thin. It's just basic dissection for us," Sadie said.

"HA!" Jill laughed. "Do you realize every time you get a bunch of freshman chiropractic students together, all they can talk about is their cadaver?"

"It's true." Jeff smiled. "We did the same thing when I was a freshman." He leaned forward before continuing. "At our freshman welcome party, Ed Gaines was sitting at the bar describing his cadaver, a slender female—they called her Kathy. Some guys next to him were listening in on the conversation. Then, he casually mentioned that Kathy was hanging on a meat hook."

"Really?" Jill asked.

"Yeah," Jeff nodded. "The guy next to him actually fell off his bar stool!" "HA!" He laughed at the memory.

"Oh, my. I can just imagine that!" Sadie joined in the laughter, as did the rest of the group.

Ellen's loud horse laugh had met its match with Danny's. At his loud bark of a laugh, he met Ellen's eyes, causing them to both to laugh even harder. (Ellen had never met anyone with a laugh as distinctive as hers.) Sadie watched them laughing together. *Perhaps the two of them would be well suited.* She knew that Ellen was usually shy when she met new people, yet she seemed perfectly at ease with Danny. Both Jill and Becky had turned to look at her. Apparently they were thinking the same thing.

It was during dinner when Danny mentioned that he rode gaited horses.

"Oh, I *love* American Saddlebreds!" Ellen gushed. The rest of the group sat there looking puzzled. Noticing their confusion, Ellen explained, "American Saddlebreds are very elegant show horses. The five-gaited Saddlebred does the normal three gaits—walk, trot, and canter—but also had been trained to perform two additional gaits—the slow gait and the rack."

Danny sat smiling at Ellen during her explanation. Although Ellen wasn't aware of it yet, his interest had just shifted—away from Sadie and onto her.

"Did you ever go to the World's Championships?" Ellen was referring to the World Championship Horse Show held annually in Louisville, Kentucky.

"Yes." Danny nodded. "I took third place with my gelding two years ago."

"You did!" Ellen now had eyes only for Danny. She couldn't help but continue their conversation on horses.

"Excuse me," Sadie got up, heading for the ladies room. Jill followed.

"Do you think they'll miss us?" Jill whispered as they wove their way across the crowded restaurant.

"Not at all," Sadie answered. As the door closed behind them, she turned, smiling at Jill. "They are perfect together!"

"They are, aren't they? You don't mind?" Jill reapplied her lipstick.

"Oh, no!" Sadie pushed an unruly curl behind her ear. "I'm so happy for Ellen. It's good to hear her laugh again."

By the time Sadie and Jill returned, Danny and Ellen had just finished their horse show discussion.

Turning to Jeff, Danny asked, "Are you really working for Dr. Dana Andrews?" He looked suitably impressed. Dr. Andrews was something of a legend among the students.

"Yes, Jeff nodded. "I'm there on Saturdays."

"That must be awesome!" Danny leaned his lanky frame forward, eager to hear about her clinic.

"It is! She had a huge practice," Jeff said proudly. "She has an M.D. and a P.T. working for her as well as a massage therapist. Her clinic is state of the art."

Before Jeff could praise Dr. Andrews any more, they were interrupted by the waiter checking to see whether they'd saved room for dessert. It was a good thing because Jill had begun to chew off her newly applied lipstick at the mention of Dr. Dana.

Ellen looked at her watch. "Oh, no. It's later than I thought. I have to get home. Mom's hoping to get some new test results on Troy."

"Don't worry, Ellen. I'll get a ride back with Jeff. Tell Troy 'hello' for us." Becky gave Ellen a hug.

Sadie jumped up to give her friend a hug, too. "He likes you," she whispered in Ellen's ear. Ellen looked down at her and grinned, hugging her back even harder.

"Go," Jill commanded. "Give Troy our love."

"Thanks, you guys. I had a great time." Danny stood, watching her as she left the table. Turning, Ellen's eyes connected with his once more before she swung the door open and headed for home.

"Bye." Danny mumbled, staring at the door for a moment before finally sitting down. "Who's Troy?"

"Her brother." Sadie filled him in on the details.

"I didn't know he was sick." Jeff was in his clinician mode now, striving to figure out a problem.

"Oh, Jeff, I don't know why we didn't think to ask you." Sadie frowned. "I guess we've all been so busy."

Jeff looked deep in thought as he considered the possible causes of Troy's mysterious symptoms. "Adrenal problems could contribute to the fatigue. You could look into supplements. Ginseng is good, too, but I'd get organic. They put lots of chemicals on it otherwise."

Sadie watched Jill as Jeff was talking. She never took her eyes off of him. It was easy to see that she was proud of him.

Jeff scratched his chin. "It sounds like there's some type of environmental component, some toxicity that hasn't been handled."

"Thanks, Jeff." Becky flashed him her wholesome smile. "*Brought to you by milk*" would have been an appropriate caption. "I'll be sure to let Ellen know what you said."

Well, the group outing was a hit—even if it had turned out differently than expected. Leave it to the Hill to come through for them. Food. Fun. Family. There was definitely something to be said for the Italian way of life.

— • • • —

RING. RING. RING. The ringing of the phone had disturbed Jill's sleep. It was Sunday morning. She heard Sadie answer it in the kitchen. The muffled conversation lulled her back to sleep.

"Jill!" Sadie called. "Mark is on the phone."

Mark! Jill sprang out of bed, putting on her satin robe. Sliding her slender feet into matching slippers, she hurried downstairs.

Sadie smiled. Fresh out of bed and she still looks like a model, she thought, pouring her a cup of coffee. She made it just the way Jill liked it—with chicory and cream. The smell filled the kitchen.

"Hello?" Jill sat down, giving Sadie a grateful smile as she took the cup that Sadie offered. Sipping the coffee, she listened attentively. "Really?" Jill jumped off the chair, ignoring the coffee. Eyes wide, she nodded her head. "Are you sure?"

Sadie stopped drinking her tea as she watched Jill. After the events of her childhood, she was still strongly affected by surprises. Even now her pulse was quickening. Maybe Mark has some good news about Jennifer, she thought, striving for optimism.

"Thanks, honey, you're the best!" Jill hung up the phone. "Sadie, we're going out for brunch." With that said, she turned heading for her room.

"What did he say?" Sadie followed her. "Is it about Jennifer?" She was now standing at Jill's doorway, watching her go through her wardrobe. Suitable brunch clothes were landing on the bed. "Is there something I can tell Greg?" She was now begging for news.

Taking pity on her, Jill turned, stepping out of her closet. "Honey, it's the best news. I'm going to share every juicy morsel with you over brunch. Champagne brunch," she added as an afterthought.

Jill's idea of going out was definitely not Denny's. Sadie soon found herself seated at one of the most prestigious restaurants in the Central West End—Balaban's. It was like being transported to a French bistro. Once inside, she was so awed by the amazing art collection and the beauty of her surroundings that she temporarily forgot to pepper Jill with more questions.

"You're never going to believe what Mark found out," Jill said after ordering.

"What?" Sadie leaned forward in nervous anticipation. Her heart was pounding—beating out its own brand of Morse code. She tried swallowing, but her mouth was too dry.

"That girl isn't even pregnant!"

"What?" Sadie exhaled. She'd been holding her breath, waiting for the news. Although this new information hadn't been too surprising to Jill since she'd had that suspicion all along, it came as quite a shock to Sadie. She sat for a moment, speechless. "Are you sure?" She was still having a hard time believing what she'd just heard.

"I most certainly am." Jill sipped her coffee. Since she'd had the time to get used to her brother's news, she was able to relay the facts fairly calmly. "A friend of Mark's saw Jennifer at Walgreen's pharmacy . . . " Jill paused for another sip of coffee. She was definitely *not* a morning person.

"What does Walgreen's have to do with it?" Sadie interrupted.

"She was getting her prescription filled—for birth control pills!"

"No!" Sadie shook her head. "I can't believe she wasn't pregnant."

Then the bomb dropped. "She was." Jill, too, had been surprised by this bit of information.

"What?" Sadie's mouth dropped open. Feeling as though she were on a roller coaster making a rapid descent, her surroundings blurred. Unaware of the waiter's actions, a plate of eggs Benedict sat in front of her—untouched.

Jill watched with some concern as the color drained from Sadie's face. "Honey, you need something to eat," she said pointing to Sadie's plate.

Sadie took a bite of food, chewing mechanically. It was tasteless. Gradually, the shock wore off. Her surroundings came back into focus. She took another bite of eggs, which tasted surprisingly good. Taking a deep breath, Sadie looked over at Jill. "Okay, I think I'm ready for some more bombshells."

"Good, because I have a few more to give you. Jennifer *was* pregnant but she had an abortion."

Sadie shook her head. "How did you ever find this out?"

"One of Mark's friends knows one of her friends. It's complicated. Besides, it doesn't really matter. What does matter is this—not only is she no longer pregnant, but the baby wasn't even Greg's!" Jill speared a stalk of asparagus. By now she, too, needed some nourishment.

Even when you think you're ready, news like this still hits you. Sadie shook her head, dumbfounded. "You're kidding!" she finally managed to say.

"No." Jill shook her head. "One of Mark's friends was in one of the same classes as the guy she used to date. He dumped her when he found out she was pregnant."

"Wow!" Now that some of the shock had worn off, Sadie realized she was hungry. Picking up her knife and fork, she cut through the English muffin.

After seeing Sadie's smile, Jill poured herself another cup of coffee. Her brother had really come through for them. Just like always, she thought. She'd never told anyone how Mark had come to her rescue when her prom date had decided that a good night kiss wasn't enough of a reimbursement for his expenses. She shivered at the memory.

"Are you cold?" Sadie started to take off her sweater so that Jill could wear it.

"No. I'm fine, really." Pushing the unpleasant memory aside, Jill searched through her purse, pulling out her cell phone. "Here," she said handing the phone to Sadie. "Call Greg."

Sadie smiled. Jill had thought of everything. She quickly dialed his number.

"Hello?" Greg answered.

"Greg?"

"Hi, Sadie!"

Sadie smiled at his obvious pleasure to hear her voice. "Can you meet me sometime today?" She listened, nodding her head. "Okay. I'll see you then. Bye."

"Well?" Jill dropped her phone back into her purse.

"He's meeting me at Starbucks in two hours."

Jill smiled, lifting her champagne glass.

Sadie lifted her glass of sparkling cider.

CLINK. Their glasses touched. "To finding the truth," Jill said.

"To the truth," Sadie replied.

— · · · —

If Starbucks was famous for anything besides its coffee, it would have to be for the music it played. Inside, the senses were stimulated by more than caffeine. Ray Charles was playing when

Sadie walked in. The mellow songs combined with the smell of fresh-roasted coffee created their own brand of urban oasis. Greg was at a table in the back. Seeing Sadie, he stood up.

Unable to contain her excitement, she rushed over, giving him a hug. After all, he *was* a free man. He just didn't know it yet.

"What's that for?" he asked.

"You'd better sit down," she said, speaking from experience.

Frowning, Greg did as she requested. He waited in suspense as Sadie took off her sweater, hanging it on the back of the chair.

She was trying to decide how to break the news to him. On the one hand, it was good news because he was free. On the other hand, it was a shocking betrayal. She decided to apply the "band aid" theory. (Everyone knew that if you pulled a band aid off quickly, it didn't hurt as much as if you had dawdled.) Biting her lip, she sincerely hoped this applied to the delivery of news as well as the removal of band aids.

"Oh, Greg. You're never going to believe what I found out!" *Might was well prepare him a bit—sort of like loosening one corner of the band aid before you gave it a good yank.*

"What?" He leaned forward, waiting for the news.

Taking a deep breath, she put her theory to the test. "Jennifer had an abortion and it wasn't even your baby."

WHOOSH. Greg's mouth dropped open and the air left him in such a rush Sadie could actually hear it. He sat staring straight ahead through blank and unfocused eyes.

Sadie waited.

Finally, he turned to look at her. No longer looking stunned, he now looked confused. "What?" He managed to say.

Sadie filled him in on everything Jill had told her.

In some ways, it was harder for Greg, hearing all the details (maybe the band aid theory wasn't such a good idea). He sat, staring at his hands, numb.

Sadie stood, patting his shoulder. "I'll be right back." She returned with a fresh cup of coffee and a scone. *This ought to boost his brain sugar.* "Here," she said, sitting the scone in front of him, "have some."

The combination of caffeine and carbohydrates kicked in after several minutes. Gradually, the color returned to Greg's face. Although Sadie was glad his skin was no longer pasty-white, there was still something wrong with his eyes. No longer resembling rich, smooth chocolate, right now they could only be described as muddy. Like swirling, turbulent, flood waters.

"It's still hard to believe," he said, shaking his head.

"I know," she nodded.

Frowning, he asked, "Why would she do something like that?"

"I don't know." Sadie shook her head.

She sat there, no longer noticing the spicy smell of cinnamon combining with coffee. Unaware of the background music, all her senses were focused on Greg. For ten minutes, (which felt like an hour to Sadie), she sat, waiting, as he absorbed the news. Gradually, she noticed that his eyes seemed to lose some of their turbulence. It was like watching flood waters recede, she thought. "How are you doing?"

"Okay."

"Let's take a walk," she said, grabbing his hand. Outside, Sadie noticed Greg squinting in the sunlight, as though that much raw energy were hard to confront. Food and fresh air, she thought, heading for a deli several blocks away. That should help him.

Instead of a regular door knob, the deli's front door had a meat cleaver embedded in it. As Sadie reached for it, manners kicked Greg out of his stupor. "I'll get that," he said. The smell of sausage spilled out as soon as the door opened.

Inside, the glass meat counter dominated the room. Black and white tiles covered the floor. Seating was around the corner, past a row of condiments. Soon, an enormous roast beef sandwich appeared before them.

"I'm glad we're splitting this," Sadie said as the smell of horseradish cleared her sinuses.

Greg nodded, once again deep in thought as he ate his sandwich. Sadie let him eat in silence.

As she was reaching for her dill pickle, Greg grabbed her hand, squeezing it. "Thanks," he said.

"For what?"

"For being my friend."

Sadie smiled at him. "You're welcome."

Walking back to their cars, Sadie noticed Greg starting to frown, once again deep in thought. By the time they'd reached his car, he began shaking his head.

"What's going on?" she asked.

Greg fiddled with his keys. "I'm not sure. Something's not right."

Sadie definitely understood the power of "a feeling in your bones," as her grandmother used to say.

"Do you feel all right to drive?" she asked.

"I'm fine." He hugged her. "Thanks to you."

Sadie watched him drive off. Something's brewing, she thought. She was not referring to Starbucks.

CHAPTER

17

"Did Greg talk to Jennifer?" Jill asked, swiveling her chair to the right so that she could face Sadie. They were waiting for the start of their Monday morning Nutrition class.

"No, she's at home until Thursday. He wants to talk to her in person."

"That makes sense." Jill nodded.

Professor Gutman walked in, ending any further conversation. "I know we've been discussing the nutritional requirements of the brain recently," he said as he began his lecture.

Sadie wasn't paying attention. She was thinking about Greg. He looked as though he hadn't slept at all last night. *How could Jennifer do something like that?* Shaking her head, she focused her attention on to what Professor Gutman was saying.

"Did anyone hear about the CDC mistakenly sending out a virulent strain of a flu virus that had killed four million people in the 1950s?"

Naturally, Peter had something to say. "I heard that a Canadian lab finally identified it correctly, causing the CDC to issue warnings to have it destroyed."

"That's right." Professor Gutman nodded.

Jackie shook her head. "Here we are spending millions to prevent bio-terrorism and the Center for Disease Control is sending out virulent strains of a flu virus!"

Professor Gutman nodded. "Thankfully, it was identified and destroyed before there were any problems." Anyway, since there's been so much talk about the flu recently, I thought that it would be the perfect topic for today's discussion. As you know, influenza actually starts in birds, with pigs serving as the intermediate host."

Sadie heard Paul mutter, "So that's why there was the swine flu scare!" Looking over to her left, she saw Jill drawing some pigs with wings. They were being chased by a mad scientist holding a huge syringe. Smiling, she turned, once again facing Professor Gutman.

"As you know, every year the warnings come out about the upcoming flu season. Advisories to get your flu shot are issued. Often, the flu shot doesn't prevent the flu."

"Why is that?" Becky asked.

"Because the different influenza viruses constantly mutate. Each year, scientists choose three strains to use in the making of the vaccine. If the virus mutates, or a new one surfaces after the vaccine has been made, then the vaccine is really useless."

Professor Gutman walked to the blackboard. "In a study done by the National Institute of Allergy and Infectious Diseases, it was found that after examining death rates among the elderly from 1968 to 2001, the so-called lifesaving value of flu shots is virtually nonexistent. This study clearly shows that flu shots did not reduce death rates as much as the public is led to believe."

Sadie wrote that down in her notebook, knowing that studies were always on the exam.

Turning away from the blackboard, Professor Gutman continued, "In addition to the possibility that the vaccine won't offer protection, there is also the very real possibility that it could backfire. It can cause very serious illnesses by damaging the immune system. Guillain-Barre Syndrome has been known to have been caused by the flu shot."

"It's like playing Russian roulette with your health!" Jackie exclaimed.

"It is." Professor Gutman nodded. "Do you know why the elderly, in particular, are urged to get their flu shots each fall?"

"Medicare pays for them?" Paul blurted out. The class burst into laughter, with Ellen's horse laugh echoing among the rest.

Professor Gutman's lips curled into a smile. His eyes twinkled as he shook his head. "Actually, it's called immunosenescence— aging of the immune system."

Sadie raised her hand. "So, instead of doing things to naturally boost the immune system, they offer a vaccine that may or may not work."

"That's right," Professor Gutman nodded. "Unfortunately, the only method of protection offered by conventional medicine is the flu shot." He shook his head before continuing. "The best way to decrease your risk of disease is to keep your immune system working as efficiently as possible. Can anyone tell me some of the possible ways to boost the function of the immune system?"

Peter Burger started talking about a 2001 study using purified bovine thymus protein. He was cut short, however, by a disturbance in the back row. Apparently, anything dealing with bovines was too good of an opportunity to waste. Wadded up notes saying "Milk Maid" and "Bovine Queen" were reaching Becky, one actually hitting her in the back of the head.

"Is that any way for future doctors to act?" Professor Gutman was clearly upset with the juvenile antics occurring during his lecture. The snickering from the back row quickly stopped. Professor Gutman seemed appeased.

Now that the class was back on track, Sadie raised her hand. "Antioxidant vitamins and minerals are very important. Vitamins A, C, and E as well as selenium and zinc are beneficial for the immune system," she answered with a list of some of the vitamins she took on a daily basis.

"Good job, Sadie Jo." Jill whispered in Sadie's ear. Recently Jill had given her the nickname, officially adopting her as an "honorary southern gal." Sadie caught a glimpse of her arched eyebrow. Something was coming.

"Echinacea purpurea stimulates macrophage activity as well as inhibits the ability of bacteria to proliferate," Jill said. Then, she pointed to Peter, whose color was beginning to rise at being shown up by two girls.

"You did that on purpose," Sadie whispered, "just to make him upset."

Jill grinned. Although it was always fun to irritate Peter, she really wanted to distract Sadie from worrying about Greg.

Unfortunately, Peter was a bit of a chauvinist, believing that men were intellectually more qualified than women to become doctors. Therefore, it was doubly hard for him to be upstaged by the girls. He now felt honor-bound to take up the challenge. "In a study published in the *Journal of Clinical Epidemiology . . .* "

"Ooh, *Clinical Epidemiology,*" Jill whispered sarcastically, obscuring Peter's comments on glutathione.

Sadie grinned.

"That's right, Peter."

Sadie looked up, realizing she'd just missed something important.

"In a study from . . . " he was writing an abbreviated journal name, *Free Rad Biol Med*, on the blackboard as he spoke. (In the back row, they were now occupied with *taking* notes instead of throwing them.) Professor Gutman continued, " . . . the study found that adequate levels of glutathione could inhibit production of active influenza virus."

Ellen raised her hand. "How can you increase your glutathione levels?"

"Cruciferous vegetables such as broccoli, cauliflower, brussel sprouts, cabbage, kale, bok choy, turnips, and kohlrabi are the richest source of glutathione."

The bell rang before Professor Gutman could write down another study. Sadie closed her notebook. Looking up, she saw Greg waiting in the aisle. The dark circles under his eyes were prominent.

"Do you have a minute?" he asked.

"Sure," she said. "Let's go to the cafeteria."

As soon as he sat down, he said, "I don't think this was all Jennifer's plan."

"What do you mean?" Sadie leaned in closer.

Greg frowned. "My dad was really pushing us together."

Sadie's heart beat faster. Greg had just given voice to her suspicions that something wasn't quite right with his father. "Do you think he had something to do with it?"

Greg nodded. "I was up all night thinking about it. I mean, all of a sudden Dad's okay with my being a chiropractor and he's supporting my decision to marry Jennifer." Greg paused, frowning.

"What?" Sadie asked.

"Actually, now that I said it out loud, marrying Jennifer was his idea." Shaking his head, he continued. "What an idiot! I was acting like some misguided kid, still trying to win my father's approval."

Sadie grasped his hand, offering support. "That's only natural. After all, you were just trying to do the right thing."

"Thanks," he said, giving her a ghost of a smile.

"Why would your dad want you to get married?" Sadie didn't realize that she was still holding his hand.

"I don't know." Greg sat staring at the chipped Formica table, deep in thought. Suddenly, he looked up.

Sadie leaned forward, releasing his hand. "What?"

"He found me in his study! That's when it all started—he blew up about Chiropractic School, threatening to disown me!"

"So you think there's a link between school and marriage, and something about his study?" Sadie asked, trying to piece together the information.

Greg nodded. "There *has* to be."

"Did you find anything in the study?" Sadie shifted in her chair, resting her elbows on the table.

"No." Greg shook his head. "I wasn't in there searching for anything except the cat. Dad usually keeps the door to his study shut. Mom couldn't find Fluffy, so when I saw the open door I thought she might be hiding inside." Greg paused, recalling the incident. "Wait!" His eyes opened wide. "Dad's a fanatic about this desk—no loose papers and the drawers are always locked!"

"Yes?" Sadie said, prompting him to continue.

"The bottom desk drawer was open—not much, but I remember thinking how unusual that was. The corner of one of his files was sticking out. Then he walked in and started yelling."

"He must have thought you found something."

"I think you're right." Greg scrunched his eyebrows together. "I wonder what it could have been?"

Sadie shook her head, deciding that now would be a good time to share the facts of her own independent investigation of Zena Pharmaceuticals. "I don't know, but your dad's company has a long history of dealing with dangerous drugs." She filled him in on her research findings.

"I can't believe my dad works for Zena and I didn't know that!" Greg shook his head. "You're amazing!"

Sadie smiled at the compliment. "Now we have to find out what was in the bottom drawer."

"You're right." Greg nodded.

Side by side in the cafeteria, they began to devise a plan.

CHAPTER

18

"What did Jennifer say?" Sadie asked Greg the question that everyone wanted answered.

It was Friday morning and they had a few minutes before the start of their Nutrition class. Today, instead of waiting in their assigned seats, the group was huddled together. Becky and Ellen were sitting on the table in front of Sadie and Jill. Greg was standing in the aisle next to Sadie. Looking up at him, she could still see the shadows under his eyes.

"She told me everything," Greg said in a hollow voice. "My dad was in on it, just as we thought." Greg frowned.

"I'm sorry, Greg." Sadie reached for his hand. She couldn't imagine being betrayed by your own father.

Jill shook her head. "Why did he do it?"

Greg knelt down. It was easier to talk when he was on the same level as everyone else. "Jennifer was dating Alan when she got pregnant. When she told him, he dumped her. She was back home in Indiana, crying and all upset—really worried about telling her parents. Well, that's when my dad dropped by to see her dad."

"Let me guess: She was the only one home, right?" Jill wanted to get the facts straight.

"Right," Greg nodded. "When Dad saw her crying, he offered to help her. Jennifer said he was really nice and said he'd fix it so she would never have to tell her parents. He offered to pay for an abortion."

"Wow!" Jill exclaimed.

Becky shook her head. "I can't believe it!"

Sadie sat in stunned silence.

"What does that have to do with the two of you?" Ellen frowned, confused.

Greg shook his head sadly. "He wanted her to date me so that she'd interfere with my studying. He was hoping I'd either drop out or flunk out."

"But you didn't!" Sadie squeezed his hand. She was proud of him.

"No, I didn't." Greg's lips curved, attempting a smile for Sadie before continuing. "That's when Dad stepped up the plan. He figured if we were married, she'd have more control over me."

"So would he," Jill pointed out.

Greg nodded. "Dad told her to tell me she was pregnant and threatened to tell her parents about the abortion if she didn't."

"Oh, my God!" Sadie's jaw dropped. She'd said it so loud that several classmates turned, staring at her.

The entire group sat, silent, as they digested the news. After a few moments, Greg continued. "Jennifer said that after a while, when he realized his plan wasn't working, Dad started pressuring her to have a baby."

"But she had just had an abortion!" Becky was horrified.

"I know." Greg nodded.

Jill frowned, looking confused. "Then why was she on birth control pills?"

"She was starting to feel guilty. She said I was being so nice that she didn't want to trap me with a baby. She was actually relieved when I confronted her." Just then, Professor Gutman walked in. Reluctantly, Greg, Ellen, and Becky headed for their seats.

Today, Sadie didn't open her notebook at the start of the lecture. It sat in front of her, unopened and ignored. As though from far away, she heard, "Turmeric and garlic are both beneficial." Okay, she thought, we're still on the immune system. Her notebooks, however, remained closed.

I can't believe his dad. How could someone bribe another person? And pay for an abortion, too! Sadie shivered. Life was precious to her. Biting her lip as tears welled up, she felt a deep sadness for the unborn child. She was so caught up in the sadness, she actually began to hear the buzzing of flies. She shuddered.

Jill looked over. "Are you all right?" she whispered.

Perhaps it was Jill's concern that banished the other memory. Whatever the reason, Sadie was grateful. She managed to give Jill a weak smile of reassurance.

"Reduce your intake of refined sugar. Excess sugar can make the immune system sluggish," Professor Gutman carried on.

For Sadie, listening to the lecture was like listening to a radio trying to pick up a distant signal—only bits and pieces could be heard. Instead of struggling to pay attention, her thoughts turned to Jennifer. She seemed to be a victim, too. *I was probably too hard on her. I wonder if there's something I can do for her?* Deep in thought, she chewed on her bottom lip as she sought to put things into perspective.

Bit by bit, more of the lecture was beginning to reach her. "Nutrition can drastically influence infection. First, deficiencies make it easier for organisms to invade the body. Second, deficiencies slow recovery time." As Sadie began to take notice of her surroundings, she saw that Professor Gutman was pacing back and forth in front of the podium as he continued with the lecture. "A study in The *Lancet* described a woman responding to drug treatment only after receiving zinc supplements." *Well, that came in loud and clear.* Still, she sat staring at her notebook.

Then she heard, "The essential fatty acids play an important role in regulating immune function." *There has to be something connecting those two statements.* Idly, she wondered how much of the lecture she'd missed. Right now, it didn't matter as her thoughts shifted to Greg's dad.

What kind of person would betray his own son? A poor excuse of a man, that's for sure. She shook her head. *There must be something awfully important in that bottom drawer (not that anything could possibly justify his actions, of course). I still can't believe anybody would do that!*

I really should catch some of this lecture, she thought, looking up.

"There have been many documented studies supporting natural alternatives to antibiotics. For example, St. John's wort prevents viral growth. European doctors have successfully used Echinacea to treat whooping cough, bronchitis, and tonsillitis."

Sadie took notes as Professor Gutman continued bullet-pointing the available research. "Tea tree oil has many anti-microbial properties. High doses of vitamin C, given intravenously, have been used to successfully treat meningitis and pneumonia as well as many other infections."

Professor Gutman walked to the front of the classroom. "Let's spend a bit more time on vitamin C. There is an interesting book written by Dr. Archie Kalokerinos called *Every Second Child*. Dr. Kalokerinos was a physician with the Australian Health Service during the 1960s. He noted that when Australian Aborigine children were given DPT immunizations, a very sad thing happened—half of the children died."

"Oh, my God," Sadie muttered to herself. Her attention was now fully on the lecture.

"Dr. Kalokerinos deduced that they had poorly functioning immune systems due to their diet. They ate mainly white bread and canned goods. Before giving the children their second round of immunizations, he supplemented their diets with vitamin C—between 1 to 3 grams, depending upon their age."

"I can't believe that they'd even think to give a second round of DPT immunizations if the first round killed half of the children!" Sadie was outraged.

"I know," Professor Gutman nodded, "but the results were much better—this time, none of the children died."

Professor Gutman continued his lecture, talking about a report published in the *Journal of the American Medical Association*, which showed that children with Pertussis (whooping cough) treated with vitamin C instead of the vaccine actually recovered well before the children treated with the vaccine.

Normally Sadie would have been fascinated by this research. Today, however, it faded into the background. The sadness she had felt earlier had vanished. The combination of Greg's news and the story of the Aborigine children had gotten to her. Now she was angry. Thinking about Greg's father as she stared at her notebook, she came to a decision. *He's not going to get away with it!* Her eyes narrowed and her lips pinched together. The blood of generations of Celtic warriors was coursing through her veins. *He's not going to get away with it!*

CHAPTER

19

St. Louis was blooming. Emerald-green grass was generously covering Mother Earth. Masses of sunny-faced daffodils were greeting the day. Lemon-yellow forsythia blossoms flourished along the highways. Birds were singing and red-breasted robins were searching for worms. It didn't matter what the calendar said; it was spring in St. Louis. Better yet, it was St. Patrick's Day! The wearin' o' the green had begun. The local brewery was sponsoring a race and the downtown was hosting a parade. Inside the bars, the green beer was flowing.

"I'm sure none of the beer drinkers will be thinking that America was first known as 'Great Ireland' long before Columbus," Sadie mused. Years ago, her grandmother had told her the story of St. Patrick.

"Ooh, lassie, he was a great man, one of the greatest of Celts. He first came to Ireland in the year 389," she had said.

Sadie sat at the kitchen table recalling that long-ago day with her grandmother. They'd both been walking barefoot through the lush grass. It had felt so soft underfoot. Deep in thought, she burrowed her toes deeper into the rug. She had learned of Tara, the home of the High Kings. Great kings had ruled Ireland long before there was a Rome or an Athens. These fair and handsome kings ruled a land of poets and legends, mystery and music. Ireland—the land of druids and priests, truth and beauty. Sadie sighed.

"Ooch, dearie, 'tis remembering you are, isn't it?" Elsie made one of her special appearances.

Sadie smiled. How appropriate, she thought, to have her grandmother show up today. "Happy St. Patrick's Day."

"The same to you, dearie. 'Tis a grand thing to remember who you are and where you've come from. Don't be forgettin' you come from the land of Brian Boru, who united Ireland; Fiona the great druidess . . ."

As her grandmother recounted the legends, Sadie clasped her hands around her tea mug, savoring its warmth. It seemed that she felt a chill whenever Elsie chose to make an appearance.

"What's that?" Jill called out. Her question put an abrupt end to Elsie's visit.

"Nothing. Just Grandma," Sadie replied. As she sipped her tea, she thought how good it was to have friends who accepted her—grandmother and all.

She remembered when she had first noticed that she was different. Other children didn't share her "hunches" or "feelings." It had been Elsie who had nurtured her intuitive nature. Elsie who had made her proud of her perceptions, unlike most of her classmates, who called her a freak. To Elsie, she was fey—a product of that hopeful land of the High Kings valiantly fighting for truth. Although she had chosen schoolbooks instead of a sword, she was on the same quest for truth as her Irish ancestors. For Sadie, these truths were within the health care field—every bit as bloody a battleground as any ancient Irish battlefield.

SWISH. SWISH. SWISH. The sound of Jill's silk robe and slippers interrupted her thoughts. The combination of the sounds of conversation with Elsie and the smell of fresh coffee had lured her out of bed.

"Mmmm, smells good." Jill poured herself a cup. "I'm so glad we don't have to go to school today."

"Me, too." Sadie poured herself another cup of tea and joined Jill at the table.

There were no classes today because all of the faculty were busy proctoring the upperclassmen's National Boards tests. Everyone knew that National Boards made finals look like a cake walk. They were broken down into four parts. Each part had to be passed, in addition to State Boards, before they could be licensed to practice. Luckily, Sadie and Jill didn't have to worry about National Boards yet. Instead, they served as the perfect excuse to enjoy the beautiful weather.

"Well, Sadie Jo, what are your plans for today?" Jill suppressed a yawn as she stretched her slender arms above her head. Twisting left, then right, she moved with grace of a ballerina.

"I thought I'd take a walk in the park and then do some studying. Finals will be here in three weeks." Sadie shook her head at the thought, causing a riot of red curls to spill out from the confines of the green scrunchie, bravely trying to hold them in place. "How about you?"

"Jeff is taking me downtown to see the parade. You're welcome to come with us if you'd like."

"Thanks, but I think I'd better get some study time in."

Sadie marveled at Jill's generosity to her friends. She knew that Jill wasn't able to see Jeff as much as she'd like and would probably rather be alone with him. She also knew that Jill's invitation was genuine and that she'd extend one only to herself, Becky, or Ellen.

Jill had told her once how she envied Sadie's ability to befriend other women. She had even remarked that she might never have had the chance to bond so strongly with Becky or Ellen if she hadn't had Sadie as a roommate. "I just hang around you and I get all the friends I could ever need or want," she had said.

Sadie was still thinking about her friend as she was driving to the park. "I think she sells herself short. She could have all the girlfriends she wanted. I think some girls are just intimidated by her looks." Sadie had grown accustomed to talking to herself as she drove. She felt it made it easier for Elsie to make an appearance.

If Elsie had been planning on a second appearance today, she would have been scared off by her granddaughter's sudden pounding of the steering wheel.

"That's it!" Sadie shouted, turning the wheel of her green Volkswagen. She was now heading for the library.

In less than twenty minutes she was sitting in front of a computer screen typing away. A modern-day Celtic warrior doing battle against the enemy—in this case, Troy's mysterious illness. Perhaps she was drawing on some inspiration from her forebears on this special day. Whatever the reason, Sadie was definitely feeling the luck of the Irish.

"Now, let's just hope it pays off," she murmured as she surfed the Internet.

"That's my fey girlie." Elsie stood well back, not wanting to break Sadie's train of thought. Very gently, she gave the computer screen a psychic nudge.

Sadie sat transfixed as the new screen appeared. "That's it!"

Elsie smiled fondly before leaving her beloved granddaughter.

Sadie was viewing a computer screen showing the different manifestations of environmental illness. Job risks were included.

In the car, she had remembered that Troy worked with seed corn and ginseng—both at friends' farms. Jeff had mentioned the high use of chemicals in ginseng when they all had been eating dinner at Gian-Tony's. Now it was all starting to make sense.

"Hmm, mercury chloride is a common fungicide used on corn. Elevated levels could cause kidney, neurological, and immune problems." She spoke to herself as she wrote: DETOXIFICATION NEEDED! MERCURY CHLORIDE?

"Wow, this is interesting . . . the average American consumes roughly 40 milligrams of pesticides each year in food alone. They also carry about 100 milligrams permanently within their own body fat. YUK!" She was definitely glad she had skinny Leroy as a cadaver. She continued writing: FIND WAY TO DETOX FAT CELLS, TOO!

"HA! Wait until I show Tom this," she muttered as she read how environmental illnesses invade so many body systems that the medical community often declares one to be a "psychiatric illness." Sadie shook her head as she recalled Ellen telling her how furious her dad had been when they wanted to "treat" Troy with Prozac.

"Hmmm, what if Troy's total toxic load became too great for his immune system to deal with?" CLICK. CLICK. CLICK. She flipped to the screen on ginseng. CLICK. CLICK. CLICK. She typed on, advancing down her own modern-day battlefield.

Before she began studying the chemicals used on ginseng, she made sure to write down the symptoms of a toxic overload: FATIGUE, DEPRESSION, HEADACHES, MUSCLE ACHES, CHRONIC INFECTIONS, FREQUENT COLDS, NERVOUSNESS, IRRITABILITY, and SENSITIVITY TO PERFUMES AND ODORS.

"Wow, this sure sounds like Troy's symptoms. Okay, let's check on the ginseng."

"Hey, Sadie."

Sadie swiveled her chair around to see Greg. She smiled. "Hi, Greg. Take a look at this," she said before turning to face the screen again. "Remember when Ellen told us that Troy started having headaches after visiting his friend in Wisconsin and helping in the ginseng fields?"

Sadie was so caught up in her research, she didn't think to ask Greg what he was doing in the library. What a shame, since he'd come to talk about the two of them. She seemed so focused on her computer that he decided not to bring up the subject. Probably just as well, he thought.

"Yes." Greg's answer was hesitant. He didn't know whether she'd still be interested in a relationship, anyway.

"Well, I've been researching environmental illnesses. Look at this . . . " she gestured to the computer screen, " . . . fungicides alone are applied to ginseng 9 to 12 times per season!"

Greg's eyes opened wide as he grasped the implications. "I see," he nodded. "Troy's toxic load could have simply gotten too high for his body to handle."

"Exactly!" Sadie's red curls bounced as she nodded her head for emphasis. "I remembered Becky saying that ginseng naturally grows in the shade. When it's grown commercially, they cover it up with tarps. That's a prime environment for all kinds of pests, so they really use a lot of chemicals on it. Anyway, that's why I decided to research possible environmental toxins."

"That's a great idea!" Greg rubbed her shoulders as he stood behind her, staring at the computer screen. "Hey, look at this," he said, pointing to the paragraph he'd just read. "It looks like you're on to something. Here's a report of dead bees found near ginseng operations. And another one about nine horses found dead at a ranch that fed hay grown on land where ginseng had been grown."

"Wow! That's scary."

"Yeah," Greg agreed. "I wonder what they use that's so toxic."

Sadie was typing again. "Look at this. Here's a report showing that half of British Columbia's ginseng didn't pass the required tests for sale to Europe."

"Why is that?" Greg leaned forward to get a better view of the computer screen. What he did get was the fresh scent of Sadie's hair. He inhaled greedily.

"Something about containing too much QUINTOZENE. What's that?"

"I'll get on the other computer and find out." Grateful for a reason to escape her intoxicating scent, he sat down next to Sadie and began typing.

"I found it!" Greg looked over at Sadie. "It's used for crown rot; it contains PENTACHLORONITROBENZENE (PCNB)."

"What's that?" Sadie asked.

Greg looked back at the screen. "It's considered to be a toxic waste." Greg looked over at Sadie. "I think you've solved the puzzle."

Sadie smiled at the compliment. "What else does it say?"

Greg read on. "Well, it looks like PCNB has been proven to

cause liver problems in mice, fetal mortality, and bacterial infections in female mice . . . "

"Poor mice," Sadie murmured.

"It's not just them; there's also records of it causing liver and spleen problems in monkeys." Greg scanned down the screen. "It goes on to list the places where PCNB has been found. Wow! Listen to this: well water, cropland, nursery soils, leaves of spinach, cheese, fruits, ground grains, leaf and stem vegetables, nuts, fish, and, of course, ginseng."

"It sounds like it's everywhere!" Sadie shook her head. "It sure makes a case for organic farming, doesn't it?"

"It sure does."

Sadie recalled how supportive Elsie had been of organic farming. "It's common sense, darlin'; only natural things for nature," she had said. Sadie smiled at the memory before returning to her computer screen.

"Now we have to find a way to get that stuff out of Troy." Once again, she began typing.

CLICK. CLICK. CLICK. The library sonata had begun. Fingertips connecting with keyboards, accompanied by the whirring hum of the air vent. Both Sadie and Greg were oblivious to the birds chirping outside as well as the far-off sounds of *Danny Boy* currently being mangled by a local high school band.

"I've got it!" Sadie whirled around in her chair. "Look at this." She pointed to a picture of a book on the computer screen. On the cover was a picture of a waterfall with a blue background. It wasn't the beauty of the cover that attracted Sadie; it was the title: *Clear Body, Clear Mind. The Effective Purification Program*, by L. Ron Hubbard. "Look, it says over 250,000 freed from the harmful effects of drugs and toxic substances!" Sadie couldn't resist a squeal of delight. Luckily, she and Greg were the only people in that section of the library. The rest of the student population was either sweating over National Boards or swilling green beer. Jumping up from the computer, she threw her arms around Greg and then danced a bit of an Irish jig. "Let's go to the bookstore and get this for Troy."

— • • • —

With book in hand, they headed for Troy (the geographical location, that is). Sadie was driving, since Greg had ridden his bike to the library.

"The turn-off is just a mile or so ahead," she said. Sadie had been telling Greg all about spending Thanksgiving with Ellen's family.

"Here it is," she said as she turned onto the gravel road.

Woof, woof. The sound of barking reached their ears before they actually saw Andy, Ellen's beloved golden retriever. Sadie parked and quickly jumped out of the car.

"Hi, Andy." She was greeted with a riot of barking and tail wagging. Bending down to pet him, she got her face licked in the process.

"Hi, boy." Greg, too, got his face licked as Andy joyfully greeted them both.

Andy's barking had alerted the rest of the family to their arrival. Ellen came running out the front door. "Sadie! Greg!" Ellen said, looking from one to the other. "What are you guys doing here?"

"We've got something for Troy," Sadie said. Giving Andy a final pat, she stood and they all went into the house.

"Sadie! Hello!" Ellen's mom was working in the kitchen.

"Donna, this is Greg." Sadie made the introductions.

"Hi Greg. Ellen talks about you so much, it's nice to finally meet you," Donna said.

"Thank you." Greg smiled. "It's nice to meet you, too."

When they were all seated at the kitchen table, Sadie and Greg shared their research findings. Greg handed Donna the *Clear Body, Clear Mind* book that they had just purchased.

"This makes perfect sense!" Ellen reached for the book, paging through it. "I can't believe it," she said shaking her head, "an actual program to get rid of toxins!" First, she gave Sadie a huge bear hug, and then Greg. "You guys are the best!"

Donna was overcome with emotion. "Thank you both so much for all of your help." Wiping her eyes, she got up to prepare food as a further sign of her gratitude.

Greg stood up. "Let me help you with that."

"Thank you." Donna gave him a grateful smile.

"Let's show this to Troy!" Ellen grabbed Sadie's hand, pulling her toward Troy's room.

Sadie was shocked. Troy looked so different than she remembered. He was thin and pale. His once lively, twinkling eyes were now flat and dull. It was hard to find any traces of the vibrant seventeen-year-old who she remembered.

"Hey, Troy." She sat down next to the bed.

"Hi, Sadie." Troy gave her a wan smile.

"I've got something for you." She handed him the book,

watching as he thumbed through it. Doing so, a ray of hope seemed to spark within him.

"This is the first thing that actually makes sense to me!" Troy grasped Sadie's hand. "Thanks!"

"You're welcome, Troy." Sadie kissed his cheek before leaving the room.

Walking back to the kitchen, Ellen paused, turning to Sadie. "Thanks again. Troy already seems better, just from looking at the book."

"You're welcome." Sadie smiled. "Wait until he actually *does* the purification program."

"Yeah." Ellen nodded.

As soon as they entered the kitchen, Ellen grabbed a slice of corned beef. "Mom, I think this is really going to help Troy!"

Donna smiled. "I think you're right."

"You guys will have to find a sauna so that Troy can sweat out some of those toxins." Sadie helped herself to some slices of apples and cheese that Greg had finished slicing. Noticing the artful arrangement of the cheese tray, she turned to Greg. "You're pretty good in the kitchen."

Greg smiled. "I can hold my own."

Ellen reached for a slice of cheese. "Once Troy gets better, we'll have to have you come over and train him."

Greg laughed. "I'd be happy to."

Tom walked in to a kitchen filled with laughter, which was quite a change from the past few months. "What's going on?"

"Sadie and Greg found a way to help Troy," Donna said. She brought a steaming dish of corned beef and cabbage to the table. Over dinner, they filled him in on all the details.

— • • • —

Later that evening, Sadie was still thinking about her remarkable day when Jill came home, joining her in the kitchen.

"How was your day?" Jill grabbed a handful of almonds and sat down next to Sadie.

"It was one of my best St. Patrick's Days ever!" Sadie filled her in on the detective work at the library and their trip to see Troy.

"That sounds great! I can't wait to tell Jeff about your discovery." Jill kicked off her shoes.

"Oh, Jill, it was great! I really think the purification program will help Troy. You should have seen him when we gave him the book—he looked so happy and hopeful." Sadie smiled at the memory. Then, she continued her St. Patrick's Day recap. "We had such a good time on the way home."

What did you do?" Jill asked, hoping for some sort of romantic news.

"We sang every Irish song we could think of at the top of our lungs."

Although it wasn't the answer she had hoped for, Jill did have to smile at the image of Sadie and Greg singing along in her little car. "So, you and Greg were together all day?" she asked, hoping for more intimate details. "Any talk of getting back together?"

"No." Sadie shook her head. (This was the only blight on her otherwise perfect day.) "I think he's had too much betrayal recently. He probably doesn't want to get emotionally attached to anyone for a while." Deep down, Sadie hoped things would work out for them in the future.

"Maybe." Although Jill decided not to challenge Sadie on the subject, she wasn't buying her idea at all.

"How about you?" Sadie asked, changing the subject. "How was your day?" She leaned forward, resting her elbows on the table.

"It was fun!" Jill smiled, telling her all about the St. Patrick's Day parade."

"How are things going with Jeff?" Sadie, too, wanted intimate details. "Are you okay with him working for Dr. Andrews?"

Jill frowned before answering. "I guess they're going all right. I mean, I really like him, Sadie. I just wish he didn't talk about Dr. Andrews so much. I'm starting to feel jealous." Jill shook her head. "I've never felt jealous before! I don't like it."

Sadie patted Jill's shoulder. "I don't think you have anything to worry about. He's probably so excited to be working there that he doesn't realize he talks about her so much. He probably thinks of it more like sharing clinical data with you."

"I know, honey," Jill nodded, "I'm sure you're right. I'm surprised that we didn't find thick skulls on all the male cadavers—men do seem thick-headed sometimes."

BUZZ. BUZZ. BUZZ. The doorbell chimed in with their laughter. Sadie was still chuckling when she opened the door.

"Becky!" Sadie was surprised to see her. "Come in."

"Hi." Becky's face was flush with excitement. "I just got off the phone with Roger," she said in a rush. "We both decided that we don't want to wait until after Chiropractic College to get married. We're getting married in June! I had to come by. Will you two be my bridesmaids?"

"Becky!" Sadie squealed in delight. "Of course!" she said, giving her a hug.

Jill joined in, "I can't think of anything I'd rather be doing in June than attending your wedding! I'm so happy for you, honey."

Becky was beaming. Her milk-white teeth actually sparkled. "I'm so glad! Now the wedding will be perfect. Ellen said that she'd be my maid of honor. I'm so excited!"

"Do you have any ideas about the wedding plans or dresses yet?" Jill quickly moved to her favorite subject—fashion.

"No. With finals coming up, I'm not sure how I'm going to handle all the details." Becky nervously chewed on her bottom lip, thinking of all the preparations.

"Well, that will be part of my wedding present to you. I'll help with all the details—you won't have to worry about a thing." Jill's eyes gleamed in anticipation; she was in her glory.

"Oh, Jill, that would be wonderful!" Becky hugged her. "What a perfect St. Patrick's Day!"

Sadie smiled at her friends. "You know, I was thinking the same thing myself."

Somewhere in the heavens, or perhaps on the grassy hill of Tara, Elsie Shaunessey was smiling. On this special day, she recalled the history of her people. The terrible Penal laws of William of Orange during which, for more than a century, Irish Catholics were forbidden to receive an education and prohibited from entering a profession. Her great Celtic heart swelled with pride as she looked down on her granddaughter. Seeking an education. Pursuing a profession. She sighed in contentment.

"Brrr, it's cold in here!" Becky briskly rubbed her arms.

"It is." Jill reached for her sweater. "It's weird—sometimes we get really cold drafts in here."

Sadie smiled, lifting her eyes upward. "Happy St. Patrick's Day," she murmured.

CHAPTER

20

Rushing to class through raindrops, Sadie narrowly avoided a puddle. It was hard to see. She brushed the wet curls from her eyes. *There, that's better.* The moist, humid air made Sadie's hair even curlier—if that was possible. April showers had descended on St. Louis in full force.

Grateful to be out of the rain, Sadie sat down for the last Nutrition class before finals. Easter and spring break were fast approaching. She looked around the room as the students were settling into their now familiar seats. *Jill's hair doesn't seem to be negatively influenced by the humidity.* Sadie turned further, observing her friend. *Ellen looks good, too. That new cut really suits her. Now that she's found Danny, she looks even prettier.* Turning further, she saw Becky. *She looks positively radiant these days. I can't wait for the wedding.* Behind Becky was Greg. Sadie smiled at him, glad that the dark circles were finally gone from under his eyes. *I love these people!* The intensity of the emotion took her by surprise. After all the sorrows of her childhood, she felt blessed to have such dear friends.

CLICK-CLICK. CLICK-CLICK. That was a different noise. Definitely not the familiar SQUISH, SQUISH sound made by Professor Gutman's rubber soled shoes. Sadie turned to see a very pregnant woman in heels making her way to the podium. What was even more surprising than the unfamiliar face was the fact that she was holding a briefcase in her left hand and a can of diet soda in her right hand. By the murmurs she heard from the rest of the class, she wasn't the only one who was surprised.

"What's up with that?" Jill whispered.

"Maybe it's just for a demonstration," Sadie offered hopefully. Surely a pregnant woman wouldn't be drinking a diet soda—especially one teaching a class on nutrition!

"Good morning class. My name is Dr. Morgan. I will be substituting today because Professor Gutman is attending a conference." With that said, she briskly opened her brief case, setting several papers on the podium. The diet soda? On the podium as well. The class learned that she was a medical doctor and taught at the nearby medical school.

Sadie was watching with fascination—the diet soda, not the doctor. *Maybe she's going to talk about the dangers of aspartame.* That had to be it, she thought, especially since they had all read Dr. Blaylock's book, *Excitotoxins. The Taste that Kills.* What an amazing book that was, linking aspartame and MSG to Alzheimer's, Lou Gherig's disease, depression, multiple sclerosis, headaches, strokes, and ADHD.

CLICK. POP. FIZZ.

Sadie looked up. "My God, she's actually drinking the stuff!" She was so amazed that she didn't realize she'd actually spoken out loud.

Jill turned, giving her a thumbs-up sign.

"Excuse me?" Dr. Morgan's pinched brows revealed her irritation.

Sadie felt a moment of panic before replying. "I'm sorry, Dr. Morgan, it's just that aspartame is really bad for your health and it's devastating for a developing fetus."

"I do not tolerate interruptions in my class." Dr. Morgan glared at her.

Sadie felt a sudden chill in the room. Not the pleasant kind that let her know Elsie was nearby; no, this was decidedly different.

Dr. Morgan gripped the podium. "Aspartame has been approved by the FDA. It is perfectly safe, comprised of two amino acids, aspartic acid and phenylalanine."

Sadie couldn't believe her ears. "Excuse me, Dr. Morgan, but according to Dr. Blaylock, those amino acids can become deadly toxins."

The class, who had taken an instant dislike to Dr. Morgan, now came to her defense. Becky was the first to respond. "Dr. Morgan, you only mentioned two of the components of aspartame. What about the other one? It's perhaps the most dangerous part—breaking down into methanol, a known nervous system toxin. As you know, methanol is rapidly released into the bloodstream, where it's metabolized into formaldehyde."

Paul spoke up next. "Yeah, methanol was the main ingredient in the moonshine made during Prohibition. Everyone knows it causes blindness."

Sadie shook her head. Trust Paul to bring up a mob-related subject. She looked over to see that Jill was doodling a cartoon stick figure wearing concrete boots. She also had a biohazard sign and a pregnant stick figure (which was pretty funny looking all by itself) next to a gigantic can of diet soda.

"Good job," she whispered.

Jill grinned and continued drawing.

"Do you know whether that can of soda was stored in a warehouse that reached 86 degrees?" This came from the back row, from Ken Davis, the resident ski bum. "If so, you might as well be drinking moonshine."

Dr. Morgan frowned. She was losing control of the class.

Jackie chimed in, "That's right. Aspartame degrades readily into methanol at temperatures exceeding 86 degrees."

This was becoming too much for Peter. At first, he hadn't felt the pressure to respond since it was just a substitute teacher, and, in his opinion, the class was being disrespectful. But now, when it looked as though the rest of the class knew more than him . . . well, he felt compelled to respond.

"During the Gulf War of 1991, the soldiers were given free soft drinks sweetened with aspartame. As you know, temperatures in the Gulf region exceeded 86 degrees. It is theorized that methanol poisoning from aspartame is one of the possible causes of 'Gulf War Syndrome' affecting over 50,000 soldiers."

Surprisingly, the back row was not through with this topic. Terry Hart had something to say. "Some airline pilots are in danger of losing their flying licenses because of seizures caused by aspartame."

Ken continued the debate. "My dad's a pilot. He knows a dude (Ken's term for another pilot) who had blurred vision so bad he couldn't read the instrument panel. He almost crashed when he was trying to land the plane. He had only two cups of Nutra Sweetened hot chocolate. Anyway, after he landed, some other dudes (translation: co-workers) said the same thing happened to them. That stuff will rot your brain, lady."

That was probably the most Ken had ever spoken in class—except for snide remarks, that is. Everyone knew that he was a licensed pilot and that his dad flew for a major airline. Actually, both Ken and Terry were licensed pilots—often taking their friends up in the small planes available at the location airport.

Dr. Morgan was shaking her head, clearly irritated with the class. Perhaps medical students didn't question authority. That wasn't the case in this classroom. Here, practically every student had been touched by some type of medical negligence or had been the victim of an FDA cover-up. Some had sought a chiropractic career after the failing health of a loved one had been "miraculously" helped by chiropractic. Whatever the reason, this was health care's equivalent of "born-again Christians." It was a class full of born-again chiropractors—except for Peter Burger, who was still straddling the proverbial health care fence.

Sadie was shaking her head, her fiery Celtic temper igniting. Sitting here listening to one reason after another that the FDA should never have approved the use of aspartame was getting to her. It wasn't just the aspartame—one thing, she could handle. No, it was that one thing on top of Vioxx, statin drugs, Prozac, ADHD, flu shots, you name it! It was too much! All in the name of "help"—that *really* bothered her. She clenched her teeth in frustration.

Jill looked over at Sadie. She'd never seen her this agitated. But then, with her history of being lied to by the medical establishment, it was really no wonder she'd be upset by yet another greed-provoked lie. As a matter of fact, now that she thought about it, it's a wonder that Sadie hadn't blown her stack long before this. (Jill was right, and she only knew part of Sadie's history.)

Sadie's frustration mounted. Right now Dr. Morgan represented the combination of ignorance and defiance that she'd been battling for too long. This combined with jeopardizing the health of an innocent unborn child, with no voice to protect it, was too much for her. Her eyes narrowed, "Dr. Morgan, 80 percent of the complaints to the FDA are about aspartame. Why haven't they alerted the public?"

Terry Hart cut in. Holding up a *Flying Safety* Magazine, he read from it. "In pregnancy, the effects of aspartame can be passed directly on to the fetus, even in very small doses."

Apparently, Sadie wasn't the only one who was upset. The class was definitely as irritated with Dr. Morgan as she was with them.

"Why did they approve it in the first place?" Paul asked.

"That's right. Why would the FDA approve this?" Greg asked. "As a matter of fact, *Omni Magazine* asked the very same question. It even warned its readers that over half of all the drugs the FDA approves have such serious health risks that they could be fatal."

Jackie added, "Just because the manufacturer of aspartame makes over a billion dollars a year doesn't mean the stuff should be approved."

Since entering Chiropractic College, Sadie had compiled folders of data on various health controversies. Topics included vaccines, MSG, Prozac, Ritalin, Vioxx, statin drugs, antibiotics, aspartame, and cancer. She carried these with her and reprinted them for classmates. She referred to her "Aspartame Controversy" folder now.

"It's amazing to me that aspartame was ever approved at all! When they did the preliminary tests, animals suffered seizures and some of them died. Dr. Olney found that it caused holes in the brains of mice. He even filed a petition after it was approved, prompting an FDA investigation of the laboratory practices at Searle. The investigators said they had never seen anything as bad as Searle's testing—full of inaccuracies and manipulated test data."

Sadie was on a roll now. "Criminal investigations were brought up against Searle for knowingly misrepresenting findings, concealing material facts, and making false statements concerning aspartame's safety. Then, while the investigations were under way, Searle met with the U.S. attorney in charge—the company hired him to work for *them*! Losing their lead attorney held up the grand jury investigation, so the statute of limitations ran out."

Sadie's heart was pounding. She took a deep breath, hoping to pacify her body with more oxygen. To her, this one subject was beginning to represent everything that was wrong with the current health care system. She knew that the toxins caused by aspartame were deadly. Phenylalanine not only lowered the seizure threshold but also blocked serotonin production. Just look at America today, she thought, shaking her head. Low serotonin levels causing hostility and violence in our schools. Depression on the rise and Prozac use escalating.

As usual, whenever she thought about psychiatric drugs, her blood began to boil. She knew from experience how damaging they could be. She had all she could take. Something inside her snapped—an anger, long repressed. "It's not right," she muttered to herself. Sadie looked up. "Dr. Morgan, just look at the research.

Fetal tissue cannot tolerate methanol. Drinking that will harm your baby." Sadie stood up. "So I ask you, Dr. Morgan, is that diet soda worth it?" With that, she marched to the podium, grabbing the can and throwing it in the trash as she stormed out of the room.

"Way to go, Sadie!" The entire back row stood up, clapping and cheering.

Dr. Morgan was relieved to hear the buzzing of the bell, signaling that this class—her own personal hell—was finally over.

Sadie sought refuge on her favorite park bench. Fresh air, blue sky, green grass—she focused on that for a moment. She took a deep breath. Gradually, her heart no longer felt as though it were stomping out the beat of *Riverdance*. The oxygen was working.

Greg and Jill found her moments later, the outward picture of calm.

"Hey there, Sadie Jo." Jill rested her hand on Sadie's shoulder. "That was some class demonstration. How are you doing?"

Sadie looked up at Jill. "Did I make a fool of myself?"

"No, honey." Jill patted her shoulder. "You said what everyone else was thinking."

Greg sat down beside Sadie, putting his arm around her shoulders. "I'm proud of you." He pulled her closer. "The back row gave you a standing ovation!"

"Wow!" Sadie was amazed that the back row would do something like that. "At times I feel so betrayed. After trusting the medical establishment, the government, the FDA . . ." she shook her head, trying to explain things to her friends. "To be so betrayed after that, that's part of the problem. Then it's the lies! One right after another. How can people, in the name of science, in the interest of public health, perpetrate such lies?" Sadie looked first to Greg and then to Jill, half hoping they'd have an answer.

"Unfortunately, money is a powerful motivator." Greg lightly stroked her shoulder.

"Honey, there's good and bad in every profession," Jill said. "It's just unfortunate that the potential for money seems to pull in more of the bad than the good."

"Yeah, you're right," Sadie agreed. Hearing footsteps, she turned to see Becky and Ellen making their way down the path.

"Hey, girl." Ellen stopped in front of the bench.

Sadie smiled. "Hi."

"I'm proud of you, Sadie," Becky said.

"Thanks, you guys." Sadie felt the bond of friendship so strongly it was as though it were a physical thing, comforting and nurturing. "What would I do without my friends?" she thought. Luckily, that was one thing Sadie didn't have to worry about.

21

It was hard to believe that another trimester was coming to an end. Here it was, mid-April and already time for finals. The girls were in their usual booth at Denny's. This time, however, they were joined by Greg as well. They had decided to start a tradition: The night before finals—head to Denny's. There was nothing like food and friends to take the sting out of studying.

"Troy has been doing the saunas and exercising," Ellen said, between bites of her pancakes. "He's feeling a lot better. Thanks again, you guys."

"I'm glad he's doing better!" Sadie smiled as she picked up her fork.

The girls had decided not to break tradition, so the table was covered with Grand Slam breakfasts. (Even Greg had been persuaded to order one.)

Ellen speared a sausage link. "Yum," she said. With her empty fork in hand (using it like a conductor with his wand), she made an announcement. "Danny is going to be showing his horse at a local horse show on Saturday. I know it would mean hanging around a few extra days after finals, but I'd really like it if you all could be there."

"I'd love to go to a horse show!" Sadie replied.

"Me, too." Greg nodded.

"Count me in!" Becky said.

"Honey, I'd love to go!" Jill smiled as she spread strawberry jam on her toast.

Ellen looked around the table. "Thanks, guys," she smiled. "It will be a lot of fun."

Becky looked over at Jill. "Maybe we can go over some wedding plans, too."

"You bet." Jill poured herself another cup of coffee. "Honey, this wedding is going to be beautiful."

Becky smiled. "I hope the weather is nice. I want to have it outside."

Sadie patted her hand. "I'm sure it will be lovely," she said, hoping to give Becky some emotional support. With both finals and a wedding to prepare for, she'd been under a lot of stress lately.

Smiling at Sadie, Becky nodded. "I'm sure you're right." Turning to Greg she asked, "Would you be an usher at my wedding?"

"I'd love to!" Greg grabbed her hand, squeezing it. "Thanks for asking me."

Becky sighed with contentment. "It really is going to be perfect."

"Of course it will," Jill said.

Becky laid her fork down and continued with her wedding discussion. "I love your idea of simple sundresses and daisies for the bridesmaids."

Jill smiled at the compliment. "Thanks."

Meanwhile, Ellen was continuing to consume her Grand Slam breakfast. "I'll be glad to be finished with Anatomy lab. Leroy's getting a little ripe." Ellen stated this so matter-of-factly, as though this were common restaurant discussion, that it struck everyone as funny.

Sadie began giggling. Soon the entire group was laughing. "Do you guys realize we're doing it again?" she said as the laughter died down.

"What?" Ellen asked.

"Talking about cadavers during a meal," Sadie replied.

"Oh," Ellen grinned, "I thought you meant laughing in the back booth at Denny's before finals."

"That, too." Sadie toasted her with her water glass.

"Well, it worked for us last trimester." Becky raised her glass. "Let's hope it does for this one as well."

CLINK. They all touched their glasses together.

— • • • —

Finals *did* go well. Another trimester was finished. Today was Saturday—horse show day. Neither Sadie nor Jill had ever been to a show before. Greg had seen show jumping. Becky and Ellen, however, were both veterans of the horse show world.

The show grounds were only minutes away from the Chiropractic College. The auditorium was the same one used by the St. Louis Chiropractic hockey team. Greg was one of the team's star players.

"It looks a lot different for a horse show than it does for a hockey match," Greg said upon entering the auditorium.

Not only was he referring to the obvious—dirt instead of ice—but also the many other changes, for instance, the flowers. There was a small army of potted plants surrounding a square in the middle of the arena. An organist was set up in the center. Three judges and a ringmaster were watching the horses perform.

"Let's go see if we can find them in the barn." Sadie led the way, walking by bleachers filled with families and fans. It's a bit like being at a carnival, she thought, taking in the sights and sounds. To her left was the arena, full of beautiful horses trotting in precision. She could hear the pounding of their hooves on the tanbark. Shouts rang out, too, as trainers on the rail called out instructions. All the while the organist played on. She continued walking. To her right were the bleachers. Looking over, she saw a little blue-eyed, blonde-haired girl pointing with joy at the "horsies." Sadie smiled at her.

The smell of the tanbark was prominent this close to the arena. Sadie sniffed. It smelled good—kind of a moist-dirt-and-shavings smell combined with the smell of horses. Nearing the concession stand, she noticed that more smells began competing for her attention—coffee, popcorn, hot dogs. The show grounds were a feast for all the senses.

As Sadie left the arena behind, the swirling sights and sounds calmed down. Now it was the crunch, crunch, crunch of footsteps on gravel and the nickering of horses in the background. The bright sun was causing Sadie to squint before she entered the shelter of the barn.

"Hi!" Ellen greeted them. She was polishing one silver stirrup.

"Hi, guys." Becky was working on the other stirrup.

"Hi!" Sadie said.

"Hey, cool saddle." Greg walked over to look at the saddle more closely.

"Is that real silver?" Jill asked.

Ellen shook her head. "No."

"That saddle isn't very big," Jill said.

"English saddles are supposed to be small; that way, they don't distract from the horse," Becky said as she continued with her polishing.

"This is amazing." Sadie watched in fascination as they prepared for the competition. "Where's Danny?"

"Hi, everyone." Danny's voice came from behind a sixteen-hand chestnut Saddlebred gelding with four white stockings. For the uninitiated, that means a tall, reddish-brown horse with white on his legs.

"There you are," Sadie said, turning toward the stall. "Hi, Danny."

Greg walked into the stall. "He's beautiful, Danny," he said as he let the gelding nuzzle his hand.

Jill chose to stay outside. "What are you doing back there?" she asked as she looked through the bars on the stall to get a better view.

"I'm picking out his tail." Danny continued the slow process of smoothing the individual tail hairs with his fingers.

"Why don't you just brush it out with a comb?" As usual, Jill was fascinated with anything dealing with fashion or grooming.

"That would pull out too many hairs and break them. We want the tails to look long and full," Danny explained.

"Oh. That makes sense." Jill nodded in understanding. "No one wants split ends."

Sadie joined them in the stall, petting the horse on the neck. "What's his name?" she asked as she continued stroking his silky coat.

"He's got a long registered name, but I call him Carter. That's the name of the trainer I bought him from." Danny finished picking out Carter's tail and then looped it into a loose knot.

"Why did you do that?" Jill asked.

"So it won't get dirty and drag on the ground. Carter's tail drags the ground about a foot when he's standing." Danny gave Carter an affectionate pat. "Wait until you see him in motion. His tail flows behind him."

"Sounds beautiful," Sadie said.

"Like a wedding veil." Becky came over to join them, having finished cleaning the saddle.

"I can tell where your mind is," Ellen teased. With the tack all cleaned, it was time to finish getting ready for their class. She and Danny quickly put the saddle and bridle on Carter.

Now it was time to get Danny ready. "Here's your number." Ellen was holding the number "215" printed on a square of white cardboard.

"What's that for?" Jill was intrigued by this new sport.

"That's my exhibitor's number." Danny was now pinning it to the back of what looked like a suit coat. "We all wear one on the back of our coats. That's how the judges identify us."

"Isn't it hot in that outfit?" Jill was looking at the vest, hat, and coat that Ellen was holding for Danny.

"It is, but I'm so focused on the class that I don't really notice it until afterward." Danny was putting his tie tack on as he talked.

The humming of fans used to keep the horses cool could be heard in the background. The soft drone of the fans was interrupted by a voice on the loud speaker. "Class Number 8 is in the line-up. Class Number 9 should be in the warm-up area."

"That's us; time to go," Danny said, putting his derby on and grabbing his riding crop.

"I'll give you a leg up." Ellen led Carter out of the stall. "Here, Sadie, can you hold his bridle while I help Danny?"

"Sure." Sadie grabbed the reins.

Ellen helped Danny into the saddle and gave his boots a final wipe with her polishing rag. "Good luck."

"Thanks." Danny rode out of the barn and into the warm-up arena. Ten other horses, riders, and trainers were already there. Some were trotting in circles while others stood quietly as their riders received last-minute instructions.

"It's like being behind the scenes of a fashion show—only for horses." Jill watched in awe at all the primping being done.

"It is," Sadie agreed.

Ellen was standing in the center of the warm-up arena watching Danny as he trotted in a circle around her. "Use a little more curb rein to tuck his nose," she advised.

"He's beautiful." Sadie admired the powerful beauty of the elegant horse with his perfectly arched neck and flowing mane. "It's like watching a ballet."

"He is a beautiful horse." Greg was standing beside her. "Danny's a good rider, too."

"The results from Class Number 8 are in. The winner is . . ." The loud speaker could be heard throughout the warm-up arena.

Becky cut in before the announcement was finished. "Let's go inside. We don't want to miss the beginning of the class."

They all hurried inside in time to see the winner of Class 8 making his solo victory pass. The show photographer was scrambling to get a good shot.

"Class Number 9, Gentleman's Five Gaited." The announcer called the class. Horses began trotting inside to the accompaniment of the organist.

"I'll bet she gets tired of playing by the end of the weekend," Jill said as she turned her attention to the organist in the center of the ring.

Sadie smiled, leaning forward for a better view. "I don't see him yet." So far, eight horses had entered the arena.

"Here he comes." Greg's height was an advantage in spotting the horses as they entered.

"Yea!" They all cheered as Danny rode by.

"Judges, that is your class," the announcer informed them. The entrance gate closed and the class was on. The arena that had once looked so big suddenly seemed to shrink in size.

"That's it." They heard Ellen's encouragement as Danny made another pass. She was leaning over the gate along with the trainers, who were shouting instructions each time their rider passed by.

"He's looking good." Becky, too, was leaning forward, eyes riveted to the competition.

"Walk. Walk your horses." In unison, the horses slowed to a walk. Tails were no longer flowing behind them but now dragging on the ground.

Sadie exhaled. She'd been holding her breath with excitement.

"They have to watch out so they don't step on those tails," Jill said.

"Slow gait. Let your horses slow gait," came the command from the announcer. Immediately, the horses and riders responded.

"Oh, my. That's so beautiful." Sadie watched in awe.

"It looks so smooth, doesn't it?" Becky pointed out how quietly the riders were sitting while their horses paraded around the ring.

"Rack on." With this, the horses went into overdrive. So did the organist. The notes coming from the organ at the furious pace, however, couldn't keep up with the speed of the horses.

"Look, he's passing them!" Sadie observed, as Carter passed two horses in front of the judge. "Yea!" she screamed as he came around the turn in front of them. She wasn't the only one screaming. It seemed that the entire audience was cheering for their favorites.

"Walk. Walk your horses."

Sadie wasn't the only one to exhale at this command. The entire crowd seemed to relax. The calm didn't last long, however.

"Canter. Canter your horses." They were off again. Wait! One of the horses was picking up speed, suddenly starting to gallop. It was out of control!

"Heads up." Ellen's booming voice rang out, warning Danny. He turned to his right, cutting the ring in half, just before the other horse charged by.

"Time out." The horses slowed to a walk. The runaway horse's trainer leapt over the fence, entering the ring. The combination of the familiar sight of his trainer and the fact that the other horses had all stopped calmed the horse. He slowed to a walk. The trainer led him out of the ring. The young boy riding him looked visibly shaken, wide-eyed and very pale.

"I'm glad he's okay," Sadie said.

"Yeah," Greg agreed.

"Number 200 has been excused. Reverse and walk your horses." The horses turned, heading in the opposite direction. After performing all the gaits in this direction, the announcer called them to the line-up. One by one, the horses stopped in the middle of the ring, facing the audience. Nostrils flaring, sides heaving and soaked with sweat, they stood proudly. The judges walked beside them, all the while making notations on the cards they were carrying.

Sadie watched the judges walk behind Carter and look up at Danny's number, writing it on their cards. "Hey, that's got to be a good sign."

"I think so." Becky nodded in agreement. "He did really well."

The riders continued to sit, still as statues, awaiting the results from the judges.

"The results are in. The winner of Gentleman's Five Gaited Class is . . . " Sadie held her breath in anticipation. " . . . number 194. Champion Dun Haven's Commander, ridden by Nick Barnes." The crowd clapped as the winning team trotted over to receive their trophy. Meanwhile, Danny's fans let out a collective sigh of disappointment.

"Second place goes to . . . " They waited expectantly. " . . . number 215. Valleyview's Supreme Heir, ridden by Danny Durbin."

Sadie jumped to her feet clapping her hands. "Yea!"

"Way to go, Danny!" Greg, too, was on his feet, clapping loudly.

"Yea, Danny!" Becky joined in.

"All right, Danny!" Jill yelled. Turning to Sadie, she added, "No wonder they call him Carter."

Sadie shook her head and smiled. Typical Jill, she thought.

The atmosphere in the barn was relaxed. Danny, now wearing jeans and a T-shirt, was giving Carter a well-deserved bath. "He seems to like it." Sadie watched Carter sticking his tongue out to the side, catching drops of water from the sponge.

"He does." Danny continued sponging him off.

"You guys did a great job." Ellen was standing behind Carter, braiding his tail.

"I never knew a horse show could be so much fun," Sadie said, stroking Carter's neck.

"Me, either." Jill quickly stepped back as Carter started shaking, causing water droplets to be sprayed all around.

Sadie laughed as both she and Becky were included in Carter's shower. "I'm definitely cooled off now." Becky smiled, giving Carter a pat on the neck.

"I'll put the tack away." Greg grabbed the saddle and bridle.

"Thanks," Danny said.

The rest of the afternoon was relaxing. They sat on the bleachers watching the remainder of the show. After listening to Danny's tips, Sadie and Greg were getting pretty good at picking out the winners. Taking her eyes off the horses, Sadie spent a moment looking at her friends instead. Jill and Becky were discussing wedding plans. Danny and Ellen were devouring hot dogs, all the while pointing out the horses they liked. She watched as Danny leaned forward, gently wiping a dab of mustard from the corner of Ellen's mouth. She smiled at the intimate gesture. I'm so happy for them, she thought before turning her attention back to the horses.

— • • • —

With the relief of finals being over and the fun of the horse show experience, tonight would seem an unlikely time for the dream to intrude on Sadie. The dream, however, was seldom polite. Drenched in sweat, she sat up. "Katie!" she cried.

TRIMESTER THREE

"If only there were evil people somewhere insidiously committing evil deeds, and it were necessary only to separate them from the rest of us and destroy them. But the line dividing good and evil cuts through the heart of every human being, and who is willing to destroy his own heart?"

—*Alexander Solzhenitsyn*

CHAPTER

22

It was hard to believe that spring break was over already. Today, Monday, May 10, marked the official beginning of Trimester Three. As usual, the class schedule was grueling, with Microbiology, Physiology, Neurology, and Chiropractic Techniques—known to the students as "adjusting lab." Finally, they were going to start the long process of learning how to perform a chiropractic adjustment. That's where they were right now—in the adjusting lab. Dr. Anthony Cantiko was calling out the names for roll call.

"Dr. Burger?"

"Here." Peter managed a whisper. He had a bout of laryngitis.

"It's cool that he's calling us 'doctor,'" Sadie whispered to Jill. "Too bad about Peter's voice."

"Yeah." Jill nodded. "Too bad it's not Cathy with laryngitis. It's going to be hard for me to think of calling her 'Dr. Muncie.'" Jill directed her attention to the petite blonde. Cathy was wearing a tight, short skirt. She had neglected to button her long lab coat in order to display her legs. Paul was grinning at something she had just whispered in his ear.

"Well, they're obviously still together," Sadie whispered.

"Amazing, isn't it?" Jill shook her head.

"Dr. Jensen?"

"Here." Sadie smiled. *I like the sound of that.* She turned her attention to Dr. Cantiko. He was in his late thirties. In some ways he resembled an older, taller Paul Santini. An Italian-American, originally from New Jersey, he had been teaching here at the college part-time since he'd graduated ten years ago. The decade spent in the "Show-Me" state had not dulled his New Jersey accent.

"Hey, Jill. He was sitting next to us when we had dinner on the Hill," Sadie whispered.

"Yeah, that's right, and it's Dr. Jones to you," Jill joked.

Sadie grinned. "Excuse me, doctor."

Their joking was interrupted by Dr. Cantiko. "I want you to pair up. One person lying on the table, the other standing by the head piece. We're going to practice cervical set ups."

Jill jumped onto the adjusting table. Sadie stood beside her.

"Sadie, don't mess up my hair or makeup," Jill whispered with a smile.

"It's Dr. Jensen to you," Sadie joked.

"Ha!" Jill laughed.

Learning set ups meant learning the exact position to hold the head and neck for each type of adjustment. It was very precise. Right now, Dr. Cantiko was stressing the importance of the correct line of drive. After demonstrating the set up, he walked to the first adjusting table to watch and critique the student doctor. Apparently Jill had jumped onto table number one.

Sadie bent over, placing her right hand under Jill's head for support while placing her left hand on Jill's neck, showing the correct set up for correcting a rotation of the fourth cervical vertebrae.

"That's good." Dr. Cantiko moved her arm. "Just a bit more to the left; move your elbow; that's it." Dr. Cantiko went to the next table as Sadie helped Jill into a sitting position.

"Good job, Dr. Jensen." Jill gave her a thumbs-up sign.

"Wait until you try it, Jill. Heads are a lot heavier than I thought."

"So, that's why you started shaking. I thought you were just nervous."

Dr. Cantiko continued walking from table to table. Then the partners reversed positions, giving everyone the opportunity to practice.

Jill leaned in closer to Sadie. "How's Greg doing?"

Last night, Sadie had shared Greg's news with her. His mom had decided to leave his dad.

"He seems to be doing pretty well." Looking over, she saw that Greg was now with Dr. Cantiko.

"Just from the little bit Greg's said about his dad, I'm surprised that his mom stayed with him as long as she did." Jill shook her head.

"Yeah, I know what you mean." Sadie had the feeling that his mom had made a good decision.

"I wonder what made her do it after all this time?" Jill mused. "Maybe she caught him cheating."

"Maybe," Sadie said. Somehow she thought there was more to the story. Ever since Greg had told her about it, she couldn't stop thinking about that paper in the bottom of his dad's desk drawer. She had a feeling that it was a key to the puzzle. The problem was, she didn't know where it fit.

BUZZ. BUZZ. BUZZ. The bell caught them by surprise. The two-hour adjusting lab had gone by very quickly.

Microbiology was their next class. "Let's go outside for a few minutes before Micro starts," Sadie suggested.

"All right," Jill readily agreed. The St. Louis climate in May was more agreeable to her Southern blood. Becky, Ellen, and Greg joined them, deciding to take advantage of the thirty-minute break between classes.

Sadie grabbed Greg's hand as they made their way down the winding path to the park benches. With one thing after another happening, there never seemed to be a good time to talk about the two of them. Now it seemed that the longer they put off the subject, the harder it was to bring up. Sadie tried to put her unresolved feelings aside, wanting instead to offer her support if Greg needed it.

The park benches were now shaded by a canopy of leaves overhead. Dappled sunlight filtered through, creating an ever-changing kaleidoscope of light on the benches. At 10:00 in the morning, the temperature was a perfect 75 degrees. The full brunt of the summer humidity was still several weeks away. Three robins were hopping along the well-manicured lawn. Purple irises were waving in the sun. A perfect day—perfect for catching up on all the spring break news.

Jill turned to Greg. "How's your mom?"

Greg frowned. "She's going through a tough time right now. I wish she'd open up so I could help her."

Sadie squeezed his hand. "I'm sure she knows you're there for her."

"I hope so." Greg nodded before changing the subject. "Becky, how are the wedding plans coming along?"

"Great! Thanks to Jill." Becky smiled. "Roger loved your ideas for the wedding!"

"I can't believe it's only four weeks away." Jill sat down next to Becky. "I found my bridesmaid's dress; it's perfect!" She pulled a photograph out of her Gucci purse and handed it to Becky.

"It's beautiful! Oh, I can't wait!" Becky passed the photograph around so that everyone could see it.

Sadie looked over at Ellen. "What's up with Troy?" she asked. "The flowers he sent me were so beautiful." (Troy had sent her a bouquet of flowers when he had completed the purification program.)

"I've been thinking about him, too. How is he?" Greg asked.

"Oh, you guys, he's doing great!" Ellen smiled. "He even entered a rodeo last week!" She was standing next to a large maple tree instead of sitting with everyone else on the park benches. When asked about her habit of standing, she'd replied that (except for riding horses, of course) she didn't like spending that much time on her butt.

"That's great!" Sadie said.

Greg turned, whispering in her ear, "Good job, Sadie."

"Thanks." Sadie smiled, savoring the intimate moment.

"How about you, Ellen?" Jill asked. "How was your vacation with Danny?"

"We had a great time! Danny spent a weekend with us. Troy even got him on Cutter for some roping practice. Ha!" Ellen laughed at the roping memory.

Sadie was aware of the fact that Jill was directing the attention onto everyone else, thereby keeping the conversation away from her. Sadie and Jill had stayed up late last night discussing, among other things, Jill's concerns about Jeff. Primarily that once he graduated, he wouldn't have time for a second-year chiropractic student.

BUZZ. BUZZ. BUZZ. The break was over.

Microbiology lecture met in the morning. Its two-hour lab was held after lunch. Dr. Adni, the Microbiology professor, was now walking to the podium. He was a short, bespectacled man from India. The buttons of his lab coat strained over his stomach yet somehow managed to hold the ends together.

"I think he needs a bigger coat," Jill said, eyeing the mighty buttons.

"I think you're right," Sadie whispered.

Dr. Adni cleared his throat. "Good morning, doctors."

"This must be a third trimester custom—calling everyone 'doctor,'" Jill observed.

Sadie nodded. "It's kind of cool."

Dr. Adni's heavy Indian accent added interest to the now familiar roll call. It was during his discussion of thick- and thin-walled viruses that it was most evident, sounding more like "tick- and tin-walled wiruses." After the novelty of his accent wore off, the class settled down to learn this new subject.

As they had with the preceding trimesters, the days fell into a pattern. The rhythm of lectures, labs, and library was as regular as a heartbeat. As with a heartbeat, it sped up before tests, returning to normal afterward. Right now, they were in a normal rhythm.

Neurology fascinated Sadie. She loved learning the cranial nerves and tracing their tracts or pathways. She now thought of the brain as one big puzzle that she was piecing together—and she loved puzzles.

Today, instead of studying cross-sections of the brain, Dr. Grant initiated a discussion on vaccines. The change in lesson plan was prompted by a recent magazine article exposing one of the many tragedies relating to the DPT vaccination.

Sadie had read the article, which talked about Michael Jonas, a one-month-old baby who had received a routine DPT vaccination that caused a severe allergic reaction. Michael suffered more than one hundred seizures as a result and now, at age ten, is confined to a wheelchair, legally blind, and still suffering from seizures. She shook her head; it was such a sad story.

The magazine had coupled Michael's story with an excerpt from *The Lancet* concerning the ineffective pneumonia vaccine. They revealed the fact that a Swedish study had followed 700 elderly patients who received the vaccine. Their findings were startling. Not only did they conclude that the vaccine was ineffective but also that the vaccinated group actually developed a 23 percent *higher* incidence of pneumonia!

"Can anyone tell me what goes into a DPT vaccine in addition to the toxoids and whole cells?" Dr. Grant waited expectantly. He was a kind, round-faced man in his early sixties. He wore wire-rimmed glasses that would frequently slide halfway down his rather bulbous nose. (Luckily, that large bump prevented his glasses from further descent.) He was short on hair and long on knowledge. For all his scientific acuity, however, the first word students usually used to describe him was calm. Patient, calm, nice—those were the words that came to mind. Perfect qualifications for being one of the students' favorite instructors.

"Yes, Becky?"

"They use formalyn, which is a derivative of formaldehyde . . ."

"What?" Paul's head swiveled around. CRACK. (It swiveled noisily.) "You mean they put embalming fluid in shots?"

The back row started laughing at his outburst.

Peter Burger rolled his eyes. That was as much as he was able to do today since the laryngitis prevented any further communication.

Nodding, kindly Dr. Grant looked a bit sad. "Research from as early as 1920 has confirmed that some of the substances that are added to vaccines, such as formalyn, serve to increase the severity of disease and the probability of death, depending upon the type of bacteria or viruses that are injected along with these chemicals."

"Wow!" Sadie frowned. "I didn't know that."

"I'm afraid that's not the only additive," Dr. Grant continued. "Methanol is also added . . . "

Paul broke in again. "Embalming fluid *and* wood alcohol?"

"Oh, there's more." Dr. Grant then asked, "Does anyone know what it is?" He looked around. "Sadie?"

"Thimerosal."

"Very good." Dr. Grant nodded. He had a special way of making you feel really glad to be able to answer a question. "As you are all aware, thimerosal is a mercury compound toxic to human cells. It also produces an allergic reaction in the body. In addition, an adjuvant is added. Common adjuvants are aluminum hydroxide . . . "

Yet again, Paul cut in. "I thought aluminum wasn't good."

"Shush." For some reason, Cathy was irritated with his interruptions. Perhaps she was worried that he was looking foolish and that reflected badly on her. Whatever the reason, she was now glaring at Paul, scowling so much that her eyebrows actually touched in the middle.

Sadie looked over to see Jill sketching a picture of Cathy frowning. Instead of eyebrows, she had drawn a large caterpillar in the center of her forehead. It, too, was frowning. Sadie bit the bottom of her lip to keep from laughing out loud.

Paul was unfazed. Turning his attention to Cathy, he continued. "My mom got rid of all of her aluminum pots and pans. She said that aluminum caused Alzheimer's disease." (To Paul, if his mom said something, it was gospel.)

"Humph." Cathy turned away, ignoring him.

Before the back row's "Mama's boy" chant could take hold, Dr. Grant resumed lecturing. "Let me give you a bit of research history. As early as 1940, it was noticed that children recently injected with the Pertussis vaccine suffered from paralytic polio at an increased frequency over those who had not received the vaccine. "In 1954, a study by the Medical Research Council of Great Britain showed that Diphtheria-Pertussis vaccines predisposed children to paralytic polio."

Frowning, Dr. Grant continued, "Each year, more than 33,000 children experience acute neurological reactions to their routine DPT immunization. Approximately 9,000 have convulsions, while over 16,000 have episodes of high-pitched screaming, which, as you know, indicates brain damage in progress."

"Why don't they do something about it?" Jackie was outraged. "I mean, if chiropractors caused 33,000 children to suffer from neurological reactions each year, our whole profession would be shut down." She shook her head. "I just don't get it," she muttered to herself, having seen too many vaccine reactions in her years as a nurse.

"I'm afraid I don't understand it, either." Dr. Grant, too, was dismayed. "Over fifty years ago, two Harvard scientists, Byers and Mol, did research on DPT vaccines at Children's Hospital in Boston. They concluded that severe neurological problems followed the administration of DPT vaccines. This was published in *Pediatrics*. Thirty years after that report, an FDA scientist named Charles Manclark said, 'The DPT vaccine had one of the worst failure rates of any product submitted to the Division of Biologics for testing.' So yes, Jackie, when faced with years of research like this, it does make one wonder."

BUZZ. BUZZ. BUZZ. Luckily for everyone's rising blood pressure, the class was over.

Jackie stood abruptly, causing the now familiar swaying of her glasses, which hung at mid-chest level. (Funny, but no one could remember actually observing her with them on.) The class may have ended but, as could be heard from the lunchroom to the library, the discussion was far from over.

CHAPTER

23

The twins had arrived (heat and humidity, that is) so typical of St. Louis in the summer. It was yet another reason to have coined the phrase "the terrible two's." Today was Thursday and they were heading north for Becky's wedding. She had been promising them beautiful Wisconsin weather all week. Sadie smiled as she recalled Becky's daily weather forecasts. "You'll love it. It's not nearly as hot or as humid. It will be great!"

For several weeks now, Becky had been exhibiting an endearing mix of traits. On the one hand, she was preparing to be a proud hostess, hoping to showcase her home state to its best advantage. At the same time, she was a nervous bride-to-be, desperately hoping that the weather would cooperate.

Luckily, the weather forecast was good. Sadie smiled as she put the last of her makeup into her travel case. "Jill, Greg will be here in a few minutes."

"I'll be right down."

After pouring a fresh cup of coffee into a travel mug, Sadie went to check on Jill. After last night, she was still concerned for her. It had been the first time she'd seen her break down and cry. That wasn't normal for Jill, especially over a guy.

Sadie felt torn. She loved them both but she was also upset with Jeff for canceling his plans to attend the wedding. Oh, she knew that at this stage of the game, work came first. She just hoped that Jill did. Even when Jill had tried to brush off her unhappiness by saying "Greg can escort both of us," Sadie could hear the sadness in her voice.

"Oh, honey, thanks for the coffee." Jill took the mug and had a sip. "Ahh, coffee with chicory and cream. Nothing beats it."

HONK. HONK. HONK.

"That's Greg. Are you all right?" Sadie waited.

"Well, that's a pretty broad question." Jill smiled. "Yes, thanks to you, I can honestly say I'm of sound mind and body."

Sadie grinned. "Are we going to a wedding or writing your will?" She was relieved to see that Jill was looking better.

"Ha!" Jill started laughing. Sadie joined in. The sounds of their laughter greeted Greg as he came in to get their luggage. He quickly packed the Jeep and they started on their journey.

In spite of her earlier laughter, Jill was unusually quiet inside the car. Sitting in the back seat, she was staring out the window as the miles rolled by. Leaning over, Sadie whispered to Greg. It was time to cheer Jill up. Besides, after three hours on the road, they all needed to stretch their legs. Greg pulled over at an Illinois rest stop.

"I've never seen so much corn in my whole life." Jill shook her head. "I'm going to the bathroom." Looking at Sadie, she asked, "Are you coming, too?"

"No, I'm okay."

As soon as Jill was inside the bathroom, Sadie and Greg hurried to set up their picnic. Sadie had called Greg last night after Jill had gone to sleep. Together they had planned a surprise picnic to lift Jill's spirits. Little did Sadie know it, but she, too, would eventually be surprised as well. Apparently, Greg had done more last night than simply help to arrange their feast.

"This is perfect," Sadie said after everything was set up. The green picnic table under the huge oak tree had been transformed. It was now covered with a red-and-white checked tablecloth and laden with food. Oven-fried chicken, corn bread, and coleslaw— all of Jill's favorite foods. A jar of iced tea with lemon wedges and fresh mint was sitting in the center of the table. "Thanks for your help."

"No problem." Reaching out, Greg brushed a stray curl from her face. Their tender moment was cut short, however, by Jill's arrival.

"Oh, I can't believe this! It's beautiful! You guys are the best!" Jill hugged them both.

After their picnic, they were once again back on the road. Jill's good mood had been restored. "What's up with your mom these days?" she asked Greg.

"Well, she said she found something in dad's office when we were on the phone the other day. Before she could tell me what it was, she said she had to go and hung up the phone."

Sadie had another one of her feelings. Something wasn't right. She could feel it in her bones.

Jill apparently didn't share those feelings. "He was probably cheating on her. Maybe she found a picture."

"Maybe," Greg said.

Sadie could tell from his tone of voice that he, too, thought there was more to the story.

The story, however, would have to wait as the scenery took center stage. Having just crossed the state line, they were now officially welcomed to Wisconsin. The miles of flat cornfields gave way to gently rolling farmland. Red barns, lush green pastures, blue skies, and, of course, black-and-white cows dominated the landscape.

"Oh, look at that!" Sadie pointed to a baby calf sleeping on a bed of grass. "No wonder Becky loves it here!"

"It's beautiful!" Greg readily agreed.

Jill was more reserved. "Yes, it's nice." Although she could appreciate the picturesque setting, the stone and steel of the big city were more suited to her taste. Cows were all right, but art and architecture—now that was something!

The closer they got to Becky's farm, the more Sadie felt as though she were coming home. Her Celtic soul was soaring, right here in central Wisconsin. *I wish you could see this place, Grandma.* When the familiar cold draft hit her, she smiled, rubbing her arms. *I guess you can.*

"This is it," Greg said, turning the wheel.

Becky's farm was surrounded by white rail fencing. Their tires crunched on the red granite as they pulled into the driveway. A two-story brick farmhouse was off to their right. Sadie recalled Becky saying that it had been built in the 1850s. Various generations of Becky's family had added to it over the years. One of the newer additions was a wrap-around porch complete with rocking chairs, all of which were currently occupied by barn cats.

WOOF. WOOF. WOOF.

"Sam, hush!" Becky came out of the front door, calling instructions to their black-and-white border collie. Sam was now wagging his tail as well as the entire lower half of his body as he greeted everyone.

"I'm so glad to see you guys. Was the trip all right?" Becky reached for their luggage.

"The trip was great," Greg said. "Don't worry about that. I'll bring everything in."

"Thanks." Becky looked down. Sadie was still engrossed in petting Sam.

"Hey, Becky, I think I'm in love with Sam," Sadie said while petting his stomach.

"I'm so glad we're going to have nice weather," Jill said.

"Me, too." Becky smiled.

SLAM. The screen door hit the doorframe as Ellen and Danny came out.

"How did you do in the horse show?" Greg asked Danny as they were carrying in the luggage. Ellen and Danny had left on Wednesday so that he could ride in the Milwaukee horse show.

"We won our qualifying class."

"That's great," Greg said.

"Luckily the championship isn't until Sunday afternoon," Danny said. "That way we won't miss any of the wedding and we can still make the end of the show."

"Who's taking care of Carter?" Sadie asked.

"His trainer," Danny said.

"Oh, that's good." Sadie replied.

They unpacked and, after a tour of the farm, settled in for the night.

— • • • —

Sadie woke up early the next morning. Looking out of the second-story window, she could see millions of stars twinkling in the pre-dawn sky, winking at her from the heavens. Suddenly, the memory hit her. "Twinkle, twinkle little star . . . " she recalled Katie singing. A tear slid down her cheek, but she was too caught up in the memory to wipe it away.

Far away, Elsie shook her head. "There now, lassie, 'tis no use frettin' about what cannot be."

Thanks to Elsie's help, the pain of the memory eased and Sadie wiped the tear from her cheek. She watched as the sky changed before her eyes. Faint ribbons of pink appeared, circling the horizon. Like ribbons on a giant present, she thought. Smiling, she recalled her grandmother's comments. "It's a gift from God, child, the gift of a new day, a new beginning. Morning is special."

A breeze stirred, causing the curtains to sway. A rooster crowed. The farm was waking up. Looking out at the gently rolling pastures dotted with grazing cows, Sadie felt a sense of peace.

Then she noticed something—some motion. Looking closer, she saw Becky's pet pygmy goats running toward the fence. Yesterday Becky had affectionately introduced them as "my bad goats." Sadie watched as they raced to the fence, their little round bodies on skinny goat legs. Arriving at the wire fence, they first rubbed their right sides against it and then turned, rubbing their left sides (a modern goat's guide to good grooming). The three goats performed this ritual with the precision of a drill team. Then, one by one, they scurried under the fence. Sadie smiled as she watched them negotiate the fence. First they tilted their head to the left, to get their horns through. Then they crawled on their knees to get all the way under the fence. (This required some effort as their round bellies hindered the maneuver.) Finally, they were free! With their tails wagging, they began to graze.

"I guess the grass really is greener on the other side of the fence." Sadie grinned, cheered by the frolicking goats. She was excited for the day ahead.

Sadie wasn't the only one excited. Becky was positively beaming as they headed to a neighbor's farm to take part in an annual tradition—June dairy breakfast.

"We hosted it at our farm last year," Becky explained. "People come from all over the state and tourists who are visiting Wisconsin come as well."

"Really?" Jill was intrigued with this social custom.

"Here we are." Becky pulled in to the driveway. To the right was a large red-and-white-striped tent. The sides were rolled up, revealing rows of picnic tables inside.

"Wow, it looks like there's at least a hundred people already eating!" Ellen, too, was surprised by the large turn out.

Greg sniffed the air. "It sure smells good."

"It does!" Danny agreed as they all went inside.

In addition to pancakes, eggs, sausage, bacon, and ham, there were fresh cheese curds as well as samples of every type of cheese made in the state. There were ice cream and custard samples as well.

"This stuff is great!" Ellen waved her spoon in the air as she praised the vanilla custard.

"Look at that!" Sadie pointed to the right of the barn. "A petting zoo. Let's go to see the babies." She headed for the baby goats. BAA. BAA. A little goat looked up at her as she petted it. Greg squatted next to her. An older goat stood on his hind legs, placing his tiny, cloven hooves on Greg's shoulder.

"I think he's hungry," Greg said, scratching the goat's neck.

"He probably is," Sadie said as she continued petting the baby goat. "It's great here, isn't it?" she said, looking over at Greg.

"It is."

They walked arm in arm through the rest of the petting zoo. There were babies of all species. Llamas, alpacas, goats, donkeys, calves, kittens, chickens, and rabbits, all being fed and petted by exuberant children. There were also pony rides for the kids and hay rides for anyone interested in touring the Albrechts' large farm.

"The Albrechts are in the same organic association that we are in," Becky had informed them. The sign on their farm was the same as the one at the Holter's: "Proud Members of the ORGANIC VALLEY DAIRY ASSOCIATION."

Sadie, Greg, and Jill decided to take the hayride and learn more about organic farming. Becky and Roger were busy visiting with all their relatives attending the breakfast. Danny and Ellen went to check out the horse barn. The Albrechts also raised quarter horses.

"Isn't it beautiful?" Sadie smiled as they traveled through a meadow full of wild flowers. Yellow and white daisies, orange Indian paintbrush, and purple-topped clover added color to the swaying green grass. Ahead of them was a hay field. "It smells so sweet." Tilting her head, she took another whiff of the freshly cut hay.

"If they could bottle that scent, I know people at home who would buy it," Jill said. The hay didn't interest her nearly as much as watching Sadie and Greg did. She smiled, liking the fact that Greg's arm was draped around Sadie's shoulders and they were whispering together. It was a good sign, she thought.

Beyond the hay field was an apple orchard. To the right of that, a small stream. The sound of the water flowing over the rocks coupled with the CLOMP, CLOMP, CLOMP of the horses' hooves as they walked along their familiar path and turned for home. Far too quickly, the hayride was over.

"That was so much fun!" Sadie held her arms out as Greg helped her down from the wagon.

"It sure was," he said before turning to help Jill.

Jill grabbed a sample of cheese when they reentered the tent. "This is the best cheese I've ever eaten! Is it because it's fresh or because it's organic?"

Becky walked up beside her. (Roger was still occupied by friends and family.) "Both," she answered. "Here, try these," she said, offering them all what appeared to be ice cream bars covered in chocolate on sticks. "They're lollies from Whey-Cool—w-h-e-y, not w-a-y, that is.," she added.

"Wow! It's good," Greg said.

"It is," Sadie agreed. "What's Whey-Cool?"

"A new company we're working with. This is made from whey so it tastes like ice cream but has more protein than chicken." Becky took another bite.

"Cool," Greg said.

Becky grinned. "No. Whey-Cool."

"I have to tell my parents," Jill said. "This stuff is incredible."

Danny and Ellen wove their way through the crowds to join them. "Those horses are amazing," Ellen said before popping a cheese curd in her mouth. Once she was done sampling the cheese, she went on to describe the horses in detail.

It was early in the afternoon by the time they returned to the Holter farm. After freshening up, the girls sat on the front porch enjoying fresh lemonade. (Three orange barn cats were still upset at being removed from their rocking chairs.)

"I wonder when Roger will be back?" Becky looked at her watch. Their dinner and barn dance would be starting in less than thirty minutes. Roger had left with Danny and Greg shortly after they'd gotten home. She chewed her lip nervously. "I don't know where he could be."

"I'm sure they'll be here soon," Sadie offered hopefully. Before leaving, Greg had told her that they had something important to do. None of the girls, however, knew what it was.

"Well, I guess we'd better head out to the barn." Becky looked a bit worried as the first strains of music could be heard. The girls had been banished from the barn with strict orders not to enter it until they heard the band start to play. The Notsteads had wanted to surprise Becky. Becky, however, wasn't the only one who was surprised; they all were.

"Oh, my!" Becky exclaimed as she saw who was waiting inside.

"Perfect!" Sadie said, referring to more than just the decorations.

"Ha!" Ellen laughed. "I don't believe it!"

"You're here!" Jill rushed into Jeff's arms.

Sadie hugged Greg. "I can't believe you pulled this off."

Greg smiled. "Remember when you called me to set up Jill's picnic?"

"Yes," Sadie nodded.

"Well, I called Jeff right after that."

Sadie looked up at him. "That was such a sweet thing to do," she smiled. "Thanks."

"You're welcome. Let's enjoy the party." Greg led her further inside.

Sadie continued smiling. Now everything really was perfect, she thought as she looked around the massive barn. Luckily, at this time of year it was still empty. By next week, the hay in the fields would be baled, occupying what was currently serving as the dance floor. Strings of twinkling lights were hung on the rough-hewn timbers overhead. Tables covered with red-and-white-checkered tablecloths were set up along the side of the barn. They were topped with pitchers filled with fresh flowers including zinnias, daisies, irises, and peonies.

"Oh, my!" Sadie went to the buffet table for a closer look. The foods were artfully arranged, some in wicker baskets and all at varying heights. "Look Greg, that's so pretty." She pointed to an old watering can filled with strawberries that trailed down the side of it. Plates of strawberry shortcake were arranged all around it.

"It is pretty," Greg said, although right now he was looking at Sadie instead of the decorations.

Becky walked over. "Come on, it's time to eat," she said. "Our table is over here." She led them to a large rectangular table set aside for the wedding party.

Outside, the Notsteads had barbecue pits filled with bratwurst, hamburgers, and ribs—all grilled to perfection. As they started bringing the food in, the smoky-sweet smell of barbecue made Sadie's stomach growl. "That smells good."

"It sure does," Greg readily agreed.

After everyone had finished eating their dinner, the band began playing.

"They're pretty good," Greg said.

"They call themselves the Dairyaires," Becky informed him.

Greg chuckled at the name.

"They're all neighbors and they get together on weekends to play at local events." Roger leaned over, closer to Becky. "Come on, sugar, let's dance," he said. With that, Becky got up to join Roger on the dance floor. Becky's parents, Diane and Peter, joined in, followed by Roger's parents, Duane and Theresa. Sadie watched the couples. Becky looked radiant as she circled the dance floor with Roger. She had a huge smile on her face. Roger's normally fair complexion had been bronzed by the sun, causing his white-blonde hair to stand out in stark contrast.

"He almost matches the tablecloths," Jill whispered.

"Shush." Sadie hushed her although she, too, had noticed the contrast of his sun-reddened arms emerging from the white, short-sleeved shirt.

As Becky's parents danced by, Sadie noticed that Diane looked like an older version of Becky. Peter also had blonde hair, although his was a more sandy blonde. He had a stocky, muscular build and piercing blue eyes that twinkled when he laughed. Both Peter and Diane seemed to be glowing as they proudly shared the barn's dance floor with their only child. As the dance continued, she turned her attention to Roger's parents. Both Duane and Theresa were tall, thin, and blonde.

"They look like they could be my parents," Jill whispered.

Sadie grinned at her. (They did.) Sadie and Jill were seated side by side with Jeff to Jill's left and Greg to Sadie's right. Since both Jeff and Greg were talking to people seated near them, Jill and Sadie had some time to talk.

"I can't wait until tomorrow," Jill said. "The wedding is going to be spectacular."

"I'm sure it will be." Sadie knew how much time and effort Jill had put into the planning of tomorrow's events. She had been on the phone with Diane on a daily basis.

"I'm so glad the weather will be nice," Jill said with a smile.

"Me, too," Sadie agreed. The weather was predicted to be a carbon copy of today's, with highs in the mid-seventies, lows in the fifties, and low humidity. Perfect for an outdoor wedding and perfect for Jill, since that was the only detail that had been out of her control.

"Excuse me," Greg interrupted. "I'd consider it a great honor to dance with the most beautiful redhead in the room."

Sadie grinned at Greg. "I'm the only redhead in the room," she laughed as she got up to join him on the dance floor. The Dairyaires had begun a lively polka. Soon Jill and Jeff, as well as Danny and Ellen, were all whirling around the dance floor.

The Dairyaires played for several hours, including everything from slow country ballads to lively polkas. At Becky's urging, they even included an Irish jig for Sadie.

Later that night, after the feasting and dancing, Sadie thought about how happy she felt. It's friends and family that really matter, she thought. She sighed contentedly as her head hit the pillow. Thankfully, there was no sudden interruption of the dream to spoil her perfect day.

— • • • —

If Friday had been Sadie's perfect day, today was destined to be Becky's. Jill had been up since dawn, working on the final preparations until every last detail had been completed. Now all the girls were in their room getting ready.

"I still can't believe you were up before me this morning." Sadie shook her head before putting on her pearl earrings—a gift from her grandmother.

"Don't worry, it will never happen again," Jill laughed.

"I can't wait to see everything!" Becky ran her hands down her sides, smoothing her slip.

"It's beautiful out there." Ellen said as she combed her hair. "You'll love it."

"I can't believe it's almost time!" Becky looked at the clock and then at her friends. "Thank you all so much for being here!"

"Thanks for having us, Becky." Sadie gave her a hug.

"You all have become my family," Ellen said, exhibiting a rare moment of sentimentality.

"I feel the same way," Becky said.

"Honey, watch out or your makeup will start to run." Jill dabbed under Becky's eyes with some tissue.

KNOCK. KNOCK. Becky's mom entered the room, holding Becky's wedding dress. "It's time to go," she said staring deeply into her daughter's eyes. She was oblivious to the fact that her right arm was still raised, keeping the dress off the floor.

"Here, let me help you with that." Ellen took the dress from her.

Arms unencumbered, Diane gave Becky a fierce hug. Stepping back, she smiled at her daughter. "It's time," she said again.

"Let's get you ready." Jill unzipped the dress, helping Becky with the simple yet elegant gown.

"Thanks again, Sadie, for lending me this wonderful veil," Becky said.

"You look beautiful in it." Sadie had lent her Elsie's antique Irish lace wedding veil. "Besides, it counts as something old and something borrowed." Sadie listened as strains of Pachelbel's *Canon in D* could now be heard. Diane was right; it really *was* time.

For the outdoor ceremony, guests were greeted by the sight of moss-covered bird baths topped with flowers. Jill had lined them up, forming an aisle for the wedding party to talk through. Sadie marveled again at her friend's creativity as she walked down the "aisle." Six bird baths on each side. To the side of the bird baths was the seating for the guests. For this, Jill had created makeshift "pews" consisting of wood planks supported by hay bales.

With the wedding party all assembled, Sadie watched as her friend took her last steps as a single girl. She looked beautiful. The simple, sleeveless, scooped-neck dress suited her perfectly. Sadie looked over at Roger, who was smiling broadly as he watched his future wife approach. He looked great in his khaki pants and blue sport coat. Jill had suggested dressing the men alike and keeping it fairly casual. "Nothing too stuffy," she had said.

Peter handed Becky to Roger and the ceremony began. In their beautiful meadow, overlooking the pond and pastures, Becky Holter became Mrs. Notstead.

Now it was time to celebrate. Once again, the barn had been chosen to host the reception. Jill had totally transformed it.

"It doesn't look like the same place we had dinner in last night," Sadie said as she stepped inside. A dozen round tables were set up in the center of the floor. She couldn't help touching the fabric. "Jill, how did you do this?"

"I crisscrossed the tables with strips of burlap and then I layered this crinkly white gauze over the top."

"It looks like antique linen," Sadie marveled.

"I like these," Ellen said, pointing to the place settings.

White plates were topped with simple, white, cotton napkins tied with burlap and decorated with wildflowers. Pear-shaped candles circled the table's centerpiece of wildflowers.

Sadie sniffed the air. The candles were scented as well. It was then that she noticed the small bottles of maple syrup. "Oh Jill, how perfect!"

Jill smiled. "I'm glad you like them. Not only are they cute, they're from the Holter's sugar maples. They make great place cards but they are also wedding favors."

Sadie continued to marvel at Jill's handiwork. Calla lilies were artfully draped across the seats of several vintage garden chairs. To the right, rocking chairs lined one side of the barn for those who didn't feel like dancing. Antique, two-tiered metal tables, sprinkled with daisies, served as cake stands. On the buffet table, vintage long-necked pitchers from France held masses of freshly cut peonies.

After everyone made it through the buffet lines and finished the wedding cake, it was time for the official first dance. Becky and Roger walked onto the barn's dance floor to the strains of Kenny Chesney's *You Had Me From Hello.*

"I'm really getting to be a fan of the Dairyaires," Greg said.

Sadie grinned. "Now I know what to get you for Christmas. The Dairyaires' greatest hits."

"Ha!" Greg laughed.

Sadie leaned over, whispering to Greg, "They look good out there, don't they?"

"They do," he said.

Sadie turned, observing her friends at the table. Ellen and Danny had their heads together in some private discussion. Jeff had his arm draped across Jill's shoulders and his head was tilted, whispering something in Jill's ear. It must have been funny because Jill looked up and laughed.

Greg tapped her on the shoulder. "Shall we dance?"

"I'd love to."

As the afternoon wore on, the party began to wind down. (Dairy farmers had to get home to milk their cows.) Becky wove her way through the remaining dancers. "Thank you guys so much!" she said. Then she turned and hugged Jill. "The decorations were perfect! Well, Roger and I are leaving for his cabin up north. I'll see you guys on Wednesday." Turning to her right, she then hugged Sadie. "Thanks for offering to give me your class notes for Monday and Tuesday."

Sadie smiled. "Don't worry. You won't miss a thing."

"Greg, thanks for being a great usher." He, too, received a hug from Becky.

"I had fun doing it," Greg said. "I'm really happy for you, Becky. Roger is a great guy."

"He is, isn't he." She turned, looking at the dance floor. Ellen and Danny were still dancing. "I'll go talk to them next. Bye, guys." She headed toward Ellen and Danny.

Jeff whispered something in Jill's ear.

"Wow!" Jill threw her arms around him. Turning to Sadie, she explained the reason for her excitement. "Jeff got me a ticket back to St. Louis with him."

Greg already knew that Jeff was flying Jill back with him. They would soon need to be at the airport. "If it's okay with you, Sadie, we could leave now and drop Jill and Jeff off at the Central Wisconsin Airport and then head for home ourselves."

"That's fine with me," Sadie said.

"Thanks, Greg," Jill said, happy to have some extra time with Jeff.

CHAPTER

24

Sadie and Greg were on their way home, having just dropped Jill and Jeff off at the airport.

"I must say, I'm going to miss Wisconsin." Sadie was looking out at the rolling fields, many of which are now filled with large, round hay bales. "It's so pretty here. Look at that; it's like sculpture," she said, referring to the geometrical precision of the hay bales. "Van Gogh would paint something like that!"

Greg smiled at her obvious admiration. "It *is* nice here. I've been thinking about the benefits of a small town practice lately."

"Oh, look!" Sadie interrupted, pointing to an Amish horse and buggy. "Grandma would have loved it here. She was fond of the simple, more natural way of life."

"It sounds like she was one cool lady."

"Oh, Greg, you would have loved her. She was so wise and loving." Sadie sighed.

Detecting a slight sadness, Greg changed the subject. "You know, we could start checking out towns in Wisconsin to practice in."

"You mean the two of us? Start up a practice together?" Even Sadie's natural tendency to dream up happy endings hadn't arrived at this conclusion.

"Why not? I think we'd make a great team. You could specialize in women, children, and nutrition. I'd specialize in sports injuries and accidents. Between the two of us, we'd have something for everyone."

"We really would have a lot to offer."

Sadie was amazed at how much thought Greg had put into this. She was also amazed that her feelings for him were still very much alive. Suppressing those for a moment, she considered Greg's idea.

"Maybe we could help the Amish, too," she said, looking over at Greg. "I was talking to Becky about the Amish children in the region. She told me that they are experiencing a high incidence of birth defects and rare genetic problems showing up. She said it's because of the inherent limitations of their gene pool."

"You know, I never thought about that, but I guess they all can pretty much trace their ancestors back to the initial group that came here from Europe."

"Yes." Sadie nodded. She was definitely warming to Greg's idea. "Maybe we could even work with Becky and set up something like what Dr. Golden did with Kentuckiana!" She was getting excited about the possibilities of a large, holistic health center for children with special needs.

"Wisconsiana? I don't know; you'd better come up with a different name," Greg joked.

Sadie grinned.

Greg looked over at her. "I like the idea, Sadie. I really do!"

Somewhere in Illinois, as the excitement of the wedding and the thoughts of a future children's health center wore off, tiredness began to take hold of Sadie. Slowly her head sagged forward. Then she jumped, bringing her head up and blinking her eyes rapidly.

After witnessing this for the second time, Greg reached over, laying a hand on her shoulder. "It's okay. You don't have to struggle to try and stay awake. Put the seat back and go to sleep."

"Are you sure?"

"Yes, I'm sure. I'm used to driving at night; get some rest."

Greg's permission was all it took for her to succumb to the demands of her tired body. Within ten minutes she was asleep. After thirty minutes, Greg could detect the occasional soft snoring sound. He smiled, glad that Sadie was sleeping.

Driving along, Greg felt happy. Their time in Wisconsin had been good for all of them. Miles rolled by. The drive was a peaceful one—at least it was for a while.

It was happening. Unfortunately, once it started, there was no turning back. Sadie quickly turned her head toward Greg. The sudden movement caught his attention. Briefly, he looked over to his right, thinking that she'd awakened and wanted to talk. It was like looking at a Halloween mask. Tight muscles had twisted her face into an ugly grimace. Her teeth were clenched and tears were streaming down her cheeks.

Then, she started shaking her head violently, back and forth, back and forth. "No!" she sobbed.

It was the scream that did it. A loud, tortured sound that caused his hair to stand on end. The Jeep swerved. Greg gripped the wheel firmly. At that moment, it was hard to tell who was more horrified.

Greg hit the hazard lights and his turn signal. Checking the rear view mirror, he eased the Jeep into the right lane. Luckily, there was a rest stop ahead. Turning the wheel, he took the exit. Just as he was slowing the Jeep to a stop, Sadie began thrashing her arms, struggling within the confines of her seat belt.

"Katie!" she screamed.

"Sadie, Sadie, wake up." Greg had both seat belts unfastened. Grabbing her shoulders, he commanded, "Wake up!"

She did. Her face, no longer frozen in a grimace, now looked haunted, even tortured. Although Greg had seen photographs of people who had viewed some horrific tragedy, he had never seen a person exhibit this much grief in real life.

"Are you all right?" Not really knowing how to help her, he gently wiped her tear-stained cheeks.

She nodded, although that was far from the truth.

"Who's Katie?"

Those innocent words opened the floodgates of hell. Gut-wrenching sobs racked her body. They seemed to come from her very soul. Her face screwed up in pain. She put her hands up to shield her eyes. Her fingers were so contorted, they now looked like claws.

Greg held her as her body shook. Her years of pent-up grief were now demanding a release. Finally, her sobs subsided. Greg put one hand under her chin, tilting her head up. He kissed her. Softly at first—in an attempt to comfort her. Then, more urgently—this time for his comfort. With an effort, he broke away, searching her face. Thankfully, the pinpoint pupils created out of terror were gone.

Sadie was speechless. Powerful emotions assaulted her—horror and happiness, sadness and seduction. If she'd been in her right mind, she might have been amused by this dichotomy. Tonight, however, there was no "right mind" in sight. Tilting her body to the left, she kissed Greg—seeking comfort for herself. (Was comfort possible at a rest stop in Illinois?) Perhaps.

Greg gently cupped her face with both hands, staring into her blue-green eyes. Rather than take what she offered with her body, he instead sought to soothe her soul. "Who's Katie?"

This time there were no gut-wrenching sobs as a result. Instead Sadie looked as if she'd suddenly aged twenty years. Her shoulders slumped forward. All the muscles in her face were slack. Her head drooped as though the effort to hold it up were too great.

"It's okay, honey," Greg said. "We need to get through this."

Sadie nodded. It was time to confront the horrors of her past. Taking a deep breath, she began. "Oh, Greg, I've never told anyone about the nightmares. I mean, Mom, Dad and Grandma knew the cause but they didn't know all the rest. I just couldn't add to their pain." Sadie was talking faster and faster, clenching her hands into fists at the same time.

Greg came to her rescue. "Take it easy." He unclenched her fist, holding her hand for comfort. "It will be better when you let it all out. Whatever it is, we'll deal with it together."

It was that word—together—that helped her. It wasn't until this moment that she fully realized how lonely she had felt—locked inside the terror of the dream. Gritting her teeth, she then continued.

"It was summer time. I'd always loved it, not just because of my birthday but . . . well, just the season itself. The long, lazy days, fresh fruit, country fairs . . . you know, summer." She shrugged her shoulders.

"I know. Go on," Greg urged. He didn't push the Katie question, sensing Sadie's need to sort out the details in her own mind before sharing them.

"Well, Mom was making us a cake for our birthday . . . "

Greg tensed at the word "us" but didn't interrupt Sadie. She now seemed to be reliving the event. She was staring straight ahead as though she were looking directly at that long-ago scene.

"It's German chocolate, our favorite. I go outside to pick raspberries . . . " Sadie frowned, looking down, unaware that she had a death grip on Greg's hand.

Suddenly, she lifted her head to stare at Greg, wide-eyed and horrified. "Oh, Greg, I took too long," she cried. "I shouldn't have dawdled so." Tears were streaming down her cheeks. She shuddered, shaking her head. "I shouldn't—have eaten—so many berries." The words came out sporadically, between her sobs. She gulped for air.

Greg held her for what seemed like hours. "It's okay, honey," he crooned. Finally, her sobs subsided and he felt her relax. Ever so softly, he wiped her tear-stained face and urged her to continue.

"Katie was my sister, Greg. My twin."

Sadie had finally answered his question. After the "us" slip, it shouldn't have come as such a shock. But it did. The impact of her words hit him like a punch in the stomach. He struggled to hide his emotions, focusing on her instead.

"What happened, honey?"

"I was picking raspberries for Katie; she loved them. We both did. There was a really good patch near our neighbor's old barn." She took a deep breath and continued, muscles tensing. "You see, it was our birthday. Mom was making German choco-late cake. Katie loved the coconut icing . . . " (The pressure on Greg's hand was increasing.)

"And you love chocolate." Greg finished her sentence, wiping another tear from her cheek.

"I do." She relaxed her grip and managed a weak smile before continuing. "Anyway, I wanted to get her some fresh rasp-berries to go with the cake. You know, to cheer her up."

Greg didn't know, but he figured he'd soon find out.

Sadie paused, remembering. The past she had tried to sup-press came back in vivid detail. She was there—living it again. Greg noticed the change as she continued her story, once again staring straight ahead.

"It's my birthday—our birthday," she said haltingly. "Eleven years old. It's summer. I love summer. I walk outside. BANG. The kitchen door slams when you go out. My hand is still sticky. I lick the chocolate off my fingers. Yum, it tastes like velvet—rich, creamy velvet." She smiled at the memory but her eyes were far away.

"She's been so depressed lately. Jeremy doesn't like her; he likes Angie. I told Katie he was a jerk but she doesn't care. She cries a lot. Last night I woke her; she was crying again. 'Katie, it's okay, you don't need dumb ol' Jeremy.' She looked at me. I never saw her look that way." Sadie paused, frowning.

"Go on," Greg stroked her arm.

"I'm shaking her. 'Katie?' She's looking at me, this time—not so far away and scary. 'It's the pills,' she says. 'They make me feel funny. I'm not myself.' Greg . . . " Sadie looked up, once again back in the present moment. "That's what she said, Greg." Tears streamed down her face.

Greg continued holding on to her hand for support. "What pills?" he asked with a sick feeling in his stomach.

"She was taking antidepressants."

WHOOSH. The air rushed out of Greg's lungs. He tried to breathe; his lungs were on fire. The hatred he felt was fueling it.

"Damn it!" He shouted, shaking his head. "I can't believe they give kids that crap!" Gritting his teeth, he also couldn't believe his father worked for the company that manufactured "that crap."

Then it hit him. The awful realization that his father was somehow responsible for Sadie's sadness. The guilt ate a hole in his stomach. He shook his head, "I'm sorry, Sadie." He held her. Sensing that she had more to say, he urged her to finish telling her story.

She did.

"The school counselor had her fill out a questionnaire. From that they determined that she was depressed and needed 'help.' They pressured mom and dad until they finally filled the prescription." Tears slid down her face. "Oh, Greg, she was only eleven years old!" she cried.

"Shhh," Greg cradled her, wiping her eyes. After several minutes she was able to continue.

"Anyway," she said, taking a deep breath, "Katie was right: She wasn't herself on the drugs, so I wanted to cheer her up."

"With the raspberries." Greg stroked her arm.

"Right." Sadie nodded. "Susie was with me."

"Who's Susie?" Greg asked.

"My cat." Sadie looked down, gritting her teeth as her muscles tensed.

Greg noticed the change in her; the pressure on his hand intensified but he continued holding on to it for support.

"I went to the barn. At first I was busily picking berries— eating some, too. The bowl was filling up. I was happy, eating raspberries and petting my cat. I remember I was thinking about my birthday—presents, cake, you know, kid stuff." Sadie smiled at the memory. Her smile, however, quickly faded.

"Then I stopped picking. It was the sound that caught my attention. The buzzing sound of flies and the banging of the barn door. I went around to the front of the barn to investigate. That's when the smell hit me." She looked up at Greg, unable to hide her horror. She was deathly pale. "Oh, Greg, it was awful," she cried. "That acrid stench. Sometimes at night I can still smell it."

Greg pulled her closer. She seemed oblivious to her surroundings.

"I kept walking. It was like I was being pulled forward. I remember thinking that maybe some kittens were caught and that I might need to save them." Sadie looked down, shaking her head. Gulping for air, she started sobbing.

Greg was now cradling Sadie in his lap in an effort to comfort her. She was trembling and then she started shaking her head. Reaching out, he stroked her cheek, resting her head upon his chest. "What was it, honey?" he asked quietly.

Drawing upon Greg's strength, she mustered up the courage to carry on. Taking a deep breath, she rushed through her final statements. "She hung herself! She was hanging there. The flies were everywhere . . . the buzzing . . . the smell . . . " she broke down. Trembling violently, she cried for her sister as waves of grief poured out.

Greg held her close. He felt as though he'd been suckerpunched. If he felt that way hearing her story, he couldn't imagine how horrible it must have been for Sadie. "Oh, Sadie," he sighed. Holding her close, he rocked her gently. Finally, she continued.

"I dropped the bowl and ran to Katie," she sobbed. It was like I was moving in slow motion. I tried to hold her up. I kept holding her . . . " Again, she broke down, sobbing so hard she could no longer speak.

"Shhh. It's all right." Greg held her. After several minutes of clinging to each other, Sadie swallowed hard and continued.

"I was screaming, 'Katie!' as loud as I could. Over and over— screaming—standing in a pool of urine—my arms around her lifting with all my might." The words came out haltingly. Shockingly.

Looking down, she continued quietly. "I guess I fainted when Mom and Dad arrived. I woke up the next day. At first I thought it was just a bad dream, you know, not really real. But it was. Oh, God. It was!" she cried. Her body heaved as she was once again racked with pain. Huge, gut-wrenching sobs poured out of her small frame.

Greg held her, stroking her hair. "It's okay, Sadie, I'm here. We'll get through this. It's going to be all right," he crooned. Bodies entwined, they hugged, rocked, and cried for a long time. All the while, Greg continued his efforts to comfort her. "Oh, honey, I'm sorry about Katie. I'm so sorry." Kissing the top of her head, he continued. "I love you, Sadie. We'll get through this. I promise. Together we'll get through this."

Sadie was so engulfed in sadness that Greg's words didn't fully register. The depth of his emotion, however, did penetrate her wall of grief. Slowly, her sobbing subsided.

SNIFF. She wiped her nose. "After the suicide, Mom and Dad weren't the same—they felt guilty—like they were to blame. They were so quiet and distant, I felt like I'd lost them, too." her bottom lip quivered. "Luckily, Grandma was there for me. She's the one who taught me how to garden and how to cook. I spent most of my time with her after that. We used to have the best tea parties."

Now her deep connection to her grandmother made sense. So did her fiery spirit. Greg silently thanked Elsie for keeping Sadie's optimism and joy for life intact.

Sadie looked up at Greg. "You're the only person I've told that to. Thanks." She gave him a weak smile.

Greg did the only thing he could think of. He kissed her. Softly, almost delicately, caressing the corners of her mouth, her eyelids, full on the lips—he kissed her. Pulling back, he cupped her face between his hands, staring deeply into her eyes.

"I love you, Sadie"

Those words *did* register. Staring back, she felt as though she could see his very soul. "I love you, too."

CRACK! Sadie jumped. Lightning lit up the sky. They had been so involved in Sadie's story, neither one had been aware of the approaching storm.

"We'd better get going." Greg backed out of the parking area. "There was a sign for a motel at the next exit."

"Okay."

The storm was fast approaching. BANG. A soda can hit the side of the Jeep. The wind was picking up, lifting cans from the trash barrels and flinging them everywhere. BANG. There was another. Luckily, the hotel was less than a mile away. Sadie breathed a sigh of relief when they pulled into the parking lot.

"Let's make a run for it!" Greg yelled over the wind and thunder. They were both soaked by the time they reached the door.

A balding, older man looked up when they entered. "There's a bad storm coming. Lucky for you, we have one room open."

"Great." Greg pulled out his credit card. After the paperwork was complete, they were escorted to room 131. The smell of chlorine was strong. (Room 131 was near the motel's small indoor pool.)

Luckily, the chlorine smell wasn't as strong inside the room. It smelled musty instead.

Sadie walked over to the large, metal box on the wall, turning on the air conditioning. Maybe that would help. The room was probably at the height of fashion during the seventies with its green shag carpeting and faded, paisley bedspread covering the king-size bed.

"Look at this," she said, pointing to the TV set, which was chained to the desk.

"I guess it's a good thing we don't need a television," Greg joked.

Sadie smiled. "I guess so," she said, shivering as she brushed a stray curl from her forehead.

"You're soaking wet, Sadie. You must be freezing. Why don't you take a hot shower to warm up."

"What about you? You're soaking, too."

"I'm okay; just throw me a towel."

"All right." Sadie grabbed a towel for Greg before turning on the hot water for her shower.

Greg toweled off, heading to the vending machines as soon as he heard the sound of the water running.

Sadie took a long, hot shower. When she opened the bathroom door, so much steam escaped that it took her a moment to see Greg.

He saw her, though. She looked like some Celtic goddess stepping out of the mist. She had a towel wrapped around her and her hair was wrapped in some kind of towel turban. Very impressive.

As the steam cleared and Sadie could see, Greg was rewarded with a smile. "A picnic," she said, hopping on the bed to join him.

"Only the finest," he joked at his array of vending machine entrees.

"Yum, yellow crackers with peanut butter; my favorite." Sadie tore open the plastic wrapper, stuffing a cracker in her mouth. "Cracker?" she mumbled, mouth full, as she offered one to Greg.

They sat for a while on that old paisley bedspread in companionable silence (except for the cracker crunching, of course). They both needed a moment to digest—not only the food but also their reactions to everything that had occurred.

CRACK! Sadie jumped at the sound of the thunder. Once again, she was in Greg's arms. She sighed. It felt good.

CRACK! She jumped again. Greg held her tight as the storm intensified.

"I love you, Sadie Jo," he said, using Jill's nickname for her.

"I love you, too." She lifted her face up to him, open and trusting.

This time, Greg took what she had to offer. Pulling her close, he kissed her deeply—branding her as his own. With his tongue, he continued his sensual assault, lightly at first, touching the corners of her mouth. She moaned and he took advantage of her open mouth.

Sadie felt as though he were touching her very soul. Her towel fell off as she met his embrace. She didn't care—she was on fire. Waves of emotion washed over her. Never in her life had she felt like this.

CRACK! The lights went out. The storm intensified. So did their lovemaking.

— • • • —

By morning the storm had ended. Sadie crawled out of bed. With her head under the shower, she didn't hear Greg get up. Nor did she hear him enter the bathroom. The shower curtain parted.

"Oh!" she said in surprise.

"Good morning, sunshine," Greg smiled as he stepped into the tub. "Here, let me help you," he said, grabbing the bar of soap.

Sadie felt surprisingly refreshed as they drove down the highway. It must have been the long morning shower with Greg, she thought. Looking over at him, she smiled at the memory.

"What are you looking at?"

"You," she said.

"Oh." He smiled, reaching his hand out to her.

She grasped it with her own small hand. Today she was happy, gloriously happy, finally finding the love that had eluded her since that fateful summer. The miles rolled on.

— • • • —

Moments after Greg dropped her off, Jill walked in.

"Sadie Jo, you slept with him!"

Spreading her arms, Sadie looked around for whatever it was that Jill had detected. Everything seemed normal to her. "How could you possibly know that?"

"It's written all over you—you're glowing! Tell me everything." Jill pulled her into the kitchen. (The kitchen table seemed to be the spot to hold all major discussions.)

"Oh, Jill, I'm so happy. I love him so much!"

"I know you do, honey. I'm happy for you."

Sadie paused, looking closely at her friend. "Jill, it looks like I'm not the only one who's glowing. Did you and Jeff get things all sorted out?"

"We did."

"No more Dr. Dana worries?" Sadie leaned forward, putting her elbows on the table and resting her chin on her hands.

"I can't believe I was so jealous!" Jill shook her head, white-blonde hair swirled around her.

Sadie smiled. "It looks like we're all doing pretty good."

"It does—Becky is married, Ellen and Danny are together, you've got Greg . . . "

"And you're with Jeff," Sadie finished.

"Yeah." Jill nodded.

"What a great trip!" Sadie sighed contentedly.

CHAPTER

25

Certified letters were uncommon for Greg. He and Sadie were at the post office now, signing for it. "Who's it from?" Sadie asked.

"It's from Mom." Greg took the envelope from the postmaster.

"What does she say?" Sadie couldn't wait to find out. She was the same way about her own mail and even worse with presents—tearing the paper to bits in her enthusiasm.

Today was Monday and they'd just finished Microbiology lab. Sadie had taken copious notes all day long so that Becky wouldn't miss out on too much information. Their next stop was Whole Foods to pick up groceries.

"Let's eat at Whole Foods before we do our shopping. We can open it then," Greg said. On matters such as this, he was infinitely more patient than Sadie.

"All right," she agreed.

They had each made salads and were sitting in the Whole Foods dining area. Greg was sipping organic decaf. Sadie had chosen fresh carrot juice. "Okay, what does your mom have to say?" she asked as she took the plastic top off of her salad.

Greg put his coffee down and opened the envelope. There were several documents inside. Greg frowned. "Sadie, these are internal memos from Zena Pharmaceuticals."

"What?" Sadie put her fork down. "Let's see," she said, moving her chair closer to Greg.

Together they reviewed the documents. Then they sat in stunned silence. Greg's coffee had long since grown cold.

Sadie couldn't imagine how Greg must feel. It was one thing to suspect that your dad was up to something; it was quite another to have it confirmed. "So *that's* what was in your dad's desk drawer," she said breaking the silence.

Greg nodded. "I can't believe he knew about this and did nothing!"

Sadie reminded him, "He *did* do something—he covered it up."

Greg shook his head, scowling.

Sadie was referring to an internal document from Zena showing that they had fifteen years' worth of data indicating that patients on their antidepressant were far more likely to attempt suicide and show hostility. For years, the company had attempted to minimize public awareness of these horrific side effects.

Greg was furious. If there had been any familial thread that still attached him to his father, it was now completely severed. "Dad hid these documents." He shook his head, thinking about Katie. In his mind, his dad was now responsible. Even though he had the evidence right in front of him, it was still hard to believe. He pointed to a paragraph. "Look, patients on their antidepressant have a twelve times higher suicide rate . . . " he read from the study.

Sadie gritted her teeth.

Looking up, Greg noticed her tension. He put his arm around her. "I'm sorry, honey."

Sadie nodded. "I know."

She read further. They both did. They'd initially been so shocked by what they'd found that they hadn't fully grasped the enormity of the contents. "Oh, my," Sadie said. "Look, Greg, all this information disappeared in 1994. It was during a trial in which a man in Kentucky killed eight people at his workplace before killing himself. He'd been taking one of Zena's antidepressants."

WHOOSH. All the air left Greg's lungs. He looked white as a ghost.

"What's wrong?" Sadie was concerned.

Greg couldn't talk. He looked down shaking his head. Sadie could see the muscles in his face tighten. When he finally looked up, his eyes were full of pain—he looked tortured. "Sadie," he said sighing, "1994 was the same year Dad was promoted to Vice President."

Sadie's jaw dropped. "Oh, Greg, I'm so sorry." She reached for his hand, squeezing it.

Absently, Greg took a sip of his cold coffee. His thoughts were miles away.

Sadie picked up the documents to return them to the envelope. "Greg, there's something else in here," she said, pulling out another piece of paper.

If they had been shocked before, they were now horrified. "Oh, my God!" Sadie stared at Greg, wide-eyed as she read the horrific report of a young girl's suicide. "She was only nineteen years old!" Tears slid down her cheeks.

Greg reached out, wiping them away. As he did, an anger burned deep inside. He made a decision.

Sadie sniffed, her tears replaced by a steely resolve. She, too, had made a decision. "We can't let him get away with it," she said, voicing Greg's own thoughts.

"We won't." Greg promised.

"Let's talk to Jill," Sadie said. (Both of her parents were prominent attorneys.) She felt certain that they would know what to do.

"Good idea."

Groceries forgotten, they left the market.

Jill listened intently as Greg told her the details of the company's cover up.

Sadie shared the other story. "She was staying at the Zena lab," she said, referring to the nineteen-year-old student.

"What's that?" Jill asked.

Greg knew all about it. "That's a hotel-cum-clinic in Indiana where people who are taking part in trials for new drugs stay. They call it the Zena lab."

"Oh," Jill nodded. "Go on."

Sadie continued, "She was perfectly healthy, not depressed at all. The only reason she enrolled in the clinical trial was to earn money to pay for her college tuition." Sadie shook her head.

"What was she taking?" Jill asked.

"One of Zena Pharmaceuticals' new antidepressants," Greg said.

Jill leaned forward. "Did it make her sick?"

"Oh, Jill," Sadie said, "she was found hanging from a shower rod in one of Zena's laboratories!"

"What?" Jill's eyes popped open even wider. "Oh, my God!"

"She killed herself on February 7, 2004," Greg added. "Even after her death, they continued with the drug trials."

"You're kidding!" Jill said.

"I'm afraid not." Greg shook his head. "You see, their antidepressant went off-patent in August 2001. It accounted for one-quarter of Zena Pharmaceuticals' 10 billion dollars in revenues. They had to find a replacement."

"The FDA couldn't possibly approve of something like that!" Jill looked to Sadie for confirmation.

"But they did," Sadie said quietly. "You see, they consider it a trade secret, so her death is not linked to the drug. Unfortunately, others died, too.

"No!" Jill was shocked.

Greg nodded. "It's now on sale here. It's also being sold in the UK and Europe under a different name."

Jill felt compelled to act. "I'll call my parents right now. They'll know what to do."

"Good!" Sadie said.

"Thanks, Jill. Would you mind if I call Mom first, before we start up any sort of investigation? I want to give her a heads-up."

"Okay," Jill agreed. "That makes sense.

By now it was very late. Stifling a yawn, Greg looked at his watch. "I'd better go," he said. "I'll call Mom first thing in the morning." He kissed Sadie good night before leaving.

Greg was already gone when Sadie noticed the envelope. He'd forgotten it. Oh well, she thought. I'll give it to him tomorrow. Reaching out, she grabbed the envelope and headed for her room. She had just fallen asleep when the ringing of the phone woke her.

"Hello?"

"Sadie," Greg said, "my apartment was broken into."

Now she was wide awake. "Oh no, Greg," she said sitting up in bed. "Are you all right?"

"Yes."

"Did they take anything?"

"Not as far as I can tell. They really made a mess of the place, though. The police just left."

"Don't stay there! Come and spend the night here."

When she hung up the phone, the envelope sitting on her nightstand caught her attention. She shivered. Getting up, she put on her robe and grabbed the envelope. *Where to hide it?* Sadie looked around the room. *Under the bed? No. In the desk drawer? Definitely not.* She shivered again. Putting on her slippers, she decided to make a cup of tea. Stepping into the kitchen, she recalled something Elsie had once said about hiding in plain sight. Looking at her teapot, decoratively placed in the center of the kitchen table, she smiled. "Perfect," she said, taking the lid off. Carefully she folded the envelope before placing it inside.

Sadie was glad when Greg arrived. She felt better knowing that he was safe. Hopefully, the envelope would be safe, too.

Jill was surprised to find both Sadie and Greg in the kitchen the next morning. "I thought you went home last night."

"I did." Greg told her about what happened.

"Oh, no!" Jill exclaimed.

"Greg, you'd better call your mom," Sadie reminded him.

"Use our phone." Jill sat down beside Sadie.

Greg dialed her number. He didn't tell her about the break-in, just about Jill's parents setting up an investigation. He listened, nodding his head. "Mom, come stay with me." Then, after a moment of silence, "okay," he said, hanging up the phone.

"What did she say?" Sadie asked.

"She told me to be careful."

Sadie shivered, hoping his mom's instructions didn't have anything to do with Greg's break-in.

Greg sat down. "She doesn't want us to do anything to tip off Dad while she's there. She's afraid he'll get angry. She's coming here, but not until after the Fourth of July holiday."

Sadie looked over at Greg. "Why is she waiting?"

"My little brother, Eric, is away at school. Mom will see him over the holiday. She hasn't told him anything about Dad—he doesn't even know they're separated. She wants to wait to tell him in person."

"Oh, I guess that would be best for Eric." Sadie nodded.

Greg turned to Jill. "Talk to your parents, Jill, but have them hold off on doing anything until Mom gets here."

"Okay." Jill glanced at the clock. "We'd better get ready for school."

Sadie found it difficult to pay attention in class. She did her best, however, to take good notes for Becky. As the shock of the documents and Greg's break-in faded, they once again resumed their familiar routine of school and studying.

As the Fourth of July holiday approached, Sadie was experiencing the fireworks of her new relationship. The only thing keeping her from feeling perfectly happy was the nagging worry she still had about the break-in. Unfortunately, the police didn't find anything, so there was not much they could do. Oh well, she thought, pushing aside her worries. It was time for the Microbiology lecture to start.

Dr. Adni, in the lab coat still straining at his mid-section, was taking roll. "Dr. Jensen."

"Here." Sadie smiled, her thoughts shifted to Greg.

"Dr. Notstead."

"Here."

Sadie turned, smiling at Becky. When she turned back, she noticed that Jill was drawing a picture of Becky in her wedding dress. It was really good.

"Good morning, doctors."

Sadie turned her attention to Dr. Adni. Before he could begin the lecture, she saw Jackie Adams raise her hand. On her desk she had a book, *THE BURZINSKI BREAKTHROUGH: The Most Promising Cancer Treatment . . . and the Government's Campaign to Squelch It*, by Thomas Elias.

Dr. Adni turned to Jackie. "Yes, doctor?"

"Dr. Adni, can you tell me what antineoplaston therapy is?" Jackie leaned forward in her chair. She had just gotten the book and hadn't had a lot of time to study it yet. She was hoping for an opinion as well regarding its contents.

"Ah, Dr. Burzynski's work." Dr. Adni rubbed his chin with his left hand. "Very interesting," he said nodding his head. This, of course, came out as *"Wery Intawesting,"* but the class had long since grown accustomed to his accent.

Placing his hands on the sides of the podium, he continued, "Antineoplastins promote the body's innate healing powers. In antineoplaston therapy, these synthetic protein particles are administered either orally or intravenously. They then alter the functions of specific genes involved in cell growth and replication, forcing cancer cells to either revert to normal or self-destruct."

Moving away from his customary position behind the podium, Dr. Adni began to pace in front of it. "I know that Dr. Burzynski has treated thousands of patients in his clinic in Houston since 1977. He has had particular success in treating infants and children with aggressive brain tumors."

Becky looked up, raising her hand. "If he has been successful in treating cancer patients this long, why don't more people know about it?"

Becky had just asked the million-dollar question. Murmurs could be heard throughout the room. The class was coming to life, and it wasn't an early morning jolt of caffeine that was causing it. No, it was righteous indignation, a guaranteed waker-upper.

Dr. Adni shook his head sadly before answering. "I'm afraid it all comes down to money."

"I read that the FDA harassed his patients." Jackie flipped through some pages in her book. "It says here that on March 23, 1995, Martin Biegelman, a postal service inspector, and Thomas Hansen, an FDA inspector, arrived unannounced at the home of one of Dr. Burzynski's patients, demanding to see the packaging of his medication and saying, 'Dr. Burzynski's treatment was ineffective . . .' and that ' . . . he was offering false hope . . .' and that ' . . . they had been trying to "get him" for the last 10 years.'"

"I'm afraid that is true," Dr. Adni said. "Current cancer therapies such as surgery, chemotherapy, and radiation are a multibillion-dollar industry. Dr. Burzynski is a threat and that is why he was aggressively persecuted by the FDA. His office was raided and his medical records seized. He was brought to trial, not for endangering patients or malpractice but for engaging in interstate commerce." Dr. Adni shook his head. "Of course he was completely vindicated."

"I remember hearing about one of his patients, an Australian girl. She carried the Olympic torch for the 2000 summer games." Ken Davis blurted out this new piece of information. Ken's sporadic contributions usually surprised the class when they occurred. This one was no exception. It even surprised Terry Hart, who turned to stare at his friend.

Ken's memory banks were working overtime to retrieve this data. "That's right," he nodded as he recalled the rest of the information. "Shontelle is her name. She was 18 when she carried the torch, but what's cool is that when she was around twelve, she was diagnosed with a brain tumor. The doctors said it was so bad that she had only three months to live."

The class was giving Ken their full attention. He appeared to enjoy it. While he "puffed-up" in his chair, Peter Burger was turning an ugly shade of red.

With a dramatic pause worthy of a theater actor, Ken continued his story. "Well, Shontelle's parents heard about Dr. Burzynski, and the whole town helped raise the money to send her to Texas. That dude's therapy caused the tumor to shrink and in three years it was totally gone!" He nodded his head, emphasizing the word *gone.*

Sadie shook her head in outrage. "I can't believe that a nontoxic, effective cancer treatment isn't among the *first* things an oncologist would recommend!"

Dr. Adni echoed her concerns. "Antineoplastins have been tested in FDA-controlled clinical trials. They have been investigated by the National Cancer Institute as well as being written up and discussed in major medical journals. It is very sad that it is unlikely that most oncologists would recommend them."

"Wery sad indeed" was the thought on everyone's mind as the class ended. *Wery sad indeed.*

— • • • —

The vaccination debate had heated up in Dr. Grant's Neurology class. Before he could begin to cover the spino-thalamic tracts, Peter Burger had asked about the connection between polio vaccines and AIDS, while Jackie Adams wanted more information on smallpox statistics. It was a very effective "one-two punch" that could have disrupted most teachers. Dr. Grant, however, took it all in stride.

"Peter, your question was first, so we'll talk about the AIDS controversy."

Peter nodded. "I saw a paper titled *What happens when science goes bad. The corruption of science and the origin of AIDS. A study of spontaneous generation.* What do you think of it?" Peter looked up at Dr. Grant.

The class noticed the change in Peter. For the first time he was actually *asking* a question. Usually he raised his hand to add data—irrelevant facts, as Jill called it—to the class discussion. Jill and Sadie looked at each other in surprise.

If Dr. Grant was in any way surprised, he managed to hide it well, answering in his usual calm, professional manner. "Yes, Peter, in that paper published in 1991, Louis Pascal showed that AIDS originated as a direct result of mass oral polio vaccination that had been contaminated with simian immunodeficiency virus."

"So it's true," Peter interrupted, "that AIDS originated in the Belgian Congo as a direct result!" For the first time, Peter actually looked shocked.

Sadie heard Paul Santini muttering something about monkeys.

Dr. Grant ignored the outburst and continued. "I'll direct you to a book by a research scientist that will help to answer your questions. The book is called *Vaccination*, by Viera Scheibner, Ph.D. Dr. Scheibner has published nearly 100 scientific papers as well as three books. I think you all will find it quite interesting."

Dr. Grant then turned his attention to Jackie. "You had a question regarding smallpox."

"Yes," Jackie nodded. "After our last class, I was doing some research that has really created more questions than answers. The statistics I reviewed showed that smallpox is five times as likely to be fatal in those who have been vaccinated as opposed to the unvaccinated."

Jackie paused, frowning. "Then I was looking at different countries. In Germany, the most vaccinated country, there were more deaths in proportion to the population. I also looked at the statistics of places like Bombay and Calcutta. What seemed odd is that those are highly vaccinated areas and yet smallpox is abundant, while in some towns that aren't vaccinated, smallpox is virtually unknown."

Dr. Grant listened patiently.

"Then I looked at data from cases admitted to smallpox hospitals," Jackie shook her head in disbelief before continuing, " . . . 80 percent of the cases admitted had been vaccinated."

"What?" Paul sputtered.

"I can understand your confusion," Dr. Grant said.

BUZZ. BUZZ. BUZZ. The bell interrupted Dr. Grant. "Read Dr. Scheibner's book," he said as everyone was leaving the room.

Sounds of the student parade could be heard in the hallway. CLICK. CLICK. CLICK. (The sounds of heeled shoes.) SQUISH. SQUISH. SQUISH. (The sounds of soft-soled shoes), marching on their now familiar path from one class to the next. CLICK. SQUISH. CLICK. SQUISH. On and on, in a familiar rhythm. Above it all, the voice of Paul Santini could be heard over the steady drone of foot beats.

"Monkey pox" echoed in the hallway.

CHAPTER

26

The Fourth of July holiday had passed and Greg's mom was on her way to St. Louis. In some ways it was a typical summer day: a hazy blue sky streaked with white, wispy clouds; green grass; chirping birds. Of course, Jill was still asleep. The beauty of the summer morning was the typical part—the part Sadie had loved so much as a child—she still loved it. It was the other part of the day that she dreaded.

Today was her birthday, and she hadn't celebrated it for years. Instead of celebrating, this day was usually suffered through in silence. This one was going to be different. With Greg's help, she was going to celebrate. Fate, it seemed, had decided to lend a hand. This year her birthday fell on a Saturday. No classes to attend, and finals were, thankfully, several weeks away.

KNOCK. KNOCK.

Sadie pulled her hair back into a ponytail as she went to open the door for Greg.

"Hey, sweet Sadie, Happy Birthday!" Greg hugged her, twirling her around in circles. She started giggling. After he set her down, he gave her a lingering kiss. That quieted her.

"Umm," was the only sound she could manage as she clung to him. Greg's kisses had the effect of making her go weak in the knees. She knew for a fact that the lips-to-knees pathway had not been covered in Neurology class. "Hmm, I'll have to research that."

"What?" Greg looked down at her.

"Nothing," she smiled.

"Okay. Let's go." Greg led her to his Jeep Cherokee.

"Oh, Greg!" (A bouquet of daisies was on the passenger seat.) She gave him a hug before getting in. Turning to her left, she looked over at him as he backed out of the drive. "Where are we going?"

"That's a surprise," he said, grinning at her. His smile faded as he asked quietly, "Did you sleep all right last night?"

Sadie smiled, "Oh, Greg, it was the first time that I didn't have the dream on the night before our birthday!"

Greg's grin was back in full force. "All right, then, let the celebration begin. First stop—breakfast." Greg pulled into a Cracker Barrel restaurant. "I thought you might like it here."

She did.

They walked inside to a replica of an old-time country store. Sadie turned full circle, taking in the sights. "Wow, this place is great!" Sleek, modern styles had never appealed to her. Maybe it was because she'd been raised by her grandmother. Whatever the reason, she found them too stark and cold for her taste. This, however, was perfect. It felt warm and "homey."

Reaching in to one of the displays, she picked up a sample dispenser of goat's milk hand cream. She smiled, thinking of Becky's goats. Pressing the pump dispenser, she put some on her hands, rubbing them together as she followed Greg in to the restaurant.

"Yum," she said as the smell of ham greeted her. "I'm hungry."

"Me, too."

They both decided on ham and eggs. Greg sipped his coffee as he watched Sadie make her tea. It was more entertaining than any Japanese tea ceremony, he thought as he watched the familiar ritual. Tea bag, honey, hot water, lemon, always in the same order.

Holding her white mug in both hands, she continued to look around in fascination. "I'll bet that's great in the winter time," she said, referring to the large stone fireplace. "Thanks for bringing me here. I love the music, too." The Appalachian hymns currently being played suited the country décor.

"I'm glad you like it."

Sadie stopped looking around as the waitress placed their food in front of them. Steam was rising from the large plates. "That is the biggest slice of ham I've ever seen." She cut a piece. Within seconds of placing it in her mouth, she was slicing another. "This is the best ham!" She looked over at Greg. "Thanks for this."

"You're welcome." Greg knew that "this" meant more than the breakfast. When he thought of the rest of his plans for the day, his stomach lining felt like a trampoline with little pieces of ham jumping up and down on it. He desperately hoped that she'd like his plans.

After lingering in the gift shop, they were once again back on the road. Sniffing her flowers, Sadie said, "It's too bad we don't have a vase for them."

"We don't need one. Each stem is in a tube of water; they'll be fine until we get back."

"Wow, you really do think of everything!" If possible, Sadie was even happier now, knowing that her beautiful flowers would last beyond the day.

When Greg turned the Jeep, Sadie realized where he was taking her. "The zoo!" she said excitedly. She loved the zoo because it reminded her of happy times. As children, both she and Katie had loved C. S. Elliott's *Narnia* books. As a result, they were fascinated by lions and had constantly begged their parents to let them go and visit them.

AAAOW. AAAOW. Sadie heard the peacock's greeting. Surprisingly, the St. Louis zoo is free ("forever free," declared state legislation in the early 1900s). With no admission fees, it was a popular place to go among the students. Together, Sadie and Greg took in the sights. Hand in hand they walked, shaded from the July sun by hundreds of huge trees.

"Look at that!" Greg pointed to a polar bear plunging into the water.

"Oh, Greg. This is so much fun!" Sadie threw her arms around his waist.

"That's how birthdays are supposed to be." Greg smiled at her. "I'll get us some bottled water. Why don't you have a seat on this bench. I'll be right back."

"All right." Sadie sat on the forest-green bench under the shade of a maple tree. Both the temperature and the humidity were climbing. Ice-cold water sounded really good. She sighed contentedly as she watched the polar bear. She shivered, suddenly feeling a chill.

"Ooch, my sweet dearie. 'Tis a fine way to be a-spendin' your birthday. Fine, indeed."

Sadie smiled. "Oh, Grandma, I haven't had a nice birthday in such a long while."

"I know. 'Tis glad I am for ya, child. I'm fond of your young man. Just be rememberin' that a day is fine but a lifetime is better. Two can handle what's ahead better than one." With that advice given, Elsie left.

Sadie shivered, frowning a bit. *What did she mean by that?* She didn't have time to figure it out because Greg was returning with the water.

"Here you go." Greg handed her a bottle. "Are you ready to walk some more?"

He looked so cute standing there, she thought. Looking up at him with a big smile on her face, she answered, "You bet I am."

They walked through big cat country, rode the zoo train, visited the primate house, and were headed toward the next ivy-covered brick building when Sadie stopped.

Greg looked at the sign: REPTILE HOUSE. "Oops, let's keep going." He'd been so engrossed in their conversation that he hadn't realized that was where they were heading. He knew that Sadie didn't like snakes. They went to see the hippos instead.

"Greg, look." Sadie pointed to a young girl in blue shorts and top standing next to the huge glass wall. She was mesmerized by the large hippo on the other side. Its eyes, ears, and nose were above the water line. Its large mouth was at the little girl's eye level. Just then another hippo jumped in the water. The little girl squealed with delight.

Together they watched the hippos for several minutes before Greg turned to her. "Are you hungry?"

"I am," Sadie nodded.

"Follow me." Greg led her to the Forest Park picnic grounds.

Sadie was walking on Greg's right, so she didn't see it right away. All the while, though, she'd been wondering what they were doing going to the picnic grounds when they hadn't brought anything for a picnic.

Then she saw it. "Oh, Greg!" To her left were two picnic tables pushed together. At least half a dozen helium balloons were tied to each corner. Behind the picnic tables and balloons were her friends.

"Happy birthday!" she heard, and they started singing to her. She was overwhelmed. Wiping a tear from her eyes, she looked at her dear friends, now singing at the top of their lungs. Smiling, she listened as they belted out the refrain. Jill and Jeff, Danny and Ellen and—*wow*—even Troy was singing. Then she turned to see Becky—*wait*—make that Becky *and* Roger.

Greg put his arm around her as he, too, joined in the singing. Sadie swallowed—there was a lump in her throat. Instead of singing the final word, "you", Greg bent down and kissed her instead.

Looking up at him, she was surprised to find no words to adequately express her emotions. Instead, she gave him a fierce hug. He seemed to understand.

Then she made the rounds, hugging all her friends. "Roger," she said when she stopped by him, "I can't believe you came all this way!"

"I wouldn't have missed it for the world!" Roger said with a smile.

Danny put some brats on the grill while Becky and Ellen unloaded their picnic baskets.

"Honey, you'd better sit down," Jill said to Sadie.

Still overwhelmed that her friends had done this for her, Sadie gratefully sat down on the picnic bench. The smell of brats was in the air. She sniffed appreciatively. Roger had brought them from Wisconsin.

She watched as her friends prepared the feast. Bowls of fresh fruit appeared on the table. No raspberries, though. Greg must have mentioned that. Looking over at him, she saw that he was helping Danny and Roger at the grill. Her heart swelled with love. Then she grinned, shaking her head.

"What?" Jill asked.

"It's funny," Sadie replied, "I just got a mental picture of the Grinch with his heart growing three sizes. That's how I feel right now."

"Ha!" Jill laughed. "Not that you'd be the Grinch, though. You're just someone with an oversized heart—that would mean you have cardiomegaly."

"Oh, great," Sadie joked," My best birthday ever and I have a heart condition."

Jill grinned. Then she reached out, grabbing Sadie's hand. "It *is* kind of wonderful, isn't it?" she said, looking at everyone bringing food to the table. Before she could be taken too seriously she added, "Our very own Who-Feast."

Now it was Sadie's turn to laugh.

"Sadie," Troy tapped her shoulder.

She turned. He looked good—healthy—as she remembered from their first meeting. "Yes?"

"I wanted to give you this." He handed her a package.

"Thanks!" she said as she tore off the wrapping. Inside was a framed picture of Troy with his horse Cutter. He was holding a silver belt buckle and a check.

"That's from when I won the rodeo after doing the purification program." He gave her an awkward hug, reminding Sadie of just how young he was.

"Thanks for the picture, Troy. It means a lot to me."

"I'm glad you like it," Troy said. "I wanted to thank you again for your help. I feel like I was never even sick." He smiled before continuing. "I found out that some of the 9/11 firefighters also used the purification program to get rid of toxins."

"Really?"

Troy nodded.

"That's cool." Sadie recalled reading about the pollution at ground zero and was glad the firefighters had found a way to regain their health as well.

"It's time to eat!" Greg announced.

Seeing him take out a package of whole-wheat buns from Whole Foods, Sadie smiled. He really knows me, she thought. Becky and Ellen dished out the salad and deli items—all from Whole Foods—all her favorites.

"This must be what it's like to be a princess." She didn't realize she'd spoken aloud until Greg leaned down and whispered in her ear.

"Get used to it, princess."

When they finished eating, she found that Troy wasn't the only one who had brought her a present. Sadie tore the paper off a large package. "Oh, you guys!" she said as she lifted a handmade teapot carefully out of the box. "It's beautiful!" She blinked in an effort to hold back tears.

"It's Irish," Becky said.

"You've got cups, saucers, a tea ball, and some loose tea," Ellen informed her.

"We thought you'd like it since we know Williams Sonoma is one of your favorite stores." Jill smiled at her.

Sadie held the teapot next to her heart. Looking down at it again, she shook her head. After so many years of being haunted by this day, it was such a relief to actually celebrate it. "I love it!" she said, looking up at her friends.

There was more. Danny gave her a mug with an American Saddlebred horse and rider picture on it. Looking closer, she saw it wasn't just *any* horse and rider—it was Danny and Carter.

"It's from our winning pass at the Milwaukee horse show," Danny said.

"It's beautiful," Sadie said, looking again at the picture on the mug.

Roger handed her a jar of maple syrup. "Becky said you liked it."

"I do! Thank you."

Jeff walked over carrying a book. "Oh, Jeff," she said when she saw what is was: *Applied Kinesiology, Volume 1.*

"Study hard," he said, handing her the book. "You're going to be a great doctor."

Sadie looked down at the book and then back up at her friends. "Thanks again, you guys!"

"I'd love to stay here all day," Jill said after they'd finished eating, "but finals are coming up."

Danny nodded, "I've got a lot of studying to do, too."

So her friends said their goodbyes, packed up, and left. Sadie turned to Greg. "Shouldn't we be heading back, too?"

"Probably." Inside the Jeep, however, Greg passed their turn-off, heading for the Arch instead. Sadie looked over at him. "Let's take a look from on top of the Arch," he said. "That way, we can remember this day."

"I'll remember it anyway, but that does sound like fun."

CLICK. The door to the inside tram closed behind her and they started their 630-foot ascent. Greg helped her out of the tram at the top of the Arch, escorting her to the windows. "Greg, look!" Sadie pointed out the window. "Isn't that sweet?" On the ground below, about fifty people were lying on the lawn, in the shape of letters. They were spelling out two words: MARRY ME.

Sadie looked around, searching for the happy couple. The look on Greg's face stopped her. Her jaw dropped when he got down on one knee, holding a tiny box in front of him. Reaching out with his other hand, he swung open the top, revealing a Celtic love knot engagement ring. Her eyes opened wide.

"Will you marry me, Sadie?" Greg looked at her searchingly, all the while holding the ring in front of him.

"Yes!"

Greg stood, wrapping his arms around her.

CLAP. CLAP. CLAP. They were both surprised when the people in the Arch viewing area began clapping for them. Breaking their embrace, they turned to smile at the onlookers. Reaching for her hand, Greg slid the ring onto her finger.

"It fits perfectly," she said, surprised.

"Jill helped me. She sized one of the rings in your jewelry box."

Sadie smiled, looking at her ring.

"I love you, Sadie."

"I love you, too."

Greg held her, dipping her as he kissed her. (This earned cheers from the onlookers.) "Thank you," he said to the spectators as they entered the tram for the ride down.

"Who are all the people?" Sadie asked, referring to the human "marry me" sign.

"Our classmates," Greg said.

Those classmates were now assembled at the base of the Arch. Jill, Becky, and Ellen were standing in front of the group with big smiles on their faces. "Congratulations!" they shouted as Sadie and Greg exited the tram.

Sadie looked at her friends, overcome with emotion. Before she could say anything, she was surrounded by her classmates, asking to see her ring and wishing her well. Throughout the excitement, Greg stood by her side. She recalled her grandmother's words, "When two become one." How appropriate, she thought, feeling the steady warmth of Greg's hand on the small of her back.

"Roger wants to try Ted Drewes while he's here," Becky said, referring to the famous frozen-custard store. "He wants to see them turn the cup upside down." At Ted Drewes, the custard was so thick you could hold the cup upside down and nothing would run out. Their ads featured a smiling employee in a yellow uniform holding a cup of custard upside down. Even the spoon and the straw remained buried inside the thick, frozen creation.

"That sounds good to me," Ellen said.

"Me, too," echoed Danny.

"Let's all go to Ted Drewes," Greg said, pulling Sadie next to him.

If she thought it strange to have an engagement party at a frozen-custard stand, she didn't mention it. Actually, she was still so overwhelmed by the events of the day, she didn't think to question where they were going.

Luckily, Ted Drewes was used to serving crowds. Soon everyone was enjoying his or her dessert. Sadie was sitting with Greg at one of the many outdoor picnic tables. She was happier than she could ever remember. It was summer—they were eating frozen custard with all their friends—she'd just had the best birthday of her life and—*wow*—she was engaged! Looking over at Greg, she smiled. All the love she felt came shining through. Greg smiled back and leaned over, kissing her. His lips were cold, tasting like custard. She shivered. Then she pulled back. "What's that?" Looking up, she tried to identify the source of the rumbling sound.

"It sounds like a plane," Greg said, as the sound grew louder.

Then she saw it. Smiling, she turned to Greg. "So *this* is why we came here."

Greg nodded.

A single-engine plane was flying directly overhead with a banner streaming behind it: CONGRATULATIONS SADIE AND GREG! At the sight of the banner, all their classmates started cheering. Their enthusiasm was overwhelming, and soon perfect strangers were joining in.

Sadie threw her arms around Greg. He whispered in her ear, "Ken and Terry are flying the plane."

"No kidding!" Sadie shook her head.

Greg smiled as his final plan was pulled off without a hitch. "I wanted to give you special memories for your birthday."

That he had.

Later that night, as Sadie was nestled in Greg's arms, Elsie's words came to mind, "Just be rememberin' a day is fine, but a lifetime is better." She smiled. *Now I know what she meant.* Then the rest of Elsie's words came back. "Two can handle what's ahead better than one." Idly, she wondered what Elsie had meant by that. Oh well, she thought, much too happy to dwell on it. She was still smiling as she drifted off to sleep. She'd find out soon enough what Elsie had meant.

CHAPTER

27

With finals only a few weeks away, the library was no longer just a room full of books. It was now a room full of students as well. In addition to being a helpful place to study, the library also had the best air conditioning. Jill had once joked that they kept it like a meat locker to prevent people from falling asleep.

Today, the cold was a welcome relief from the current 102-degree temperature outside. If they would have had time to read the local newspapers, the students would have seen "Record death toll caused by record heat" in the headlines. Instead, Neurology chapters had become their headlines. Although they'd all managed to successfully navigate the finals threat twice before, they still loomed as a large obstacle ahead. No one wanted to be caught in the potential riptide of being unprepared.

Even Paul Santini knew that if you were pulled too far away from the normal bell curve, you could kiss your chiropractic future goodbye. That is why, at this very moment, he was sitting in the back row of the library next to Cathie Muncie.

Two rows away, where Sadie, Greg, and Jill were seated, Jill passed a note to Sadie. It said, *This is a multiple-choice question: What is keeping Paul awake?*

    A.   *fear of finals*
    B.   *meat locker temperature*
    C.   *Cathy's black bra—visible under her white tank top*
    D.   *All of the above*

Sadie grinned while reading it. She passed it to Greg. They both marked "*D. All of the above*" as the correct answer.

After looking at her watch, Sadie leaned over, putting her hand on Greg's thigh to get his attention. She showed him the time on the watch. He nodded and started collecting their books. Leaning to her left, she tapped Jill's arm. "Time to go," she whispered.

In the cafeteria, they met Jeff, Becky, and Ellen. This was the time for their study group. (Danny was in the Anatomy lab,

studying for his own finals.) As they entered, they saw that Jeff
was putting some files into his briefcase.

"What are those papers for?" Jill asked.

Jeff looked up. "I've been helping with Jurisprudence
recently."

Because her parents were lawyers, Jill was interested in
this legal class. "What are you investigating?"

"We've been researching radiation safety in hospitals."

"What did you find?" Jill asked quietly.

Sadie looked over at her. She knew how much Jill wished
that Mark had chosen a chiropractic career.

Jeff had hoped to have all the papers locked away in his
briefcase before Jill arrived. He gave her only a brief answer. "A
study showing that about one-third of all x-ray machines were
found to be giving off too much radiation."

Jill shook her head.

Ellen didn't stop to think that Jill might be upset because
her brother was a radiologist. She was simply interested in the
study. "What does that mean for cancer patients?"

"It's not good." Jeff shook his head. "People have died. We
found one mistake in a Texas Cancer Center that was picked up
by the Associated Press."

Then, deciding that the details would be too upsetting, he
changed the subject. "There's a study on girls receiving the Milwaukee Brace treatment for scoliosis . . . "

"What did they find?" Becky asked. She wasn't a fan of the
Milwaukee Brace. It was even worse that it came from her home
state.

"The girls were exposed to twenty-two x-rays in a three-year
period, causing a 110 percent increase in the number of them at
risk for breast cancer."

"That's terrible!" Becky said.

"We need to have chiropractors doing scoliosis screenings at
schools," Ellen said.

"We sure do," Sadie agreed. As she looked around the table
at everyone, she realized that over the course of the year, she'd
begun to consider them all as so much more than friends. They
were family. She smiled, feeling fortunate to have met them all.

Jill looked up. "You're in an awfully good mood, Sadie Jo."

Sadie nodded. "I am. I was thinking about all we've been
through this year and how much you all mean to me."

Greg put his arm around her, pulling her close.

"We *have* been through a lot," Ellen agreed. "Remember my makeover?" She grinned at the memory.

"I thought you were going to fall over when you stepped inside Saks," Jill joked.

"HA!" Ellen laughed. "You have to admit, all that gold can be pretty intimidating."

Sadie looked over at Ellen. "I had a great time at your home."

"Me, too," Jill nodded.

Becky smiled. "I remember that it was almost like celebrating Thanksgiving at my own home."

Ellen smiled, recalling the memories. "I want to thank you again for finding a way to help Troy."

"You're welcome," Sadie nodded. "I'm happy he's doing so well."

Jeff looked over at Becky. "How about my surprise visit to your wedding?"

Becky seemed to light up with pleasure as she recalled her wedding. "That was great!" Looking around the table, she continued. "I'm so glad you all were there." Turning to Jill, she added, "Thanks again, Jill, for doing such a great job planning the wedding. Everything was perfect."

Jill smiled at the compliment. "I loved doing it."

"I thought that listening to the Dairyaires was the best thing we did all year," Greg joked.

"Oh, you," Sadie playfully slapped his arm.

Jill looked over at Sadie and Greg. "I think you two take the prize."

Greg and Sadie looked at each other. Reaching over, Greg tucked a stray curl behind her ear. "It *was* pretty special, wasn't it?"

Sadie smiled, "It was."

Ellen shook her head. "I still can't believe Terry and Ken did a fly-by."

Greg smiled. "That was one of my better plans."

They all sat in companionable silence as they recalled their first year at the St. Louis College of Chiropractic. So many things they'd learned. So many memories. So many more adventures to look forward to.

Sadie broke the silence. "What are you guys doing for summer break?"

Summer break wasn't long. Trimester Four officially started right after Labor Day. It was going to be tough. Twenty-nine credits consisting of Adjusting Techniques, Physiology II, Microbiology II, Pathology, Physical Diagnosis, and Clinical Studies. Although they'd already begun addressing the students as "doctor," Trimester 4 was where the real "doctoring" began. Sadie was already looking forward to it.

"I'm helping Roger on the farm," Becky said. "We'll have to put up hay."

Sadie smiled, recalling those gorgeous, sweet-smelling, round bales.

Ellen looked up, "I'll be working at home. I'm also going to some horse shows with Danny."

"That sounds like fun," Sadie said.

"I'm going on vacation with my family," Jill announced. "It's a summer tradition."

Jeff had been saving his news. So far he hadn't told anyone, having just finalized his plans. "I'm opening up a satellite clinic with Dr. Andrews."

"Oh, Jeff, that's great!" Sadie smiled at him.

"So, you'll be around here next year," Ellen added. "That's cool."

Becky smiled. "I'm happy for you, Jeff."

Greg patted him on the back. "That's great news!"

So far Jill had been silent, staring at Jeff in surprise. She'd been worried that he would be returning to the East coast to set up his practice. Jeff looked at her. "I couldn't be away from you," he said.

"Oh, Jeff!" Jill hugged him.

Finally, after several minutes, the reality of finals set in. "Well, I guess we'd better get to our actual studying," Jeff said, returning to their normal routine. "Have you all been drinking water?" he asked.

Jill looked up in surprise. "What does that have to do with studying?"

Jeff smiled. "Well, first of all, it's hot outside and a small drop in body water—just 2 percent—can trigger short-term memory loss as well as difficulty focusing on a computer screen or on a printed page."

"Oh," Jill said. "We don't want that before finals!"

"No, you don't," Jeff agreed. Looking around the table, he continued, "You'll also have some adjusting theory questions related to water. When the body doesn't have enough water, it doesn't work properly and there is also a greater potential for injury."

"And that sends people to the chiropractor's office," Jill concluded.

"That's important for our athletic patients," Greg said.

"Yes," Jeff nodded. "You definitely want your patients to be properly hydrated."

"Muscle testing doesn't work as well if you're dehydrated, either," Sadie added. (She had been reading her *Applied Kinesiology* book every night.)

"That's right, Sadie." Jeff praised her. "It's also important to know that roughly 75 percent of the weight of the upper body is supported by the water in the fifth lumbar disc."

"That's definitely important for patients with low back pain." Sadie started writing in her notebook.

"Lack of water is the number one trigger of daytime fatigue," Jeff continued bullet-pointing information. "Even mild dehydration will slow down your metabolism by 3 percent."

Jill looked up. "Water, the modern, healthy way to weight loss. I'll bet that would get people to drink more water."

"It probably would," Jeff said.

"Okay, now I'm thirsty." Sadie got up. "I'll get us all some water." The cafeteria's vending machines were stocked with bottled water.

"I'll help." Greg joined her, bringing back bottles for everyone before they resumed studying.

Ellen waved her water bottle as she questioned Jeff. "I know the adjusting lab will go over set ups for adjustments, angles of the joints, numbers of bones, all those sorts of things, but can you tell me more about the theory questions?"

"Yes," Jeff said. "Dr. Cantiko will have a lot of patient histories on the test. He might ask about the patient who complains about fatigue or the patient who asks about losing weight, that sort of thing. That's why I went over those tips on water. Pain is also a big topic, so be sure to study all the natural pain and anti-inflammatory agents. I'll never forget my final exam with Dr. Cantiko. He based it on Kenny Easley."

"Who?" Jill asked.

Greg knew who he was. "The University of California's All-American defensive back. He led the National Football League for pass interceptions for the Seattle Seahawks in the 80s." Greg looked over at Jeff, "Whatever happened to him?"

"Well, he was a unanimous Pro Bowl pick. Then he hurt his ankle . . . "

"That shouldn't be too difficult to fix. Right?" Becky asked.

"It wasn't his ankle that permanently side-lined him," Jeff said. "It was his kidneys."

"What? I don't understand," Jill said.

"His kidneys were destroyed by ibuprofen."

"Wow, I didn't know that." Greg shook his head.

"Anyway," Jeff continued," Dr. Cantiko used that as a framework for questions on ibuprofen. He asked for brand names . . . "

"Advil, Nuprin, and Motrin," Sadie answered.

"Very good," Jeff smiled. "He also wanted to know how much Americans spend on these over-the-counter medications each year."

"Oh, I remember him talking about that." Becky flipped through her notes. "Here it is. About $500 million."

"Correct." Jeff nodded. "Then he had something about a nephrologist estimating that 20 percent of the cases of end-stage kidney disease are caused by those supposedly harmless pain killers. With that, he went into a whole line of questioning on natural alternatives to pain killers."

"Okay," Ellen nodded. "I see the type of test to study for. I guess he'll ask about cherries."

"That's a safe bet," Jeff said. "I'm almost certain you'll need to know that cherries contain natural anti-inflammatory compounds, anthocyanins, that work on the same pathways as NSAIDs and aspirin." Jeff scratched his cheek and then paused with his index finger pointed. "Write this down," he said shaking his finger. "Researchers from Michigan State University found that ten tart cherries have the same pain-relieving capacity as one or two aspirin."

"Plus, you get the benefit of antioxidants," Becky added.

"Exactly." Jeff nodded in agreement.

Sadie looked up from her notebooks. That's odd, she thought, seeing the president of the college standing in the doorway next to a police officer. She looked down to finish her notes but stopped when she heard the sound of footsteps approaching. Laying her pen down, she looked around the table. All eyes, she noticed, were on the unlikely pair of people heading straight toward them. Reaching over, she grabbed Greg's hand. Although she had just finished an entire bottle of water, her mouth suddenly felt dry.

"Greg?" The president asked.

"Yes."

Sadie thought his mouth must be dry as well because the word came out in a hoarse, croaking sound.

"The sheriff would like to speak to you. Can you come to my office?"

Greg nodded.

Before he could get up, Sadie recalled Elsie's words, "Two can handle what's ahead better than one." "I'm coming, too!" she stated resolutely.

The president looked over at the sheriff, who nodded his consent. "All right," he said, escorting them to his office.

It seemed to take forever to get there—as though things were now moving in slow motion. Once inside the office, they sat down, waiting.

From the sheriff's somber expression, you could tell it was going to be bad news. (It was.) "I'm very sorry to tell you this . . ." the sheriff began.

Sadie could see the muscles tense in Greg's face as he clenched his teeth. His Adam's apple bobbed back and forth as he swallowed, waiting. She held his hand, offering support.

The sheriff continued, "There's been an accident. I'm afraid your mother didn't survive."

"What?" Greg's tortured cry cut him off. He began trembling. All the color drained from his face as he sat staring at the sheriff in disbelief.

Sadie, too, was stunned. Unable to speak, she squeezed Greg's hand. In a split second, it had gone from warm and dry to cold and clammy.

It got worse. "Greg," the sheriff said as gently as he could, "your brother was also in the car."

Greg's hand tensed. Looking over, Sadie noticed that his eyes were darting back and forth, as though he were afraid to look at any one thing for too long. Then she looked back at the sheriff, who finished delivering his news.

"Neither one survived."

Eyes downcast, Greg could no longer face the sheriff. Tears spilled down his cheeks. "No!" he cried, shaking his head. His whole body was shaking.

Sadie, too, was crying.

Both the president and the sheriff stood beside the desk, silent and somber.

Greg continued shaking his head. "Not Mom and Eric," he cried. "They were coming here."

His denial quickly faded as the grim reality set in. His body slumped. Staring fixedly at the desk, he sat there. Unable to cry. Unable to speak as his world was ripped apart. Zombie-like, he sat, his eyes unseeing, his muscles slack as one crucial chapter in his life faded to black.

CHAPTER

28

Sadie felt as though she were being watched. Maybe it was due to the fact that Elsie herself had cautioned her to be careful following the sheriff's awful news. Whatever the reason, she made sure to lock the door as she left for school. Jill had left earlier, catching a ride with Jeff.

Today was the last day of classes before finals. Greg was inside resting. At least she hoped he was. He said he just wanted some time alone—to deal with things. Since the break-in, she had a bad feeling about him staying in his apartment. That's why he was staying with her. Besides, he really needed someone to take care of him right now. She had made him breakfast before leaving, which was why she was running late. Looking in her rearview mirror, she had an eerie sense of being followed.

Unfortunately, since she'd arrived so late, she had to park in the most remote parking lot. Locking her car, she looked around. No one in sight. Still, she couldn't shake the feeling of being watched. Goose bumps appeared on her arms. Hurriedly, she headed for the General Science building.

She felt a chill. Then, she heard footsteps. Turning, she saw a man in a gray suit. He was coming toward her. She started running.

UGH! She collided with Paul Santini as he emerged from between two cars.

"Are you all right?" Paul squinted, looking down at her.

It was like having Rocky Balboa come to your rescue. Turning, she looked behind her. The parking lot was empty. With a sigh of relief, she turned back to Paul. Since her heart felt as though it were in her throat, she didn't risk opening her mouth. Looking up at him, she simply nodded. Together they walked to class.

Somehow, Sadie made it through the day, making sure to have Jill ride home with her. It wasn't until they were actually driving home that Sadie had a chance to tell Jill what had happened.

"What?" Jill turned to her left, staring at Sadie in surprise.

"It could have been nothing," Sadie said, hoping to downplay the event.

"But it wasn't." Jill looked at her sharply. "There's something going on and you know it."

Sadie frowned. Deep down, she knew Jill was right. Nodding her head, she acknowledged, "Something *is* going on. We just have to figure out what it is."

"We have to stay together," Jill said firmly.

"You're right," Sadie nodded.

It dawned on them both at the same time. "Greg's home alone," they said in unison. Sadie pressed her foot down on the accelerator. The last few minutes of the drive were spent in silence.

"Everything looks okay," Jill said as they pulled in to the drive.

Sadie rushed to the front door. Her hands were shaking. Fumbling with her keys, she dropped them.

"I'll get it," Jill said. She opened the door.

"Greg!" Sadie called, starting to go upstairs.

"Yes?" He walked out of the kitchen.

"You're all right." Sadie threw her arms around him. "Thank God you're all right. I was so scared." She clung to him.

That got to him. Her powerful emotions of both fear and relief were palpable, jarring him out of his apathy. Now, his feeling of hopelessness was replaced by a very masculine need to comfort and protect his sweet Sadie. "What happened, honey?" he asked.

Sadie and Jill filled him in on the details.

Greg agreed that they needed to stay together. They also had to come up with a plan. Unfortunately, the planning had to wait. Tomorrow was the first day of finals. After that, the funeral. Then they'd plan.

— • • • —

Looking down at her Neurology exam, the words seemed to blur together. As she blinked rapidly, they came back into focus. Sadie didn't know how Greg could do it, yet somehow he was. He hadn't had a chance to grieve, and now here he was, taking finals— all the while keeping a sharp watch to make sure they weren't being followed.

After two hours, the test was over. Sadie and Greg went to the cafeteria for a drink before the start of the next exam. As Sadie was sipping her tea, she felt a chill. Looking up, she saw a man in a gray suit walking in the hallway. Her heart skipped a beat. "Greg," she said, turning to get his attention. When they looked back, the man was gone.

Thankfully, the rest of the exams were uneventful. Classes had ended. Summer vacation had begun for everyone except Sadie and Greg. This was no vacation for them; they were packing for the funeral. Becky had already left for Wisconsin, and Ellen was at home. Jill was staying in St. Louis for a few extra days, helping Jeff get set up in his new office.

As they were walking to the door, Greg's cell phone rang. "Hello," he said.

As Greg was listening, Sadie watched his eyes open wide and the color drain from his face. "Thanks," he said, returning the phone to his pocket.

"Who was that?" Sadie asked. Her heart was already beating faster.

Just then, Jill walked in to tell them goodbye. Looking at them, she stopped. "What's going on?"

"There's been an investigation," Greg said haltingly. The chilling reality of the phone call was setting in. "They found out that the brakes on Mom's car had been tampered with."

"What?" Sadie was shocked. This proved that her worries were not unfounded.

Jill's mouth dropped open. "Oh, no!" she said, realizing the implications. Her friends could be in danger.

"Oh, Greg." Sadie hugged him. This was much worse than grieving over an accident—this was murder. She trembled, worried that Greg would be the next target. Now the break-in and the man in the gray suit seemed even more sinister. So did those documents.

Greg, too, was wishing that they'd gotten rid of the documents earlier. If so, his mother and brother might still be alive. Right now, he didn't have time to wallow in guilt; he had to make sure he kept Sadie safe. "Maybe you should stay here with Jill," he suggested.

Sadie shook her head. "No," she said firmly. "I'm going with you. Besides, we're safer together."

Greg conceded that she might have a point. Hopefully two would be safer than one. "Jill," he said, "will you take the documents with you and give them to your parents?"

Jill nodded. Then she looked at Greg, worried about the possibility of a second accident. "You can't drive your Jeep!"

Greg had already realized that. "I know."

"I'll drive you to get a rental car," Jill offered.

"What if they know your car?" Sadie asked. "Maybe you should have Jeff check it out before you drive it."

Jill hadn't considered that possibility. "You're right," she nodded. "I'll call Jeff. He'll drive you to the rental center."

Greg shook his head, worried about the possibility of being followed. He knew that the contents of those documents were worth millions. He also knew that they'd stop at nothing in order to get them back. His jaw clenched as he wondered just how deeply his dad was involved.

"Do you think Jeff could pick up a rental car and drive it here?" he asked. "I don't think anyone would be following him."

"Okay," Jill said as she went to call Jeff.

Then they devised a plan. Jeff was there within the hour. They loaded the car behind closed garage doors. When they left, Jeff was driving. Sadie was sitting next to him wearing a blonde wig from Jill. Greg was lying down in the back seat. They weren't taking any chances. When they were certain that they weren't being followed, Jeff returned to his car. Sadie and Greg were on their way to Indiana.

— • • —

Walking into the funeral, Sadie was struck by powerful emotions. Not death or grief. No, those were normal in such a setting. It was evil—pure evil she felt upon meeting Greg's dad. As prepared as she thought she was, it still came as a shock to her. Oh, he *said* all the right things, smiling so that every tooth in his mouth was on display, but that smile never quite made it to his eyes. She had the feeling that, although he was smiling at you, he could easily be hiding a knife behind his back.

It was his eyes that really bothered her. There was no sparkle of life in them, no twinkle of possibility. Instead, they looked right through you, boring holes into your very soul. Sadie marveled that Greg had survived his childhood. She shivered. Noticing it, Greg pulled her closer.

Dismissing Sadie, Greg's dad focused his obsidian stare on Greg. "Did you get anything from your mother?" he asked.

"No," Greg lied. "Why?"

They already knew that his dad could lie; they just didn't realize how *good* he was at it. "She was working on a picture album for you. I thought she might have mailed it before . . . " As if on cue, a tear appeared at the corner of his eye. Feigning emotion, he shook his head. "It's so sad," he said unctuously.

Greg nodded, clenching his teeth to avoid saying anything else. He, too, was overcome with emotions. For him, it was intense sadness and hatred. It was his anger that kept him standing toe to toe with his father. Matching him stare for stare.

Sadie found the combination of his dad, the heat, and the cloying smell of roses overwhelming. She was relieved when the man left to join his co-workers, reprising his role as grieving husband and father.

When the eulogies began, Sadie reached over, grabbing Greg's hand. It began to tremble. She could actually feel his sadness, it was so intense. Looking over, she could see him blinking back tears.

His tears evaporated, however, when his dad got up to speak. He sat, ramrod straight, in total silence. His only outward show of emotion was the clenching and unclenching of his jaw. Having grieved in private, anger was now moving to his emotional center stage. As his father continued, his lips thinned and his eyebrows pressed together but somehow he managed to avoid scowling.

Sadie marveled at his restraint. She had never seen anyone like Greg's father. Just moments ago, when she was searching for a bathroom, she'd overheard him laughing with co-workers in a private room. Now here he was, seemingly overcome with grief. No wonder Greg hardly ever talked about his family, she thought, squeezing his hand. Now she could understand the reason for his countless stories about his friends in boarding school. He was lucky to have had boarding school, she thought, just as she'd been lucky to have Elsie.

Finally it was over. Sadie didn't think that Greg's jaw could have taken much more pressure. As they were leaving, Greg's dad placed his hand on Greg's shoulder, stopping him. Sadie was amazed that Greg didn't flinch at his touch.

"It was a pleasure to meet you, Sadie," he said, smiling his fake smile. Then he turned his attention to Greg. "Drive safely, son," he said softly. With that said, he turned and walked away.

Sadie got goose bumps. Her heart skipped a beat as though it, too, were surprised by those three simple words. As they walked outside into the hot August sun, she shivered. Greg turned to her but before he could say anything, his cell phone rang.

"Hello." He listened for a moment. "What?" He nodded. "Okay," he said. "Goodbye." Then he hugged Sadie. Instead of telling her who had called, he whispered in her ear, "act natural."

They mingled with relatives offering condolences. Sadie was tense but played her role as the supportive fiancé. At least that part was easy; it was the "act natural" part she had to work at. Mainly, she just nodded appropriately and shook people's hands. That was about as "natural" as she could get.

When they were safely surrounded by people, Greg called for a cab. Luckily, Greg's dad was talking to his co-workers when the cab arrived. He didn't see them leave.

"To the airport," Greg instructed the driver.

Wisely, Sadie didn't say a word. It wasn't until they were inside the airport that Greg's obvious tension began to show. Hurriedly he pulled Sadie along.

"That was Jill," he said, putting an end to the cell phone mystery. "Your home was broken into."

Sadie gasped.

Greg reassured her. "She's all right and so is your teapot."

The documents! Sadie was glad they were safe.

"She's got tickets waiting for us at the counter. We're going to Georgia. She'll meet us there."

As the plane took off, Greg turned to her, his eyes full of pain. At first Sadie thought it was because of the funeral, but he continued staring. He looked deep in thought but his eyes were so troubled, she wanted to help.

"What's the matter?"

Greg didn't mince words, "It's my dad. I know it. He's behind everything."

Sadie's heart went out to him as he fully faced the evil of his father. She knew that he was confronting the reality of the man as opposed to his childhood fantasy. She nodded, having felt that way for some time now. It was apparent that his father had hidden the documents in order to get his promotion. He'd also withheld suicide deaths under the guise of trade secrets. She shook her head. It all came down to death for a profit.

Greg continued, "From the preliminary investigation reports, it looks like he could have been behind the car tampering as well."

"I'm so sorry, honey," was all Sadie could say.

Greg nodded. "There's more," he said. "With everything going on, I didn't get a chance to tell you." He paused. "Jennifer is in the hospital. She tried to kill herself."

Sadie's eyes popped open. "Oh, no!"

With an effort, Greg added the final piece of news. "Dad had her on antidepressants."

Sadie gasped. "Oh, my God!" She shook her head, stunned. Suddenly, she looked up at Greg. "You don't think . . ."

"I do." Greg nodded. "I think he wanted her to kill herself. He was paying her; she knew about his plan to control me. I think she got to a point where she knew too much."

All Sadie could do was shake her head. She didn't know what to say. Her stomach felt as though it were in her throat, which could have been because the plane was landing or because of the news, she wasn't sure. Probably both.

Jill met them at the airport. Her flight had arrived half an hour earlier.

"Jill!" Sadie ran to her. "I'm so glad you're all right." They hugged briefly; there was still a lot to do.

"Luckily, I was out with Jeff at the time," Jill said, referring to the break-in. They continued talking as they walked toward the exit.

"I'm sorry to have put you in that position, Jill," Greg said quietly. This had been an emotional day for him.

"Honey, don't you worry about it. There's nothing a Southern girl can't handle."

Despite her casual attitude, she was glad to be back in Georgia. Here, guaranteed media coverage and the power of the legal system would keep them all safe from the contents of those documents. Looking over at Sadie, she continued, "I'm glad you put those papers in your teapot. That was inspired. The rest of the house looks pretty bad. Every cushion we own has been cut, and so have the mattresses."

"Where are the documents?" Sadie asked.

Jill grinned. "I stuffed them in my bra."

Sadie giggled. The thought of Jill going through airport security that way broke through some of her tension. Even Greg managed to smile.

A black Mercedes was waiting at the curb outside. They got in and Jill introduced them to her parents. "Mom and Dad," she said, "these are my friends, Sadie and Greg. These are my parents, Katherine and James."

"Thank you for meeting us," Greg said, shaking hands.

"Hello," Sadie said.

Jill's mom looked as though she could grace the cover of *Town and Country* magazine. She was an older version of Jill, really. Her dad looked like Cary Grant. It was easy to see where Jill got her looks.

"Hello. We've heard so much about you both," Katherine began. "We feel like we already know you. I'm just sorry we have our first meeting at such a stressful time."

She may have been a lawyer, Sadie thought, but she was also a perfect Southern hostess.

"I'm glad that you offered to help us," Greg said.

"Yes," Sadie nodded. "Thank you both so much."

James looked into his rearview mirror. "Jill told us everything," he said. "By tomorrow the contents of those documents will be front-page news."

Greg smiled. "Thank you, sir."

As they pulled into the driveway, Sadie's eyes opened wide. The grandeur of Jill's stately brick home definitely made an impression. She was glad to see that it was surrounded by a fence. At the push of a button, the gates opened, allowing them in. Sadie looked up at the brick pillars. There were surveillance cameras mounted on top of them.

Noticing her gaze, Jill informed her, "We have a top-notch security system."

Sadie breathed a sigh of relief.

"That's good," Greg said.

Jill's parents were incredible. Within minutes of their arrival, they had orchestrated a major media event. A reporter from *USA Today* was on his way over. So was a reporter from the local NBC TV station. Both were friends of the family.

Katherine brought tea, complete with scones, into the den. How appropriate, Sadie thought, English tea in a room resembling an English library. Sipping her tea, she looked around. The room was beautifully paneled and full of books and leather. It was a comfortable, cozy room. It smelled good, too, she noticed. Like beeswax and lemons. It was all so elegant and civilized—having tea and scones in the den. It made the events of the past few days seem almost unreal.

Sitting there, Sadie could feel the tension begin to fade from her muscles. She'd been so worried that something would happen to Greg, she hadn't even considered that Jill might become a target.

Now she could put those worries behind her. Within an hour, all of the deadly secrets would be exposed.

Greg and James were sitting in wing-back chairs in front of the fireplace. James leaned forward. "I'm going to start a class action lawsuit," he said. "Would you have any problems with that?" He looked at Greg searchingly. "You know that your dad will be brought up on criminal charges."

"Yes, sir," Greg nodded his head. "I understand about my dad." Then he paused, looking directly at James. "Start the lawsuit."

With that, Sadie was amazed to feel a moment of such intense peace that it almost brought tears to her eyes. At last, Katie's tragic death would be avenged, as would that of countless others. Maybe now, she thought, Katie could rest in peace.

Jill noticed the pinched look leave Sadie's face. "Are you all right, Sadie Jo?"

Sadie nodded. "I am now."

The doorbell rang, announcing the arrival of the modern-day version of the cavalry. The media had arrived. Sadie and Greg told their story to the nation. Finally, the nightmare of deception would be ending.

After everyone left, they had dinner by the pool. Sadie looked around, enjoying the beautiful surroundings. The pool lights were on. It looked as though the stars had come down from the heavens to celebrate as flickers of light seemed to dance on top of the water. Taking another bite of her shrimp cocktail, she thought again how surreal it was. After dinner, James and Katherine left them to enjoy the pool by themselves. They were starting on the lawsuit right away.

"It's hard to believe that in a few weeks we'll all be back in school," Jill said.

Sadie nodded. "I know."

Greg was quiet, staring at the pool. Sadie walked over, putting her arms around him. "Are you all right?"

Turning, he looked at her with all the love and tenderness he felt. "I am now," he said quietly.

The next day, the news was splashed across the papers.

Over eggs Benedict, Jill said, "Well, you don't have to worry about anyone coming after you anymore."

"No. We don't," Greg said.

"Jill, what are you going to do now?" Sadie asked, knowing that her family vacation had been canceled. Her parents were working on the lawsuit instead.

Jill put her fork down. "I'll hang around here for awhile. Then I'll go back to St. Louis to spend some time with Jeff. How about you two?"

"We're going to my house," Sadie said looking over at Greg. Last night Greg had looked so sad, telling her that he no longer had a family. She'd looked him straight in the eye. "You have me," she'd said, "and my family is now *our* family."

He'd smiled at that. "You're right," he said, kissing her.

As they were getting ready to leave, Katherine came in. "I have some news for you," she said looking directly at Greg. "Your father's been arrested."

Sadie looked at Greg, noticing his cheek muscles tighten as he clenched his teeth.

"Good," he said. Now for both of them the nightmare really was over. It was time for the healing to begin.

Elsie looked down from the heavens. This time, Katie was by her side. "Yes, my dearies," she said, "'tis time for the healin.'"

Sadie looked over at Greg, feeling a deep sense of peace.

He smiled. He felt it, too.

AND FINALLY . . .

Although this book is a work of fiction, it could just as easily come straight from the headlines. For example:

I.   On December 3, 2005, AOL news posted this headline from an article by Theresa Agovino, AP:
   CARDIOLOGIST ACCUSES MERCK OF MISCONDUCT

II.   On December 9, 2005, *USA TODAY* featured an article by Elliot Blair Smith, Rita Rubin, and Kevin McCoy:
   MEDICAL JOURNAL SAYS VIOXX DATA WITHHELD
   This article goes on to state that the *New England Journal of Medicine* accused the pharmaceutical giant of knowingly withholding data concerning heart attacks.

III.   The *Seattle Times* printed a series of articles from June 26–30, 2005, titled *SUDDENLY SICK: The Hidden Big Business Behind Your Doctor's Diagnosis*, by Susan Kelleher and Duff Wilson.
   The *Times* found that:
   "Pharmaceutical firms are behind the very process by which diseases are defined. Some diseases have even been redefined without the benefit of strong medical evidence."

IV.   In *Psychiatric Drugs*, Dr. Caligari writes, " . . . psychiatric drugs can make people feel so bad they want to kill themselves."

V.   *FORTUNE Magazine* printed an article on November 15, 2005, called "Prozac Backlash," by David Stipp, which started with this line: *"Can Prozac make you want to die?"*
   The article goes on to profile a man who killed himself at age 37, soon after being prescribed antidepressants for insomnia. His body was found hanging from the rafters of his garage. No suicide note was found.
   The article went on to say that sales of these drugs have grown into an $11 billion-a-year market in the U.S., and as a

nation, we are taking so many antidepressants that their break-down products in urine are now being found in fish.

VI.   On January 4, 2005, CNN.com posted this headline:
   "Internal documents from Eli Lilly and Co. appear to indi-cate that the drug maker had data more than 15 years ago show-ing that adverse-effect reports for Prozac were far more likely to list suicide attempts and violence than reports for other antide-pressants."
   The article goes on to state that CNN acquired the docu-ments from Rep. Maurice Hinchey, D-New York.
   The existence of these documents had been reported in the British Medical Journal the previous week. According to the jour-nal, the documents disappeared during the Wesbecker trial in 1994. Joseph Wesbecker killed eight of his co-workers before shooting and killing himself. He had been taking Prozac at the time.
   Congressman Hinchey then distributed the documents to other organizations and individuals, including Dr. Peter Breggin, who confirmed their authenticity.
   For more information, see the following:

   (1) *Breggin, P. Testimony in Joyce Fentress et al. vs. Shea Communications et al. [the Wesbecker Case]. Jefferson Circuit Court, Division I, Louisville, Kentucky. No. 90-CI-06033. Volume XVI. (available on www.breggin.com)*

   (2) *Breggin, P. Brain-Disabling Treatments in Psychiatry (Springer Publishing Company, New York, 1997). Note: The Lilly documents are discussed in this medical book.*

   (3) *Breggin, P. "Suicidality, Violence and mania caused by selective serotonin reuptake inhibitors (SSRIs): A review and analysis." International Journal of Risk and Safety in Medicine, 16: 31–49, 2003/2004.*

VII.   Dr. Julian Whitaker, along with Kirstie Alley, Kelly Pre-ston, and others recently testified before the Florida legislature in support of a bill written by Rep. Gustavo Barreiro. This bill would end the practice of forcing Florida children to take drugs in order to attend public schools.

Beverly Eakman also testified. She is a former teacher and author of *The Cloning of the American Mind*. She spoke about the alarming downward trends we are seeing in our schools.

Our SAT scores have dropped so dramatically that the test actually had to be changed to make it easier. Worldwide, U.S. students rank nineteenth out of 21 countries in math and science.

You may recall the *National Geographic* survey that found that 11% of 18- to 24-year-old Americans couldn't even find the United States on a map. More than 65% couldn't find France or the United Kingdom.

According to Beverly Eakman, this downward spiral started when psychiatrists began infiltrating our schools.
Today, close to 9 million school children are taking psychotropic drugs.

VIII.   Here is a quote obtained from Simpson's Contemporary Quotations, compiled by James B. Simpson. 1988.

> Number: 3009
> Author: Dr. William Menninger
> Quotation: Mental health problems do not affect three or four out of every five persons, but one out of one.
> Attribution: NY Times 22 Nov 57
> Subjects: The world: Medicine: Psychiatry and Psychology

IX.   Following are two particularly chilling psychiatric quotes:

"We must aim to make it (psychiatry) permeate every educational activity in our national life. Public life, politics, and industry should all of them be within our sphere of influence. We have made a useful attack upon a number of professions. The two easiest of them naturally are the teaching profession and the Church. The most difficult are law and medicine."
> Colonel J.R. Rees
> President, National Council for Mental Hygiene (1940)

"The reinterpretation and eventually, eradication of the concept of right and wrong, are the objectives of all psychotherapy. To achieve world government it is necessary to remove from the

minds of men their individualism, loyalty to family traditions, national patriotism and religious dogmas."
G. Brock Chisholm
Co-founder, World Federation for Mental Health (1945)

X.   Evelyn Pringle wrote an article on January 26, 2006, titled *Drug Marketing Scheme Hits Nation's School System.*

In it, she exposes *Teen Screen* as an elaborate marketing scheme concocted by the pharmaceutical industry. She reveals that although the National Alliance for the mentally ill (NAMI) clams to be "a grassroots organization of individuals with brain disorders and their family members," in reality it is a group funded by the pharmaceutical industry. According to *Mother Jones Magazine*, drug companies gave NAMI nearly $12 million from 1996 to mid-1999.

Taxpayers are the ones footing the bill for the mass drugging of children. An investigation by the *Columbus Dispatch* found that Ohio spent more than $65 million in 2004 on mental-health drugs for children.

The investigation also revealed that during 2004, Ohio doctors had prescribed sedatives and mood-altering medications to nearly 700 toddlers and babies. (These children were on Medicaid.)

According to Robert Whitaker, author of *Mad in America*, expenditures for psychotropic drugs were approximately $1 billion in 1987. By 2002, however, the cost to taxpayers had risen to $23 billion.

XI.   Mission accomplished?
You decide.

CPSIA information can be obtained at www.ICGtesting.com
Printed in the USA
LVOW081009300912

300894LV00005B/62/A